THE QUIET ORDER

By
Doug Joseph

Paperback ISBN: 979-8-9917265-4-2

Library of Congress Control Number (LCCN): 2025920143

First Edition

The Quiet Order series is dedicated to two of the most remarkable and fascinating people I have ever had the pleasure of knowing: my lovely daughters, Emily and Elizabeth. I pray that you know how much you are cherished and that these books remind you of some of the stories I told you as kids. I pray that you face the challenges in your life with fierce bravery and overcome them like the victors that I know you are. I love you with all of my heart.

This first book is dedicated to aspiring writers who the world has cast aside. Many agents rejected this book, but I loved the story and believed in its merit. Don't give up on what has been placed in your heart: keep honing it and turning it into your own masterpiece. If you love it when you are finished, that's what's important.

-Doug

Table of Contents

PROLOGUE

Northern Germania - Spring - 1535

◆━━━━◆◆━━━━◆

"What I wouldn't do for a fresh shirt and a real cup of coffee." Wilson said as he took a deep breath of the pre-dawn air. The smell of jasmine and fresh vegetables sprouting in his garden's well-tended soil overwhelmed everything. For a moment, his thoughts slipped back to his parents' place in upstate New York. His heart yearned to spend time there again. But that was long ago—or long ahead, he mused.

"Hey man, we gotta scoot," his friend Cody interjected reluctantly. The need to leave for this mission wore poorly on both men. Wilson heaved a sigh and headed back inside to get his bags.

The two men walked out of Wilson's modest cottage, beginning the long trek to the main road. Once on the busier path, a passing farmer's wagon splattered muck on their boots and pants. The foul smells of mud and horse manure inundated them as they met with the rest of their team. The fragrances of jasmine and youth slipped from Wilson's mind completely. The two inspected the damage, and Wilson frowned. Dirt like this was not easy to clean in this era, at least not quickly.

Wilson was still scowling as Gretta and Alex drew near. As he unsuccessfully tried to brush the debris from his trousers, he felt his shoulders tense with the burdens he carried, slumping under the weight as if it were physical. "You look angry," Gretta muttered without smiling.

Wilson realized he was sending the wrong message. The stains would have to wait. He straightened up and stretched his neck side to side. "I'm not. I just have a lot to think about."

Alex agreed. "You can't blame Wilson. It's such a terrible thing being stuck here. Nobody cares, and even if they did, they could do nut'n 'bout it. While I'm at it, I'm having a tough time grasping the stupid etiquette of this era. When do I bow? When do I step aside? When is it okay to laugh? The rules make no sense."

Gretta let out a hearty laugh, and Alex grinned.

Cody lifted his hand momentarily to interject. "The important thing to know is how to order stout!" His smile couldn't be contained as Gretta just rolled her eyes. Cody thoroughly enjoyed this region's ales, stouts, and meads, even if served warm.

Looking straight into his eyes, Alex's grin faded as he said, "Wilson, you ready for this?"

Wilson considered his response as he took a deep breath. Alex and Gretta had committed to his plan. They both had determined expressions on their face. They look set to get this done, he thought as he began to speak. "Ready as I'll ever be. It needs doing. Where is the rest of the team?" The question was directed to Alex.

"We have them scouting ahead already. I hate to tell you this, but Kelly and her gang are already onto us. I don't know how she's doing it, but she's getting intel from somewhere. We think they're already planning their reaction to our next move."

Wilson didn't respond, so Alex continued. "I've prepared papers should you encounter German or Roman soldiers. I can't believe how easy all of this is compared to back in Kazakhstan." Wilson nodded in understanding.

"It's amazing how trouble-free things are without Big Brother tracking your every move."

"You aren't kidding! Put some fictional information on an official-looking parchment, and you're good to go. "You just need to back up your lying papers with your lying responses... oh, and speak the language," Alex said while handing out their papers. His eyes narrowed on Cody, who avoided making visual contact because his German was the worst of the group. They separated the documents and put them in the proper locations in their satchels.

Once Wilson put his papers away, he burst out, "As far as Kelly goes, she better be careful, or she's going to get herself killed. We won't be the ones doing it, nor will we be able to do anything about it."

"She's pretty fearless, that's for sure." Cody smiled as he spoke about her. Wilson caught the smile, and Cody quickly looked away.

Wilson stared down at the muddy road while expressing his feelings on the matter. "There's a fragile line between bravery and stupidity. I don't think her tenacity will let her see the difference." He wanted to change the subject, so he spun around to address Alex. "You know where we're going, right?"

Alex spoke slowly through his gritted teeth. "I've made three different maps and at least four different routes to get us there."

Wilson knew he had overstepped a quiet boundary, because Alex was always prepared. "Ever on top of things, my friend," he said, patting Alex on the back. Then he led them to the stable. Wilson turned to face the group. "Let's go remake some history!"

CHAPTER 1

LAST-MINUTE PLANS

Geosynchronous Orbit - Space Station New Dallas - 2033

Kelly Rittenaugh never noticed how large this conference room was for a space station. It was also one of the few areas with leather and wood accouterments. She snorted as she considered how out of place she was in such a lofty chamber. Her jaw clenched as she scanned the outline for the meeting. The agenda caused her to stiffen her back as she gazed at her colleague, Wilson Ryken. Looking down at the docket, he scowled and nonchalantly returned the look with a slow but knowing nod. The two sat quietly, waiting for the item to be discussed.

The chairman finally arrived at the bullet point. "So the mission today, we expect to break the twenty-five-minute gauntlet. I believe you said thirty minutes. Is that right, Larry?"

An older man leaned forward to speak into the microphone. "Umm... yes, sir. As you can see, we've included the engineering auditing team from Chellos and two managers included in the crew. We want to ensure this mission goes off without any more hitches."

Kelly quickly leaned forward. "I'd like a moment to speak to this."

The chairman turned to look Kelly straight in the eyes.

He then subtly sighed before speaking. "The chair recognizes Kelly Rittenaugh."

Kelly looked to Wilson before continuing. He shrugged and raised his eyebrows. The response was not the comforting look she was hoping for. "Thank you, Chairman Embekka. I've got a few questions concerning the itinerary for the day." The chairman nodded. "Go ahead, Kelly."

"Was anyone planning on telling us about this before this meeting? I mean, you just added four engineers and two managers."

"The agenda was set five days ago."

Kelly quickly replied, "This is the first I've seen of this, and I check my mail often. I even checked it when we entered the meeting and still have received nothing."

The chairman looked down at his notes. "It was sent to your manager five days ago."

"Again, this is the first I'm hearing of it. When you say my 'manager,' I assume you mean Jason?"

"Yes, I see a receipt from Mr. Billow. Jason, why wasn't this forwarded to your team?"

Jason Billow frowned as he leaned into his microphone. "It must have been an oversight on one of my team's part. I'll have to look into it."

Kelly's blood boiled at his response. This oversight wasn't the first time his incompetence was exposed, and she knew there would be no consequence for his mistake. She spoke up without a filter. "And having Jason on our mission will ensure that it goes off without any more 'hitches'? How?"

Jason's eyes narrowed on the captain. "I need to ensure you're doing what you claim to be doing."

"Oh… you mean you'll be doing the important jobs… like holding a clipboard while looking at equipment you have no idea about?"

The chairman quickly stepped in. "Captain Rittenaugh, is that really necessary?"

Kelly felt a firm hand on top of her right knee.

She looked down and followed it to Wilson, who puckered his lower lip and subtly shook his head. The action made Kelly aware that she was letting her anger get the best of her. "I apologize for the outburst, Chairman. I'm a little frustrated that neither the crew nor the engineering team are brought in on critical decisions like this. They are made without our input or approval. It's disheartening."

The chairman nodded his head as he leaned closer to the microphone. "I can understand your frustration here. In light of that, I want to allow you and Wilson time to set up for your new guests. Unfortunately, their arrival cannot be moved at this time. Unless you have more to add, you're both welcome to leave to prepare… Oh, and Jason, I'd like a word with you when this meeting has adjourned." Jason nodded at the chairman while casting mental daggers at Kelly.

"Thank you for your understanding, chairman. Wilson and I will do our best to accommodate this plan." Kelly ignored Jason and stood. Wilson quickly followed as both exited the meeting.

When the door had closed, Wilson put his hand on Kelly's back. "That was a fine career-limiting comment."

Kelly shook her head and snorted. "You think I care about that? Still, thanks for keeping me in check. That Jason is a first-class ass."

"Yep, pretty much." Wilson shrugged.

Kelly continued to wind herself up. "That chucklehead should be fired. Why do they let him get away with stuff like this?"

Wilson donned a playful smile. "Maybe he has pictures on someone?"

Kelly couldn't help but laugh at the comment. She marveled at Wilson's ability to diffuse the ticking time bomb known as Kelly Rittenaugh. With that, her anger subsided.

Out of the corner of her eye, she noticed a few friends walking into the mess hall.

"Hey, I don't know about you, but I can't deal with team loco without an extra shot of caffeine and maybe some bacon and eggs. We have enough time. Let's make a stop."

"You had me at caffeine."

CHAPTER 2

FOLLOW THE DOT

Geosynchronous Orbit - Space Station New Dallas - 2033

The comforting *swoosh* of the mess hall doors opening tickled Keisha Bowen's curiosity. She reached out to glide her hand along the portal edge. The cool alloy calmed her as she took a deep breath of filtered air. The slightest scent of alcohol and freshly brewed coffee suppressed the expected smell of human perspiration typical on space stations. Walking through the bulkhead door and surveying the room, one specific table captured her focus. Her eyes lit up as she recognized one of her military school heroes.

Wasting no time, Keisha approached the source of her interest. Kelly Rittenaugh's pleasant confidence attracted followers, and her entourage only bolstered her persona. Her petite frame sat sandwiched between two hulking men who could have easily been mistaken for bodyguards. Kelly's contagious smile ensured that the group surrounding her enjoyed the best time of anyone in the chamber. Those gravitating toward this happy atmosphere joined seamlessly in orbit.

Keisha spoke up with an assertive tone that startled herself, "Captain Rittenaugh?"

"Yes?" Kelly turned to face Keisha. "My name is Keisha Bowen. It's an honor to meet you." Her bravery evaporated as she extended her hand to meet Kelly's.

"Nice to meet you, Keisha. You can just call me Kelly. I like the sound of that much better." Kelly shook her hand with a welcoming smile as others around the table chuckled at the young admirer's comment. "I see by your uniform that you're in Control Tower D-One. I don't think I've seen you up here before nor heard your voice on the com, and I know everyone's voice in that tower."

Keisha's eyes darted left and right, assessing the situation. "You're right. It's my first day as a civilian controller. I'm nervous as hell, but I'm excited at the same time." Her hands naturally went behind her as she stared shyly at the group around the table.

Kelly shifted in her seat to give Keisha her full attention. "Well, the good news is that Vanderwide is your commander. She's as good a commander as I've known in the private sector. She runs a tight ship, so make sure you pay close attention to her orders."

One of the massive men sitting next to Kelly spoke up. "Oh! And make sure that you have a good place to hide if you piss her off too. My name's Wilson Ryken. It's nice to meet you." He smiled at Keisha, then turned to Kelly. "Hey boss, we gotta scoot. We're already running a little late. You can bet Vercelli and Alex are goofing off with us not there." The large man turned back to Keisha and glanced at her apologetically, mouthing the word "sorry."

"Well, it was really nice to meet all of you," Keisha said. "I just wanted to introduce myself and say hello." She started backing away awkwardly.

"It was nice meeting you too, Keisha. Hopefully, you'll join us for breakfast next time," Kelly said as she cleared her part of the table.

Keisha took a deep breath as she tried to figure out how to respond to the unexpected invite, finally saying, "I'd like that very much." That was an understatement.

Having breakfast with Kelly Rittenaugh would be the highlight of her year. The clock on the wall grabbed her attention. Keisha abandoned getting coffee and headed straight to the control tower. Fortunately, it was less than a twenty-meter walk. Her adrenaline was already pumping enough that the boost of caffeine was unnecessary.

As the bulkhead door slid shut behind her, she stared out the observation windows in awe, watching the backdrop of Earth dominate the scenery. The planet's vivid details made it hard for her mind to believe it wasn't some sort of special effect.

Noticing Keisha's unfamiliar face, the tower commander walked over to introduce herself. Though in her late forties, she was physically fit and looked years younger. Her uniform fit her perfectly, and no hair on her head was out of place. "Are you Ms. Bowens? My name is Carrie Vanderwide; I'm the commander here on New Dallas-One." Carrie reached out to shake Keisha's hand. "I can tell by the look on your face that this is your first time on the station."

"It's a lot to take in." Keisha's wide-eyed gaze swept over everything. She did her best to maintain eye contact with Carrie, but the view out the window beckoned and drew her attention.

"It's pretty amazing, for sure. There isn't a more magnificent office view in the solar system, though I've heard X7-Base's around Saturn's rings is pretty impressive." The commander gazed out at the backdrop as the fresh recruit nodded. "We still have a job to do, and I'm going to need you to focus.

"We don't have near the traffic of a significant airport up here, but we have enough to keep us on our toes. I need you to stay frosty and keep to our protocols. That said, enjoy the view, but don't let it affect your duties."

Carrie gestured at a middle-aged man standing nearby. "I'm going to have you tag along with Tyrique Bashir today. He'll show you the ropes, and hopefully, you'll be up to speed in no time."

She gave a quick glance at the man as he was coming their way.

"Are you Keisha? I'm Tyrique. It's nice to meet you." He shook her hand as they made their way to a console filled with blinking lights. Everything at the workstation was pristine. No smudges were on the glass, and grime hadn't had time to accumulate on the control panel. Keisha smiled at her new office and the promises it offered.

"I'll just leave you two to get acquainted with your new post. "It was nice meeting you, Keisha. I think you're going to like it here." With a nod, Carrie moved on, leaving Keisha to study the control panel before her.

"So, I'm told you ran Air Traffic at Miramar," Tyrique began. "You'll be glad to know this gig is much easier but has perilous moments. The worst was during the conflict. Let me assure you this station was not the place to be."

Keisha was already studying and admiring the workstation. "Wow! This is a Series-8?" she queried. "I didn't even know this was out yet."

"It's not, officially. TxC gets us all the best stuff, but we're also their beta site. I think they figure that this is much lighter duty than down on the ground."

It was hard for Keisha to tell if Tyrique was sincere or sarcastic. She chose to assume it was the former.

"New Dallas-One, this is X-Ray-Charlie-One-One-Three," came a voice over a speaker at the station.

Keisha's bracelet vibrated. She realized she was expected to respond to this call. "Go ahead, X-Ray-Charlie-One-One-Three." She hoped she heard the call sign correctly.

"Requesting an immediate departure." The workstation lit up with activity. One display presented the vehicle's filed flight plan, while another showed all the pertinent information on the ship itself.

"Whoa. This bugger is a seriously modified Mite-Class cargo ship." Keisha's eyes lit up as she read the specifications on the monitor.

"Yeah, she's one of TxC's experimental projects.

"She's named *Kronos*."

Strange choice for a name. Keisha recalled, *Kronos was the king of the Titans and the god of time from Greek mythology.* "I see that. What's her purpose?"

"Don't really know, but we're pretty sure it's an Allied version of the Doppelganger, only it's way more realistic. Regardless, your job for the next hour is babysitting this ship."

"Babysitting?" "Yeah. This part'll suck, but you gotta track the ship on its run to the testing area. It's about a seventy-five-minute journey." He pulled up a sector display, showing her the secured region. "At some point, the ship will duplicate itself, and they need you to acknowledge that you can see the copy. Once it leaves New Dallas' protected airspace, you can no longer communicate with it through the intercom. We can only use the secure text channel for communication per TxC's orders. Do not record what you see, but you must follow the ship for the entire journey. When the ship duplicates, do a scan of both ships. I swear it's crazy how identical they both are. The copy even looks like it has a live crew on it. I think it would fool any radar system. So, you need to remember: When you see the copy, send them a message, okay? The duplicate usually shows up about forty minutes into the flight and disappears a little later."

Keisha nodded but didn't get a chance to respond.

"New Dallas-One, do you copy?" the voice came again.

"Yes, X-Ray-Charlie-One-One-Three. You're clear for departure." Keisha quickly responded to their request by pressing a few virtual buttons on the console. A team of barge drones responded, and the launch bay doors opened.

"Roger that. Thank you. Welcome to your new job, Keisha. Kronos out."

A smile came across her face. She thought the voice was familiar.

"That was Kelly Rittenaugh, and she knew who you were," Tyrique said with a tinge of envy in his voice. He stared at the recruit.

"How about that? I just met her in the mess hall." Keisha gazed down with a humble smirk.

"Hmmm. Well, I'm going to run to the head. You think you can stay here and not blow anything up while I'm gone?"

"I can hold my own here," she answered confidently.

"Okay, remember, it's important to let the Kronos know when you see the double."

"You got it."

Tyrique patted her on the back and headed off to use the restroom.

To her irritation, Tyrique was gone much longer than just a quick visit, leaving her unsupervised and watching a dot representing the Kronos move along her screen. Her thoughts drifted happily to earlier that morning in the mess hall and meeting Kelly Rittenaugh.

"So, how we doin' up here?" Tyrique asked, finally back from the bathroom.

"We're doing fine. This ain't too bad at all. You want boring? You should try tracking cargo planes coming down from Alaska. Talk about tedious duties."

The satisfaction in her tone was unmistakable, and she kept studying the slowly moving dot on her console.

"If you ask me, Kronos duty is the worst. That's probably why they gave it to you first. Welcome to New Dallas!"

They were both chuckling when the commander stopped by. "How's it going over here?" Carrie asked.

Their laughter stopped. "Good. Good. We've just been training Keisha on Kronos duty." He glimpsed over at Keisha, who stood at attention.

Keisha twisted up her mouth in thought. "I've got a question. Isn't the double supposed to appear around forty minutes? I've been waiting for forty-five minutes, and it's still the only one." Carrie looked at the console and confirmed they were near the target area. "You contacted them to tell them there wasn't a double, right?"

"No, sir. I was told to contact them when I saw a double."

Keisha glanced at Tyrique to confirm, but his focus was locked on the console, his eyes wide. Carrie's calmness evaporated and was replaced with a look of horror. "Contact them now and tell them to abort the mission!" Carrie shouted.

Keisha typed the message on the keypad. She feverishly scanned the console while completing the note, trying to find the encoding button. She finally fumbled onto it and sent out the urgent message:

NO SECOND SHIP PRESENT. ABORT MISSION.

She pressed 'Send' and waited. The message turned from amber to yellow, meaning it had been acknowledged. Keisha breathed a sigh of relief, as did Carrie. But then an icon on the display started flashing. Carrie's eyes darted around the console as the text declared, "Tracked Object Lost." Then the icon disappeared completely.

A beeping tone chirped from the console, informing them of a problem.

Carrie pushed Keisha out of the way and started playing with the console. "Paul, verify sector Echo-Four-Four-Three-Three-Five. I'm looking for the Kronos."

The man next to Keisha's station quickly pulled up the sector, repeating the sector name. "Nothing's there, boss," Paul said.

"Scan out," Carrie quickly replied.

"Already did. Nothing is even close."

"Do you think they could be testing some sort of cloaking device?" Keisha asked.

"Maybe, but we need to call this into headquarters." Carrie looked calm, but her heart raced, and perspiration formed on her forehead.

"I'm sorry, sir. I didn't know I was supposed to message them if I didn't see a double," Keisha said. Tyrique looked away.

"I understand, and we'll debrief this later. Let's get HQ on the line and see what we must do next. For now, we need to find this ship! Hopefully, it'll just reappear in a minute."

The room's tension remained high as Carrie directed her team to continue looking for the Kronos. But the ship never appeared as time ticked forward.

A few hours later, a team of eight individuals walked into the control room. Heading the squad was a man with a tight haircut and a military-style uniform. A subtle TxC logo adorning his shoulder patch was the only clue of rank or name on his person. "I'm looking for Carrie Vanderwide."

Carrie looked up from the tracking unit. "I'm Carrie Vanderwide."

The man headed to meet her at the workstation. "Sir, I'm Commander Mark Gilmore, and this team is TxC's emergency management division.

"We'll take over the investigation of the lost ship, Kronos." "Like hell you will! I'm the commander here, and we're fine. Who in God's name do you think you are, coming onto my deck and giving me orders?"

The man quietly reached into his satchel and pulled out a tablet. "No, sir, this is our deck."

Without any further discussion, he pulled up a page and handed her the display.

Carrie glared as she looked down to see what he held out for her. Slowly, she took it and read while the man waited expectantly. She looked up from the text twice with an incredulous frown. Finally, when she reached the end of the document, she handed the tablet back to the man.

With a resigned look on her face, she addressed her crew. "Okay, team, I need everyone to step away from their workstations. This group of TxC employees will take over. Take your personal belongings with you and consider this the end of your shift. Keisha, I'll need you to stay to catch these guests up to speed."

The officer interrupted. "That won't be necessary. We're already aware of what has happened and what you've done. We'll also run traffic control during this time. You're all dismissed now. Please exit quickly and quietly. I appreciate your cooperation."

Tyrique's nostrils flared as he stepped forward. To Carrie's horror, he started talking. "Why do we gotta leave? We're trained to be here."

"I'm not sure you understand that this stopped being a conversation thirty seconds ago. We work beyond your clearance, so you need to exit NOW! We'll inform you and the rest of your team when they may resume their responsibilities on our deck." There was nothing pleasant in Gilmore's tone. He turned to the group that came in with him. "Pull out the Parson array, and let's start setting up. We need to do this as quickly as possible.

"Every minute wasted is fewer particles to track. Look alive, team!"

Carrie shifted her jaw and walked towards the exit. The officer ignored her departure and continued his tasks as the exit doors closed behind her.

CHAPTER 3

WELCOME TO TXC

Boston - Fall - 2035

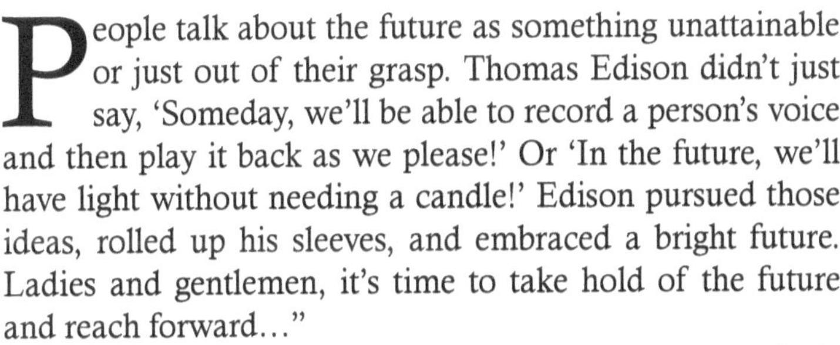

People talk about the future as something unattainable or just out of their grasp. Thomas Edison didn't just say, 'Someday, we'll be able to record a person's voice and then play it back as we please!' Or 'In the future, we'll have light without needing a candle!' Edison pursued those ideas, rolled up his sleeves, and embraced a bright future. Ladies and gentlemen, it's time to take hold of the future and reach forward…"

Colton Shaw walked up to the glass entryway of Tx Corporation's (TxC) impressive headquarters to Theseus Gell's voice on the monitors strategically and elegantly embedded around the large lobby. Jackson Tatum was waiting patiently for him inside, so he picked up his pace slightly. At twenty-seven, Colton's dexterity was at its peak. Entering the lobby, a pair of salesmen shared stories and didn't notice where they were walking. Colton effortlessly sidestepped the two, then received a flurry of apologies from them.

Colton felt his pocket buzz before his phone officially rang. He took the phone out to see who it was and answered.

"Percy, are you calling to make sure I made it on time?"

Colton's boss, Dr. Percival Adkins, snickered at the comment. "You know me well, Colton. I also called to wish you luck."

Colton grinned as he spotted his colleague. "Hey Percy, I'm going to go. I see Jackson, and we need to check in at the front desk."

"Okay. Just remember that we're only fact-finding. We aren't looking to make enemies or anything."

Colton's smile could be heard in his voice. "When do I make enemies?"

"Oh brother! Just be on good behavior, please."

"You got it, boss. I gotta go."

"Okay, buh-bye."

Colton hung up the phone and greeted his friend. "Jackson, have you been waiting long?"

Jackson shook his head. "Only about ten minutes. You're good."

Colton patted him on the back. "Have you recovered from the flight home? I know that this excavation was taxing."

"You ain't kidding. That was one hot month, but I think I'm okay." Jackson paused for a moment, then said, "Now, what exactly is the point of sending you and me to the lofty towers of TxC to meet its visionary, Theseus Gell?"

Colton ignored the cheeky comment. "First off, I discovered the artifact. It should go without saying that I need to be here." Jackson missed the humor, so Colton continued. "And you put the pieces together. Without your contribution, we would have never been here today."

Jackson smiled awkwardly. "I guess that's fair, but you know I hate stuff like this."

Colton nodded. "I do, but now you can carry the case if I get too tired."

Jackson sighed and squinted at the comment. He studied the surroundings. "Man, this place is seriously decked out."

They paused to admire the lobby, taking deep breaths featuring the pleasant scent of espresso coffee.

The designers of this facility adorned it with black granite, glass, brushed nickel, fine leather, and roasted, curly maple wood that gave it a lofty atmosphere. Suddenly, Colton felt underdressed. He looked at Jackson, who had a nicely ironed and professional-looking suit, which aided and complimented his thick glasses. Colton merely wore a sports jacket, khakis, and a blue button-down shirt with no tie. He considered his outfit and thought, It's too late to do anything now, so I got what I got! Despite this feeling of sartorial inadequacy, his attractiveness wasn't compromised. His shirt fit in all the right places, and the gentle curls of his brown hair balanced his boyish smile. Multiple onlookers noticed him and were pleased by what they saw. One young lady even did a double take as Colton passed her. It was enough to bolster his confidence as he sojourned on to the meeting.

Jackson looked up at a stealthy speaker that they passed under. "This guy has a way with words. I'll give 'em that." The media loop took excerpts from other famous talks and played them continuously. Colton chuckled. "I feel for the poor souls working in the lobby. I figure they rotate locations often, soundproof the reception desk, or they have long since grown numb to the propaganda spin of this never-ending commercial."

"Most likely the latter," Jackson replied.

The attendant at the reception desk courteously greeted them and provided personalized visitor badges. "An escort will be down shortly to take you in. You may sit anywhere in here you would like, and please help yourself to refreshments on the north wall." The attendant pointed to the wall, and the two men shuffled over.

Colton scanned the waiting area. He estimated that at least twenty people lingered, awaiting contacts within the facility. Though the number of occupants barely dented the lobby's seating capacity, lively conversations filled the room with energy that made it feel smaller than it was.

At the refreshments counter stood a young woman smiling with the perfect glint of professional hospitality.

"May I provide you with a drink? Perhaps a latte or espresso? We also have fresh fruit or bagels if you like?"

"Yeah, I'll have a plain toasted bagel with cream cheese and some orange juice, please!" Jackson blurted out. Colton looked at him in amazement. "What?" Jackson returned the look, scoffed, and bluffed an offense. Then he turned back to the attendant. "Pardon me. I didn't catch your name."

The attendant smiled at him. "My name is Megan, as the nametag says, and your food will be out shortly. Would either of you like anything else while you wait?" Colton let out a small snort at the well-crafted response, then quickly smiled, shook his head no, and thanked her for her courtesy. With no other questions, Megan nodded and tended to the next guest.

Colton waited until the attendant turned away to speak. "Well done, Sherlock! Maybe if the nametag lit up and played a little ditty, it would have helped."

As they stood talking, Megan interrupted them. "Mr. Tatum? Your bagel and juice are ready!" To Jackson's surprise, the smiling attendant handed him a perfectly prepared plate with a bagel, cream cheese, some garnish, and a surprisingly large glass of orange juice.

"Wow, thanks! How did you know my name? And you can call me Jackson."

"It's written on your visitor tag, Jackson." She pointed to his chest as Jackson blushed slightly with embarrassment. She quickly reassured him, "Don't worry. This happens all the time. People just forget that they have a visitor tag on! Thank you for asking my name. It was very polite!" His embarrassment lessened, and before he could say anything else, Megan turned and served another guest.

"We'll call that a draw," Jackson mumbled incoherently with a small smile as he moved to a small café table to eat his bagel. Colton joined him and waited for their escort. In the background, the men listened to another of Gell's famous speeches. It was the one he gave at the last Presidential Ball three months ago.

"This bagel is awesome." Jackson downed the last bites as the escort arrived to take them to their meeting.

"Dr. Shaw?" A slender man with a polished demeanor gracefully covered ground in the lobby, looking for their party.

As the two men stood up, a small piece of the bagel dropped from Jackson's mouth and careened off the lapel of his nicely pressed suit, leaving a skid mark of cream cheese for him to clean. Colton curiously watched and just shook his head in disbelief.

"I'm Dr. Shaw," Colton said as he reached out his hand to greet the escort. "This is my colleague, Mr. Jackson Tatum." Jackson reached to shake the escort's hand but quickly withdrew it, realizing he had a bit of the cream cheese residue on his palm from the attempt to clean his lapel. The other two men tried to ignore the awkwardness. Colton focused on Gell's speech to the European Union concerning advancements in alternate fuel sources and a cleaner environment.

The words inspired, but the vision he cast, backed by the technology Gell introduced through TxC, put him in a position only a few people in the world ever reached. A darling of the industry, lauded by governments, and leaving competitors in the dust, the TxC name was now the iconic symbol of high success.

Gell's humble beginnings made him the poster child for the American dream and the promise of new generations. "It's a pleasure to meet you. My name is Anton Kyrianco, and I'll be your escort for the day. If there is anything you need or want, ask me, and I'll do my best to aid you." Anton's diction conveyed polish. "Before we head up, would anyone like to use the restroom? We have a bit of a walk ahead." Both men looked at Jackson.

Jackson, who was shaking his head no, quickly changed to a nod of affirmation. He scurried to the restroom to clean his hands and possibly better clean the lapel of his suit.

Colton heard Gell's speech to the world concerning the TxC moon base opening for business.

Gell was not perfect — far from it — but the unpleasant events in his career rarely stuck in the public's mind. As his list of accomplishments grew, the people left burnt by his bad deals became merely like noise in the wind. The media had a darling who was young, eloquent, charming, brilliant, handsome, and, most important of all, a bachelor. The press often wrote of Gell's torrid relationships or took pictures and footage of a list of elite women accompanying him on one of his extravagant vacations. Rumors floated around that he dated a young TxC engineer for a while. But as with every bump in his life, these stories disappeared as soon as a new one emerged. TxC was the benefactor of a golden child, and all they needed to do was keep riding his popularity, pushing innovation, and watching their stock prices rise.

"Is that the artifact?" Anton gazed down at the case Colton carried.

Colton involuntarily gripped it a little tighter and nodded with a nervous smile.

Anton smiled back and said, "This is truly exciting. Dr. Warmouth is anxious to see it!"

Jackson returned as if on cue, looking refreshed and ready to proceed. The three men walked past the reception counter as Gell's voice warned about the government stifling innovation. Colton remembered this speech, too, from an appearance on The Late Show with Regan Terrance. It reminded him of Jackson's parents. He poked Jackson's arm. "Hey, didn't your dad buy some of those TxC original tires?"

Jackson brightened as he answered, "Oh, yeah. He was proud of those babies. He refused to give them up for as long as he could. I remember hearing this speech and feeling bad because my dad paid a lot for those tires."

A few years earlier, a division of TxC had invented a tire capable of changing its grip profile and stiffness using an embedded microchip and some electrons.

It was first introduced to NASCAR with wild success and then implemented into mainstream tires.

The tires weren't cheap but offered advantages to the savvy consumer in the four big categories: superior gas mileage, quieter ride, better handling, and faster braking. TxC had one of their most successful consumer-level products to date, but nobody realized the damage these tires caused to the roads. The tires' grip doubled the over-time wear on the streets and forced highway departments nationwide to repave more often When the Department of Transportation finally determined the main culprit, the government quietly made TxC change the design to a softer algorithm and retrofit the older tires' chip. The resulting tire performed marginally better than traditional stock tires.

Not one to take correction lightly, Gell angrily blamed the government for not keeping up with road knowledge. He even vowed to start designing better roads and publicizing his research so 'all countries could benefit from twenty-first century technology.' He quickly backed away from the promise when he realized the project's cost. No one ever expected him to follow through with it, and they just gave him a pass.

Still, many Gell fans cited this claim on social media when describing him as a fantastic, benevolent visionary. Walking down the corridor, the men heard the fading echo of Gell's voice saying, "It's time to get out of the rut of doing the same thing over and over again…" Colton and Jackson looked at each other, knowing the irony of this looping ad-nausea. The guy sure likes himself, that's for certain! Colton pondered but didn't even consider mentioning to anyone else, especially with Anton present.

As they approached the elevator, the case in Colton's hand felt as if it had doubled in weight. He considered handing it to Jackson but thought better of the moment and rested it on the floor in the elevator as they ascended.

CHAPTER 4

THE MEETING

Boston - Fall - 2035

Anton walked to another reception desk and spoke with the attendant. He quickly turned to address Colton and Jackson. "So, gentlemen, this is the end of our journey together. Doctor Warmouth should be out shortly. You can have seats right over there." He pointed to some tasteful leather chairs in a small lobby.

Colton and Jackson shook Anton's hand and sat in the provided chairs. Jackson leaned over to his friend and spoke quietly in his ear. "Do you think we're ready for this?"

Colton nodded. "Dr. Adkins wouldn't have sent us if we weren't." His mind drifted to thinking about what it had been like working for a man like Adkins.

Adkins was kind and brilliant, and Colton considered him a second father. With both of Colton's parents deceased, Adkins was a wonderful and willing surrogate. Their relationship had grown through the years as they'd discussed deep subjects accompanied by barbeque and cream soda. Adkins had personally funded most of Colton's doctorate in anthropology solely based on Colton's verbal promise to work for him upon completion.

Adkins knew he was in good company when Colton was around, and Colton knew the good doctor was proud of the progress he had already made in their shared field of archeology.

It only took a few minutes for Erin Warmouth to appear to greet them. Her golden-brown locks complemented her long, slender frame, and her laugh lines added to her attractiveness. "Gentlemen, I'm Erin Warmouth." She reached out her hand to shake, and the subtle scent of lilac perfume clouded Colton's facilities.

Colton promptly stood to meet her hand. "Dr. Warmouth, it's a pleasure to meet you!" He noticed that Erin's green eyes carried a certain brilliance. Her colleagues would quickly point out that she was incredibly intimidating despite her reserved disposition.

"I prefer just Erin." Though she didn't like titles, she appreciated that this man knew she had one. Erin had received a Ph.D. in astrophysics at age twenty-one from Notre Dame. She then rose quickly through the ranks because of her uncanny talents. She avoided credit for herself while stealthily helping solve some tricky problems with the moon base project so it could remain on schedule. At age twenty-eight, Erin had reached her current position -- quietly running things at TxC. "I'm excited to hear about your discoveries today. From what I read in the report, did you make the initial find? It's hard to tell from how it was written."

"Well... umm... Erin... it was a bit of luck, but yes, ma'am, I did stumble on the artifact.

"Our team worked for weeks to find it. Any of them could've discovered it."

Colton wasn't big on talking about himself, either. Typically, it was nice to have Doctor Adkins around because he usually could take all the attention, deflecting to Colton only for tough questions and specifics. Colton's subtle Southern accent could hinder a conversation, especially with 'elitists' from the Northeast. Erin gave no such indications of disapproval at his speech, so this was some exciting territory for him.

"True, but you did discover it. Well done!" Erin smiled, making Colton even less comfortable. His attraction to her was undeniable at this point. How could something so pleasant be so unnerving at the same time? He pondered this thought as he searched for the next thing to say, but the smell of lilacs challenged his concentration.

"I was there, too!" Jackson jumped in with his usual enthusiasm. The distraction relieved Colton and annoyed him simultaneously. "Oh? And who might you be?" Erin politely smiled. Her shoulders were squared with Colton's, but she turned slightly to allow Jackson into the circle.

"My name is Jackson Tatum, and I was an integral part of this excavation. I'm an intern but should be getting my Ph.D. pretty soon. It was my first time..." Jackson looked over at Colton, realizing he may have broken some unspoken rule, and abruptly stopped mid-sentence, lowering his head slightly.

Colton recognized his friend's embarrassment. He put his hand on Jackson's shoulder and squeezed slightly. The gesture gently relaxed his anxiety, and Erin immediately noticed the altruistic action. She made eye contact with Colton as if to acknowledge this kind encouragement.

"Well, it's also very nice to meet you, Jackson. I look forward to hearing all about this in the next few minutes. Gentlemen, if you'd like to follow me." Erin turned and headed down a long hallway.

Colton pulled his hand off Jackson's back, and they both followed Erin to a small conference room. As he looked around, he was amazed at the room's modesty.

Everything else in this building seemed larger than life, but this room was a simple table with four chairs. A pitcher of water with four glasses sat on the surface. There was a phone for conference calls on one side and an embedded monitor on the other.

What wasn't as modest was the view from the window. Colton looked out across the Boston Harbor and gulped. "Wow!" he whispered almost inaudibly. Erin noticed and smiled. "Yeah, I feel the same way. When asked what I wanted in this conference room, I wondered what I could put here to compete with this scenery. I concluded not very much. So I decided to keep it very simple."

Jackson nodded as he walked to the window to maximize the panoramic effect. "I see your point. It's nothing short of amazing."

Colton smiled as he remembered they were there for a reason. "Well, I think we can start, unless you're waiting for anyone else."

"Liam McCallister might stop by at some point, but I won't hold my breath. There's also an even slimmer chance that Theseus Gell might drop in for a visit. For now, you just have me," Erin said.

That's fine with me, Colton thought as he carefully lifted the case onto the table. "Well, let's begin, shall we?"

The three sat down around the table. Erin was the first to speak. "I read the request for your visit, and I must admit, I'm at a bit of a loss for how we can help you here. Still, history like this is so intriguing. I was excited just to get the opportunity to see something like this firsthand."

Colton nodded as he unbuckled the leather straps around the case. "I understand you don't have enough information for this meeting, ma'am, but I assure you, this will be worth your time."

Erin gracefully shifted in her seat. "Great! You have my full attention."

Colton took a deep breath before he began. "Okay… I'm sorry, but to give you context, I need to cover a bit of history.

"I hope it won't bother you if I start with what I know."

Erin shook her head. "Of course not, Doctor. We're discussing something you found in an excavation, so that seems to be the best place to begin."

Colton clapped his hands together. Why did you clap? Sometimes, you're a real goofball, he thought. "Okay. We're talking about the sixteenth century here, and there's something you need to know and understand: survival required innovation." Colton's passion for this era showed in the steadiness of his voice. He placed both of his hands on the table and continued. "Think about everything happening: rapid discovery, emerging philosophy, religious revelation, artistic freedom, new lands to plunder, and engineering innovation. The sixteenth century was loaded with significance. Two things we know from this period are that man survived and innovation prospered."

Colton reached into the bag and pulled out a few pieces of paper. The first was a map of Renaissance Europe. "About six years ago, investors approached our company regarding rumors of a series of skirmishes in what would now be northeastern Germany somewhere north of Berlin."

Colton pointed to the area on the map as Erin leaned over to see it more clearly. "Some historical texts found at three different sites corroborated that this was a conflict without the involvement of traditional governments."

Erin looked confused. "What do you mean?"

"One theory was that these were the work of a secret militia created by the Catholic Church to resolve regional quarrels. In this era, the good ol' boys of Rome had unrivaled power, so the money to fund a secret army wasn't out of the question. Another theory revolved around the idea the Moors held some unaccounted-for troops that fled Spain. The last theory involved ominous and powerful secret societies. You may have read books about some of these societies, though with that said, don't believe everything you read." Muffled laughs radiated in the room. Colton used the moment to make a request. "Would you mind if I took a drink of water?"

"Oh, of course. I'm sorry. I should have asked when we came in." Erin immediately stood and poured three glasses, handing them to Colton and Jackson and keeping the third for herself.

Colton took a cool drink. "Ahhh, that's a lot better. Where were we? Oh, yeah. All of these theories had possibility, and, in fact, it was even possible that all of them were partly true. To find the answers, we needed to examine where these conflicts occurred. Not an easy task. Remember, no one had officially heard or recalled these battles. No public records or murals commemorate where these hostilities unfolded."

Erin interjected. "That sounds impossible. How would you even know where to start?"

Colton enjoyed the interruption. "We managed to sleuth our way into some information. For example, two of the texts referenced a castle near the battles. The third text referred to it being south of water near Galenbeck. We studied maps, used satellite imagery, made three trips to the region, and determined there could only be three spots where battles of this significance could have occurred. A fourth was also considered, but political factors made us shy away from the location." Colton flipped to the next page in his pack. It revealed a small region in Germany containing Galenbeck Castle.

Erin shook her head. "That's a lot of work."

Jackson chimed in. "You've got no idea. Thank God for Dr. Adkins."

Erin cocked her head and smiled. "Dr. Adkins?"

Colton continued, "Yes, ma'am. It took Adkins almost a year of negotiation with Germany to allow us to search for this battlefield, and four months ago, we began excavation at one of the sites. Things were going poorly at first, but we stumbled on something... plum huge, actually. And that's what brings us to you." Colton reached into the case, pulled out a set of nitrile gloves, and put them on. He then carefully lifted a moderately sized box out of the case using both hands. "So allow me to show you our amazing discovery.

"All things considered, this is in excellent condition. It's not uncommon to find strongboxes when doing excavations. Generally, boxes like these secure important documents or small items of great value. We've found similar ones on many digs, but this one was unique."

Colton could see that Erin was enthralled with the box as the young executive began examining every aspect of it. He wondered if she was reverse engineering it as she turned to ask a simple question. "You said this one was unique. What did you mean by that?"

"This clever design was more likely influenced by Far Eastern craftsmen over European ones. First of all, the face of the box isn't a door, though it looks like one. It was really an elaborate security mechanism. If one attempted to pick the lock on the top, it would trigger a reaction that would have ignited strategically placed gunpowder packages within the box and destroyed the documents within. Notice the ports on the sides of the box." Colton lifted the box to show the sides, where the intricate carvings of angels blowing trumpets hid the ports.

"These ports provided the oxygen needed to assure a full burn. The gunpowder was encapsulated in sealed containers and, to our surprise, would've probably detonated if it weren't for the corrosion of the mechanical parts. We almost tried to pick the lock, but cooler heads prevailed… well, Dr. Adkins's cooler head prevailed."

Erin giggled.

"We took the box to our on-site lab, used the portable X-ray machine to determine what was happening, and discovered the rear access panel. Our team found the secret to entering the box in the back. It looked like a set of organ pipes with a ridge on the top and bottom holding the pipes in place. The pipes were removable and were six different lengths. Looking at each side of the box, you can see a single hole that allowed one of the pipes to be inserted. Each hole required a specific length of 'pipe' to unlatch its part of the lock.

"If done correctly, one of the sides popped open, and the contents would be undamaged. Other than destroying the box itself, there was no other way to open it." He looked up to see Erin smiling at him.

"Before I talk about what was inside, I'd like to make one more note, if I could. There's also an inscription on the face of the box." Colton pointed to the top.

SOCIETASILLATACITURNADATUM

"This inscription gives us an idea of its origin. Some secret society or order made this box." He paused for a moment.

"What does the inscription translate to?" "Well, it basically translates to 'The Silent Order' or possibly 'The Quiet Order.' "It's hard to say precisely, but this is as close as we could conclude."

Colton continued, "We've dated the box and its contents to the mid-to-late sixteenth century. There's no question about that. The box material, the metals used, and even the etchings are consistent with the era. The box contained two items: a multipage agreement and an item we thought was a piece of intricate jewelry or an ornate pin."

Erin smiled with glee as Colton carefully removed the items from his case. The first item was slightly larger than a legal pad and made on thick parchment. The leather-bound cover was plain but meticulously made. The rivets of the binding were the most ornate part of the face. Each one looked like some sort of seal, customarily found in wax. The other item seemed uninteresting by comparison. It was long and narrow, with three drilled holes at the top of the object. It wasn't remarkable in appearance but seemed to be a functional tool.

Colton pressed on. "Also written in Latin, the document discussed the purpose of their society, and there was a phrase in it that made no sense: 'To silence the change of history.' There was a discussion of another order called Societem ab apis custos, which translates to 'The Order of the Guardian Bee.'

"Evidently, we could conclude that this is the order they are at war with. This thing reads like a manifesto that all of the members signed."

Colton could feel the sweat forming on his forehead and lower back. He gazed at their host, who looked like she was thoroughly enjoying the presentation. He began to dislike even more what was about to come.

"So if we look on the last page, we find the signatures." Colton frowned as he turned the page. He quietly watched Erin's demeanor change from enthusiasm to dread.

Colton cautiously continued. "We didn't think much of the list, but Jackson recognized a few names. It was kind of dumb luck, but he had just read an article about a TxC transport ship that crashed on its way to the Tranquility Moon Base, killing all sixteen occupants. You see, of the sixteen names on that ship charter, eight of them show up on this list."

Erin looked numb.

"There is one more thing. I mentioned the piece of jewelry we discovered. You'll notice the narrow edge on the top near the holes. Other than that, we found no jewels or other valuable components. After examining it more closely, we realized it wasn't jewelry at all but some sort of key. See these channels on the side? We believe the years weren't kind to it, but there was some sort of circuit board capable of fitting in there."

"How can you make this sort of assumption?" Erin interrupted. Her face was neither angry nor anxious but rather curious about how the team rendered such a conclusion.

"Excellent question, Doctor... err... I mean, Erin!" Colton's face turned flush. "You can see the edge that we're talking about, and we found unidentifiable material on the floor of the box, which we now believe to be part of this gadget. What was more telling was when we looked at this key under a microscope, we found something not visible to the naked eye."

His hand shook as he presented it to her.

His hand shook as he presented to her.

Exclusive Property of TxC

Erin looked at it slackjawed. "I don't know what to say."

Like many high-tech companies, TxC devised ways to protect its intellectual property. TxC often etched its name into product components in such way to be invisible to anyone looking at it. They used these etchings in a court of law as proof of their claim of ownership. Essentially, TxC supplied a smoking gun.

Erin regained some composure. "I didn't remember seeing this in your request."

Colton nodded. "We discussed this at length at the office. We wanted to ensure you would hear us out before rejecting this. Erin, we haven't shared these discoveries with our community yet, and I think you can see why." Erin cocked her head. "What are your intentions?"

Colton did his best to defuse the situation. "We're not here trying to catch TxC in some form of cover-up, nor are we here to exact anything from you, but as historians, there is an assumption history remains static. If it's not, we must account for this in our explanations of discovery. We came here sincerely hoping you would shed some light on this and help us understand what we found."

Erin studied Colton for an unnervingly long time. Finally, she spoke. "So, let me get this straight. You made this amazing discovery and have kept this to yourself?"

Colton didn't know how to answer. Eventually, he shrugged and replied, "Ummm… yes?"

Erin was deep in thought. "Would you mind if I left the room for a moment? I need to discuss this with Dr. McCallister."

"Of course. Please know that we didn't mean to shock you with this. There is just no easy way to present something of this magnitude."

Erin emphatically nodded. "I know. I'm just glad we didn't have a whole room of employees when you presented. That would have been a nightmare.

"I'll start by saying we have some explaining to do, but I need to discuss the best way to do that, okay? I appreciate your patience, and I'll be back in a few minutes." She quickly stood and exited the conference room, leaving Colton and Jackson alone.

Jackson watched her leave before speaking. "Wow. That was intense."

"I know. I felt so bad, but I had to present everything."

Jackson looked out the window at the bay. "I don't know how that could have gone any better. You did a great job. It's not like you could look up a how-to on a subject like this."

The two men chuckled, then Colton said, "Isn't that the truth? Do you think I missed anything?"

Jackson shook his head. "No, you covered it all pretty well."

Footsteps approached, and finally, there was a courtesy knock at the conference door. Erin re-entered the room with an older gentleman. "Colton, Jackson, I'd like you to meet Liam McCallister." McCallister shook their hands and wasted no time getting down to business. "Colton, I cannot tell you how I appreciate your team's discretion on this matter." McCallister seemed sincere in his delivery, but Colton's radar was up should any misstep in conversation occur.

"Erin has briefed me, and I agree you were right not to share this news before our face-to-face meeting! I think we can all agree that we owe you all further explanation. However, we need you to sign additional non-disclosure agreements because of the sensitivity of the information. I don't want to put you all in an awkward spot, and really, it would be better to have this meeting in our Chantilly, Virginia facility. So, can we pick your team up at the municipal airport at your convenience sometime in the next few days? We'll also gladly pay for your attorney fees to review this NDA, set you up with rental cars, and fly you home at our expense. I'm sorry about the red tape, and I assure you there are reasons to do it." McCallister was nervous but not out of control.

He stood with Erin, waiting for a response. Erin continued watching Colton. "Thank you, Liam. We appreciate the difficult position this information puts you in. We really scratched our heads about the best way to approach TxC, and here we are. We can have our legal team review the NDA before we sign them, then we'll find a mutually good date to discuss this matter further." Colton was kind and cordial, which put McCallister more at ease.

McCallister quickly inserted another request. "Would you like us to secure the box and artifacts here in our facility?"

Colton's eyebrows raised at the appeal. "Liam, that's very kind of you, but I think we need to hold onto this."

McCallister smiled ruefully. "I understand completely."

Colton and Jackson began to exit the conference room as Erin approached to speak one last time with Colton. "You made an unforgettable first impression."

His body reacted without much thought as he mechanically shook her hand. "Thank you? I hope the second meeting will be much less… umm… theatrical." He smiled as he noticed she looked more at ease.

"Oh! And Jackson, it was nice to meet you as well. You, too, were… memorable." She nodded to him, and he quietly grinned while shaking her hand.

Anton respectfully approached. "Gentlemen, if you would like to gather your things, I can walk you out. Colton, I noticed your bag was somewhat heavy. May I have someone assist you in carrying it out to your vehicle?"

Colton didn't flinch. "No, but thank you. I have Jackson for help!" Jackson turned and looked like the kid whose turn it was to take the trash out after dinner.

Gell's voice echoed again as they reached the lobby, discussing the technological advancements required to make the moon base possible. Anton shook their hands, wished them farewell, as they departed the TxC building. Colton said his goodbyes to Jackson and walked to the parking garage, he could still hear Gell's garbled voice in the lobby. He looked forward to a Gell-free ride home.

On the short drive, Colton found his thoughts pleasantly drifting back to Dr. Warmouth instead of the mystery of the artifact.

CHAPTER 5

THE KRONOS

Two Years Earlier - 2033

The *Kronos* docked in a specially reserved bay with limited access to the base. Kelly and Wilson walked onto the platform as the security entry latch turned from red to green.

Kelly immediately wrapped herself in her own arms. "It's always so cold in here."

Wilson laughed. "Well, we're in outer space. It's really cold just outside that wall."

"Good point."

Wilson turned to see two colleagues standing on the ship's bow, trying to zap each other with the shielding probe. "Look at those two idiots. I told you they'd be messing around."

"Hey, bozos. Have you made it through the freaking checklist yet? Geez, it's like herding cats with you two!" Kelly's tone expressed her displeasure with their shenanigans. Immediately, they stopped and listened to their commander.

The probe tested the complex shielding system on the Kronos. In actuality, it was little more than a low-powered cattle prod. The technician's job involved poking the shield every three feet down the ship's line to verify the protection was fully operational.

Vercelli, the smaller of the two men, said semi-authoritatively, "You heard her, Alex. Get your keister moving!" He was a high-ranking engineer and preferred hanging with the maintenance crew. His slighter build, darker features, and complexion often misled people into believing he was Southern Asian when he was primarily of Italian descent

The comment drew a smarmy military salute from Alex, who chuckled under his breath while looking directly at Kelly.

"You heard Vercelli. You don't want to make me repeat that order. We got a full ship today, and you two are trying to get on my shortlist." Under normal circumstances, Kelly would have cut them more slack, but today's ride included some VIPs who were there to audit their processes.

In addition to the ten-person crew on board, four non-TxC employees and two managers were responsible for ensuring things were done correctly. No one felt the pressure more than Kelly. This mission had to go by the books, and her superiors had sent multiple emails to help her understand the gravity of this situation.

While outside the ship, Kelly and Wilson jointly did their visual inspection of the craft's hull. Their presences also ensured Vercelli and Alex continued doing what needed to be done. Occasionally, one of the two would look back at Kelly and smile or snicker, only to have her gaze suck any joy from their persona.

The *Kronos* wasn't a looker from the outside. She was merely a smaller, utilitarian cargo/passenger ship. Her lines were bulbous, and everything about her was designed to maximize carrying capacity. The designers didn't bother adding any side entry port. All was done through the aft ramp into the lower-deck cargo bay. The main modifications to this mite-class ship were larger engines and an advanced control system. TxC had spent extensive time and money upgrading the craft, but all of the improvements added nothing to the facade.

Despite this, Kelly and the crew adored their quiet giant. Kronos was comfortable on the inside and flew with surprising precision.

When Kelly and Wilson reached the entry ramp, Cody, the copilot, awaited them. "Where are we, Cody?" Kelly asked, looking up at him as he dwarfed her petite frame.

With a wry smile, Cody cocked his head to the left and said, "We're on the entry ramp of the Kronos. Oh, and look, here comes Brandon." The Kronos' chief engineering architect, Brandon Taylor, quickly walked past the impromptu meeting without raising his head or acknowledging anyone.

Kelly watched as he passed and returned her gaze to Cody. "You know what I mean, Simpy McObvious. Did you get my message about having extra passengers?" Kelly's eyes told him she didn't have time for banter.

Cody quickly straightened up. "I did. Why don't they tell us earlier about crap like that? I'm ready to send our flight plans to Control. Subsystems all check out, and some of the crew is ready to go."

"Some?" Kelly's temples pulsated at his comment.

Cody frowned. "Our guests aren't here yet."

Kelly could feel her blood pressure rising. "Oh, of course they're not. Well, if we're running late, it's on them. I'll note all that crap in my logs." She angrily tapped the tablet she was holding.

Cody took a quick glance at Wilson, who remained quiet through the engagement.

Kelly caught the look and continued. "Those prima donnas won't show up until the last second."

She showed more frustration than she wanted, and Cody ran with it. "God forbid that they'd have to do any work."

"Yeah, but let's get everything ready so they won't know some help would've been nice." She patted Cody on the back and continued down her mental checklist. "You know we got sixteen on the ship today? We just need some olive oil because it'll be as tight as a sardine can."

Before stepping onto the craft, Kelly took one more look down the line of her ship. She enjoyed flying, and had fallen in love with her assigned craft. At just over thirty meters long, the Kronos was the largest ship in the fleet that could land in the space stations' outer-ring docking bays. The ship wasn't pretty but could easily outpace fighters in the fleet with her upgrades. It could also return to Earth without external aid, though it required help leaving the atmosphere.

It took ascending two sets of ladders and walking two decks to reach the vehicle's cockpit. For as large a ship as the Kronos was, she had a cramped two-seat cockpit at the front with a blast-proof door that pilots could optionally close. A narrow hallway led through a bulkhead into the general-purpose cabin that included six other crew stations. The central computer system's primary monitor was also located in this room. Stairs led down to the forward cargo bay, which was converted into the science lab for the remaining crew stations. On the far end was the aft cargo bay, which was a full sixteen feet high. Besides a few crates of required materials for all space travel, the bay's space was reserved for the time machine.

The ship was designed to seat ten passengers. Sixteen was doable, but it would make travel less comfortable for everyone. The general-purpose room was close enough to the cockpit that a person could listen to conversations up front if they focused — With the cockpit's proximity to the main hall, there was little need for occupants to wear headsets. Instead, there was a general intercom for the ship that Kelly insisted be as loud as possible.

The *Kronos* only "needed" two people to fly, but because of the nature of the work done, TxC insisted on a crew of ten. Generally, there was a six-member mixture of engineers and scientists running tests and experiments in the cargo bay. TxC sent along two maintenance crew members and a copilot to round out the ship's complement.

As she entered the general-purpose cabin, Kelly called out to the air, "Where are we, CHAMP?"

The monitor on the main computer came to life. "As Cody said earlier, Kelly, we're on the Kronos."

Kelly rolled her eyes. "I don't have time for humor, CHAMP!"

"Sorry, Kelly. We're running behind by fifteen minutes at this point." CHAMP's smooth, even voice emanated from the main speaker on the console. The computer interface on the Kronos was also unique. Because of the mission's complex nature, Brandon designed the Cortex Help/Assist Modular Processor (CHAMP) to be a self-contained access point to the ship's massive computer system. CHAMP could control the Kronos without the need for a crew.

Early "jump tests" required the Kronos to be unmanned. Later runs carried test animals. CHAMP performed exceptionally well throughout these trials. After forty of them, it had proven invaluable. CHAMP's data resources were openly available to the crew, with self-contained search algorithms that didn't need a satellite connection. CHAMP acted as the ship medic and had access to an array of creation tools, like CNC and milling machines, and a 3D printer. As a bonus, CHAMP also turned out to be a good poker player and a heck of a bridge partner.

"I know, CHAMP, I know! Have you run your pre-launch checks yet? Maybe we can make up some time by starting a little early." Kelly followed protocol to the tee on these runs, but that didn't mean she couldn't shave some time off processes when needed.

"I can start now if you would like, Kelly." CHAMP's display came up with a diagnostics page. Though he required no human interaction, they were welcome to watch what he was checking.

"I'd like that very much, CHAMP. Thank you." Her voice drifted slightly as something grabbed her attention on CHAMP's primary monitor.

CHAMP exuberantly replied, "It would be my pleasure."

"Brandon? CHAMP's display has that weird aliasing distortion thing again. Would you mind looking at it?

"Could it be bad power from the station?" CHAMP's monitor displayed a slow-moving band of misaligned pixels. Though it might not be a big deal, Kelly felt it would be nice to understand why it was happening.

"I'm on it." Brandon was the master architect of both CHAMP and the Temporal Rift Computer (TRC). At thirty-seven, his time at TxC was nearing its end. Brandon loved what he did but was tired of management poking their heads into his projects. Jason, one of the managers boarding the flight, was notorious for aggravating engineers. One of his catchphrases was 'just fix it,' which meant he didn't understand the explanation and wanted you to go away and find a solution to a problem. All he sought to do was be able to put a checkmark on a completed task.

At this point in his life, Brandon had two options. He could become the thing he loathed: a manager. The idea that made his blood run cold. Alternatively, he could quit and run his own company, which was way more appealing. His desire to work for himself grew, even after his wife passed away six years ago. Rather than dealing with the grief, Brandon poured even more into his work and planning for his future.

No one really knew what Brandon did on these rides, but they knew he had to be here. Occasionally, he would stop missions for no apparent reason. There would be a long run of colorful language and then a shout to Kelly to take them back. He never bothered to explain much, but if you could put a few whiskey sours down his gullet, he was one of the funniest men alive. The stories and jokes he told were unparalleled.

A voice chimed in from the back, "I'm ready, in case you were wondering!"

"Athera, you were born ready!" Kelly loved Athera. She was always optimistic and happy, and she was smart as a whip. Best of all, she was always prepared. Of the science team, Athera was usually the first to arrive and the last to leave. She took her tasks seriously, and she didn't tolerate loose ends.

At forty-six, she was older than anyone else on the crew and one of the most adored and popular crew members. Her knowledge of modern physics helped every aspect of their flights and research.

"Wilson, can you help the boys with the pre-flight check? They're way too unfocused right now." "You bet, Kelly. Hey! Did you, by chance, get me those treats?" Wilson Ryken served dual purposes on the crew. As the master mechanic, he oversaw the ship's operational status. Retired from special forces, he had served multiple tours in the worst places on Earth. This earned him a second duty on the Kronos as the chief security officer. "Of course, this other job was unnecessary since the crew rarely encountered any danger, but he had been called on to break up a few "disagreements" in the past, stemming from poker games. Wilson was a can-do man who rarely talked about his time in the military.

"Right here, my friend!" She reached into her satchel and threw a small pouch to him with a few assorted treats. As Wilson caught it, the crinkling of plastic packages resonated, and they both snickered.

Her recent trip to Earth allowed her to oblige Wilson's hankering for cheap snacks. Kelly had happily purchased some "goodies" for him.

"Twinkies! The good stuff! You're a jewel. Thanks!"

Out of the corner of her eye, Kelly caught movement through one of the port windows. Four people approached the ship. The internal intercom came to life. "People, the guests are approaching. Remember, smiles, patience, be informative… but not chatty."

Having visitors on the ship was always an annoyance. Four people had joined this mission from another company's secret research facility. TxC wanted to have independent inspectors validating their processes and calculations. It was a bit of a checks-and-balances system. As such, the crew couldn't fraternize with them beyond being pleasant and answering their questions.

"Everyone seems ready. Alex and Vercelli have completed the external checks and are now returning." Cody jumped into his seat.

"Thanks, Cody, you're a good man!"

"That's why they pay me the big bucks!" He smiled and returned his attention to his monitors.

Kelly turned around to find Brandon looking at her, waiting until he got her full attention. "I think I might know what's going on with CHAMP's monitor, but I can't fix it now."

Kelly studied Brandon carefully to gauge the severity of the problem. "Is this a scrub-the-mission call? Because you have also complained about the time drift on the last three jumps. In fact, that's why we have these guests here in the first place. If we're going to call it, I need to know so I can inform Corporate." She was concerned. Brandon rarely approached her, and it was as if he wanted her to call off the mission without involving him. This project was already behind, and each delay pushed it deeper into the red. "I can't scrub this mission unless you feel these problems are big enough.

"It's your call." Kelly wasn't going to let Brandon off that easy.

Brandon clenched his teeth because Kelly was entirely correct. None of these issues were big enough to call things, but he could feel something was off with this run. Maybe it was the pressure or just the frustration of not being done. Everyone wanted to get to the next stage, and each of these missions brought them closer. Another issue was that the science team was making incremental changes to the control laws for the TRC. The last few jumps had had some time drift errors, which worried him.

"You're right. I'll keep a closer eye on things this go around, and we'll address it later this week." Both knew this wasn't ideal, but the team needed to make progress. Yet another scrub wouldn't help anything. If they chose not to proceed, it would be the sixteenth mission cancellation in the past year.

Catching the tail end of this conversation, one of the project's senior managers, Jason Billow, walked into the general-purpose room. He appeared pleasant but most people knew he would throw anyone under the bus to save his own hyde from any mishaps.

"Is there a problem here? I overheard that last statement." Jason and Kelly had run-ins in the past. The idea that Kelly was the boss when he was on the Kronos didn't sit well with the passive aggressive manager.

Kelly spoke up. "No, we have it covered. Thanks for your concern. All right, team, let's start warming things up!" She went on with her protocol, trying not to let Jason's snub eat at her. "CHAMP, set departure time to fifteen minutes. Cody, clear our flight plans with the Control Station."

"Roger that!" Cody began entering the flight plan at the console.

The humming of the engines always comforted her. She sat in the pilot's chair, strapped herself in, and took a deep breath before talking over the intercom, "Okay, team, we're locked and loaded. Everyone move to your stations and stay sharp." Kelly communicated with the control tower, informing them they were ready for launch. "Roger that. Thank you. Welcome to your new job, Keisha. Kronos out."

Cody stopped what he was doing and smiled at the personalized comment. "She seemed nice."

"Yeah, she did. Did you see the look on her face after Wilson's comment? Poor girl. I hope he didn't scare her too much. I just pray that the station is all she hoped it would be." Kelly never looked up from doing her last-minute checks, but her smile was large enough to reveal the dimples in her cheeks.

Cody leaned over so she could hear clearly. "I'm sure she'll be fine."

"Carrie will take good care of her. I do agree with Wilson, though. Run for the hills if you piss her off." The two laughed.

The airlocks of the Kronos closed, and the personnel/cargo bridges drew back. Four tug drones attached to the ship's corners and towed her to the launching point. Kelly began charging up the engines as the drones detached from the ship and the port doors fully opened. The ship's quad plasma drives purred into compliance. The ship left from Unified Space Station New Dallas, launchpad Echo-4. In seventy-five minutes, they would start the next phase of the trip.

With the crew secured for takeoff and busy with individual tasks, no one noticed the flickering second line on CHAMP's main display.

CHAPTER 6

THE MISTAKE

Boston and Chantilly - Fall - 2035

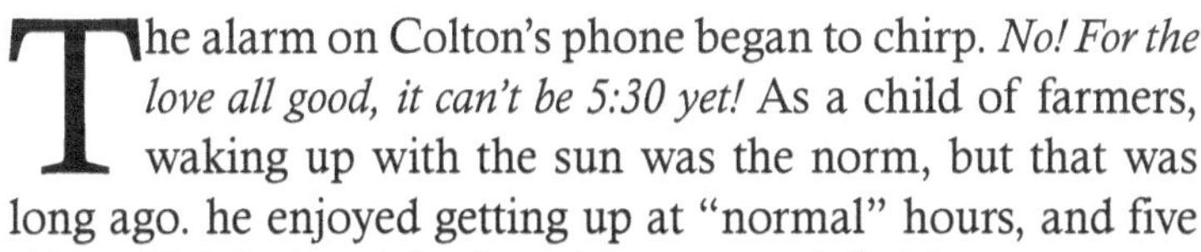

The alarm on Colton's phone began to chirp. *No! For the love all good, it can't be 5:30 yet!* As a child of farmers, waking up with the sun was the norm, but that was long ago. he enjoyed getting up at "normal" hours, and five thirty AM deviated far from his current definition.

He lurched out of bed and headed to the shower. A plane would be there to pick the team up in three hours and take them to the TxC office in Virginia, and he needed to get ready. The thought of speaking with Erin again motivated him to put more effort into his preparation.

Colton showered, shaved, and brushed his hair, taking considerably longer than usual. Before fully dressing, he went to the kitchen for a quick bite and some orange juice. He finished breakfast, returned to his bedroom to brush his teeth, and completed dressing. All that was left was the final packing of his suitcase.

It had only been three days since the last meeting, but it seemed like an eternity ago.

Though Colton and Dr. Adkins talked about what was to come, the next move belonged to TxC right now. Colton had felt his blood pressure rise as they discussed possibilities. Still, Adkins continued to be calm and in control.

With the suitcase packed, he headed out of his condominium. As he walked out of the plaza, someone hailed him. "Dr. Shaw?"

Colton turned to see who it was. A middle-aged man was waving at him from across the street. Colton lifted his head and replied, "I'm Dr. Shaw."

Though the man looked in his mid to late fifties, he jumped down onto the street like a man half his age. He quickly crossed the road and reached out his hand. "Sir, my name is Trevor Mills, and I'm an investigative reporter for the Boston Explorer."

Colton shook his hand but was confused about why this man sought him out. "It's nice to meet you, Trevor. Why were you looking for me, and how do you know where I live?"

"I'm here because I received an anonymous tip that you might be able to help me with a story I'm doing. Investigating is what I do. You weren't hard to find."

Colton snorted. "Me? Sir, I'm an anthropologist and historian. The stuff I work on is lucky to make it on the back page of your paper. It would be buried next to Dr. Xao's holistic solution to remove warts."

Trevor laughed with Colton momentarily. "No, I suspect that wouldn't be very attractive for newspapers, but my source has told me that you have some proof that TxC is hiding secrets."

Colton felt like he was in hot water. "Really? Now, who told you that?"

Trevor smelled blood. "My anonymous source."

Colton raised his eyebrows. "Anonymous. Hmmm. It seems to me like we're at an impasse. You might want to go and get your money back because I really don't have anything to say."

"I get that a lot. You know TxC has covered up so many of their accidents. It's as if they never occurred. One day, some brave soul will speak up. Would you mind if I just left you my card?

"When you realize that you do have something to say, I'd be happy to take your statement." He pulled a card from his coat pocket and handed it to Colton. Colton took the card and studied the name. "Okay, thanks." He opened up his wallet and placed the card in it.

Abruptly, the man turned and walked away.

Colton looked at his watch and realized he was late for his meeting. He quickly scaled the parking garage stairs and walked to his car. The GPS directed him to the rendezvous point for the morning. When he arrived on Airport Road, he spotted the Gulfstream jet to take them to Chantilly. The TxC logo on the tail was anything but subtle.

He pulled his car into the assigned parking area with plenty of time to spare. As he opened the trunk and took out his suitcase, Jackson's father parked next to him and honked, just in case Colton didn't notice him. Jackson jumped out of the car, acting way too chipper for such an early time in the morning. *Some people should never drink coffee, especially before noon.*

"Would you mind giving me a ride home when we get back?" Jackson asked.

"I'd be happy to," Colton replied with a smile. "You know what the best thing about this plane trip is? No security checks. It's really nice not to have to go through TSA."

Adkins had already mounted the airplane stairs. He waved and waited for them before he boarded.

Colton increased his pace until he got to Adkins. Without waiting, he blurted out, "Hey, Percy, can I speak with you a moment?"

Adkins looked slightly surprised but nodded and pulled Colton aside. "What's up?"

Colton looked over at McCallister to ensure he wasn't in ear's distance. "I was just accosted by a reporter who said an anonymous source tipped him off that we had some evidence of a TxC cover-up."

"Those reporters have spies everywhere. I think you should tell McCallister immediately.

"That NDA we signed kind of forces us to anyway."

Colton nodded in agreement. "Yeah, it's unsettling… you know?" Adkins put his hand on Colton's shoulder and replied, "I do. Let's get Liam over here."

Adkins looked over and made eye contact with McCallister, who broke off his conversation with Erin and walked over. "What can I do for you two?"

The subtle smell of lilac briefly calmed his mood. Colton didn't wait to spill. "A reporter approached me and asked for a statement concerning what TxC was hiding. He said an anonymous source tipped him off that I had information."

All humor drained from McCallister. "Did you say anything?"

Colton raised both hands. "Heck, no."

McCallister pulled out his phone. "Well done. They'll jump on anything you say, so be careful with your words. Someone in our group must have talked. I'll let our auditing team know. Who was the reporter?" Colton reached into his wallet and pulled out the reporter's business card. "His name was Trevor Mills."

"Yeah, I know him," McCallister said. "He's a real piece of work. Last year, he posted a story about how we sell weapons illegally to Third World nations. The joke was that one of our competitors made the weapon in question. Never a retraction, no apology. Just another smear with no consequences. We took him to court, and he got off on a technicality. Ever since then, he has been on a warpath. You did the right thing telling me. Now, don't worry about it. We'll take it from here."

McCallister called headquarters and passed on the information that Colton shared.

Leaving behind the conversation with McCallister, Colton decided to talk to Erin. They both walked down the aisle of the airplane.

"Have you ever been on a private jet before?" Erin's inviting smile made him unconcerned with the meeting ahead.

"No, ma'am, this will be a first for me, and what an amazing airplane to start with." Colton checked out the accouterments. Each chair had its own entertainment system, and a small crew tended to everyone's needs. Yeah, it can only go down from planes like this. I remember my first flight." She smiled with a bit of wince.

"Really? Was it bad?" His eyebrows raised as his curiosity was piqued.

"Well, the plane was nice. I was flown to Fort Worth in a Cessna CJ-3, but the ride was a bit choppy, and I ended up reacquainting myself with my breakfast burrito mid-flight."

He laughed in empathy. "Let's hope my first flight doesn't reenact that event."

McCallister walked onto the plane shortly after. He leaned over when he passed Colton. "Don't worry, Colton. My men are looking into this matter as we speak."

Colton looked up at him and said, "Thank you."

Erin looked confused. "Looking into what?"

Colton buckled his safety belt. "A reporter wanted a comment from me concerning TxC."

"Those guys never stop," Erin said with a look of disgust.

"Yeah, it made me uncomfortable, but McCallister said he would address it."

Erin's face grew apologetic. "I'm sorry about that. It happens a lot, and it's always a pain."

Colton deflected. "It really wasn't a big deal."

Erin looked concerned but nodded in affirmation. She patted him on the knee and then fastened her seatbelt.

Colton smiled. Trevor Mills wasn't going to ruin his day or his first trip on a private plane. Looking over at Jackson and Adkins, he realized he was the only one in a suit and tie on this flight. Even McCallister had on a simple sports coat. *Can I ever wear the right clothes for the occasion? Too late now.*

The plane took off, arriving at Dulles Airport about an hour later. The trip to the TxC headquarters from there took under ten minutes.

The limo rode through the TxC checkpoint to a private underground garage, where electric golf carts drove them to the facility's core.

As they approached their destination, they saw Anton waiting for them. Jackson was the first to hop off the cart and shake his hand. "I'm glad to see you again, Anton!" Colton came over and shook his hand as well.

"I trust your flight was uneventful?" Anton's etiquette remained impassive. He walked the delicate tightrope between being friendly and being involved.

"Yeah, amazingly smooth. Have you ever flown on that jet?" Colton asked, trying to make small talk.

"No, maybe someday, though," Anton said.

It surprised Colton to hear Anton hadn't been on the jet. Clearly, he wasn't just some sort of intern but rather a technical envoy. Upon a little more conversation, Anton shared that he had a bachelor's degree in engineering, chose to get an MBA, and was in one of TxC's core management tracks.

Colton concluded that someday, he'd probably see him as a principal spokesman for the company.

"It looks like things are about to start," Anton said. "I can't enter with you, but I'll remain here until the meeting has concluded. If there's anything I can help with afterward, please don't hesitate to ask." Colton nodded but was surprised their high-ranking guide couldn't attend his own company's meeting.

A matrix of small lockers stood near the door to the conference room. The sign declared the company's strict no-electronics policy in this room. Everyone, including TxC employees, emptied their pockets, removed their watches and smart rings, and placed them into personal lockers.

As Jackson entered the door, an alarm went off, and a recorded voice announced, "Unauthorized electronic device." Searching his pockets he realized he forgot to remove his earbuds. A guard quickly came over, took the earbuds, and asked him to walk through the door again.

The guard explained the earbuds would be put with the rest of Jackson's surrendered electronics. Jackson nodded, embarrassed. With no more alarms, the guard permitted Jackson to continue.

When they entered the room, Theseus Gell was already there. His perfectly groomed brown hair, iconic smile, and muscular build were easily identifiable. He rose from his chair and came over to greet the trio personally.

"Gentlemen, I'd like you to meet Theseus Gell," McCallister said, acting as the envoy.

"I'm sorry I couldn't attend the previous meeting." Gell said while bowing his head to the guests. "I heard it was a doozy, and I hope we'll all get some clarity today."

"I must admit our team is anxious to see this through. Thank you for taking the time to make this possible."

Adkins shook his hand and then introduced Colton and Jackson.

Colton mainly observed Gell, choosing to remain somewhat detached from the conversation. Gell's temperament wasn't precisely what he'd expected. Gell seemed relaxed, and there was a hint of a smile in his eyes. His comments were complimentary, and there was no great show of arrogance or bravado.

McCallister looked at his guests and apologetically said, "Gentlemen, we need to talk to our technical team about some last-minute details before the meeting starts. It was nice to see you all again." Gell and McCallister walked away together.

Colton looked around for Erin and found her talking to an older gentleman. Erin glanced over and caught him watching her. All he could do was smile and nod. Fortunately, she smiled back and returned the nod.

This room spoke of functionality. The chairs were comfortable but more utilitarian.

There were computers mounted to some spots on the table, but not at every seat, and one side of the room sported a dry-erase board with some high-tech upgrades. It didn't have the feel of an executive meeting room but more of an engineering meeting room.

Gell and McCallister returned from their brief discussion with the technical team. "Let's get down to it, everyone," McCallister spoke up first. "First of all, we wanted to thank Doctor Adkins and his team for allowing us to have this meeting here rather than in Boston. I believe you'll see the importance of having it here, giving context to your 'discovery.' "I must admit that, as with you, we're in uncharted territory. I think some of this conversation is going to be difficult. Please know we're trying our best to be as forthcoming and transparent as possible, but some of these facts might be insensitive. Let me assure you that this is the opposite of our intentions. We hope you'll see the conundrum we've been in and that you can possibly help us bring some resolution."

Colton was absorbing the gravity of this opening statement. He looked at Gell: The wrinkles on his forehead conveyed his concern with what was transpiring. Colton's mind drifted to remembering the look on his family doctor's face when he tried to tell Colton that his mother wouldn't make it past the evening. Gell's face had similar qualities.

"Before we talk more about this, we must give some historical context. One of our corporate goals is to expand human influence beyond our solar system. Newton's laws make conventional rockets impractical for any type of interstellar travel. There just isn't an easy way around this problem. We were looking for some other approach to break through. There were two main trains of thought here. The first was to find 'wormholes' in space. These only theoretically exist, but many scientists believed there might be spots in space that coexisted in dual locations across the galaxy. In other words, going through these locations would instantaneously put you in another place in the universe.

"We had a team dedicated to discovering such holes, but we haven't found any. Even if found, a wormhole doesn't necessarily get you where you want to be, but rather just to some other location. It would be like jumping on a random flight at the airport. You know where it starts, but where it lands is a complete mystery." Most of the group smiled at the relevancy of McCallister's analogy considering their recent travel.

"Another possibility was the idea of altering or bending time. There are many theories on how to alter time. Most revolve around taking advantage of either the speed of light or extreme gravitational pull. All are elements of the post-Newtonian physics pioneered by people like Einstein and Hawking. Eight years ago, a small research team in Helsinki came to us with a project they claimed could teleport small objects across a room. I could try to explain the physics, but I must admit I don't understand it fully. I'm not alone, though. The TxC scientists rejected the initial proposal because they could see no way to validate this group's claims."

McCallister rubbed his chin and smiled as he continued. "The Helsinki team was persistent. They went away, got private funding from other sources, and returned with a partially working prototype the next year. We now saw the potential, so we put our research team and money on it."

McCallister took a moment to clean his glasses. He was calm and seemed in no rush to finish the story. "In our evaluation of the device, we observed that the object coexisted in two places for a brief moment in time. In fact, the object would arrive at the target before the transportation process would begin. Our team concluded that the object wasn't just being displaced translationally but temporally.

"As promising as this sounded, it only took a few weeks to realize this wouldn't work for interstellar travel. The device, named Kairos, only allowed travel between two local points, and it only allowed travel back in time. Kairos would create a 'tunnel' that, when passed through, would instantaneously move an object to another location and time.

"There was also minimal control over the amount of time objects could jump, but it required a huge amount of computational power to render the solution. Kairos proved that objects could be moved in both time and space. At this point, the furthest we were able to travel back was about ten seconds. Not particularly practical, but still pretty amazing."

He surveyed the room. "Please join me for a walk now." He began slowly heading to the alternate exit.

"We're going to show you the surviving versions of Kairos. This project is considered highly sensitive, so I'll remind everyone of the very complete nondisclosure agreement you signed." His stern gaze met with the eyes of each his employee.

Behind the engineering meeting room were a massive set of corridors. McCallister eased over to a large door, waved a card, and a small console activated. After scanning his face, he made some non-distinguishable comment to which the door opened, allowing everyone to pass. Colton figured it was some kind of oral password or possibly a command to allow more than one person to enter the facility. Security was nothing if not tight. TxC posted warning signs every six feet. They ranged from data sensitivity to information disposal. The archaeological team suffered a little intimidation walking down these corridors, though they understood the reason for the level of security. McCallister pointed at the large signs. "I apologize for the doomsday type of security in this area, but you must understand what we're dealing with. Imagine technology like this getting into the wrong hands." The experts who had gone through training to be allowed into this area sighed loudly at the redundant mantra.

Taking a deep breath, McCallister continued speaking, "In six years, we were able to make Kairos capable of moving a small freighter through time and space. That said, we were at a point where we could see little good coming from Kairos, and there were already plans to end the project."

The group came upon a darkened lab.

One of the team members went to a console and turned on some lights in the main room.

Sitting in the middle of the floor was an unimpressive device. On the side was the name *Kairos-II*. This is our first version of *Kairos*. *Kairos-I* was the Helsinki team's design. We redesigned about ninety percent of the parts from the original one. *Kairos-II* could move an object the size of a baseball approximately ten seconds in time and one hundred feet in space. However, one of the many problems with this design was the heat generated from the tunnel. It caused the unit to break down and made it unreliable. The unreliability led us to *Kairos-III*, which was an even larger disaster. *Kairos-III* was eventually destroyed by an object attempting to move through time. Let's go look at *Kairos-IV*."

McCallister led the way down the hall to a new lab easily ten times the size of the *Kairos-II* lab.

"So, this is *Kairos-IV*. We could transport the first living thing between two points with this device. *Kairos-IV* transported small mice from one place to another. The results were completely successful. No mouse ever lost its life, but this usefulness was questionable. One of the oddest things was to see your mouse appear in the target chamber before the experiment started. It was like you knew it would work before you finished the test. *Kairos-IV* was able to transport objects about one minute into the past. It took *Kairos-IV* about thirty minutes to set up the field, so this wasn't even close to being practical." Colton was dumbfounded as he contemplated how a company could pour so much money into this dead-end project.

McCallister kept talking. "We realized we had multiple problems with this design, many of which revolved around forms of power. The electrical power consumed was too enormous to keep the field constant. Minute drops caused what we described as a temporal drift. These ripples affected the accuracy of the jump's location and time. The second type of power was computational.

"These equations for maintaining the field required unattainable processing power. The last big problem was Earth itself. Apparently, because of positional uncertainty, longer jumps would cause problems like those leading to *Kairos-III*'s demise.

"We began the process of making a cargo ship capable of traveling back in time. We named it the Kronos, and the original design allowed for a fifteen-minute jump backward. With its advanced computing ability, the Kronos created a stable field in about thirty seconds."

Colton raised his hand and said, "You needed greater cooling for the processing."

"Exactly, Colton. A very intuitive observation. Heating wasn't an issue in space, and objects were much harder to run into while navigating through space. Despite our progress, we realized there were still limited applications for this device. The pressure was mounting for the team to find a justification for the project. A few team members believed they could accurately push the time to as much as an hour, which would open some possibilities, so Corporate was willing to fund this a little longer. I want everyone to be clear on this: I made this call. I remember signing the forms to allow the allocation of more money to this project, and I remember second-guessing it back then." Liam's eyes narrowed as he stopped speaking and took a deep breath. "Before I continue, I want to explain something to those who believe I'm overdramatic."

Theseus watched and was about to stand as McCallister continued. "About every two weeks, I'd have breakfast with Dr. Athera Wallace and Dr. Rand Aurum to get updates on the project. I considered them my friends, and I believe they considered me the same. Athera attended my children's weddings, and Rand has watched my son's baseball games. We can argue the semantics of whether they died that day or were displaced to another time. Whatever the reason, they no longer are in my life, and I take that very personally. I feel like I signed their death warrant by not closing the project earlier.

"I want… No, I need to find them, and your team, Percy, has given us the first real clues since their disappearance to where they went."

The words he had just said shook him, and he needed a break. Gell walked over and put an arm around his close friend. "I think this is a good time for a break. I've gotten word lunch is waiting for us, and there's nothing more for us to see here in the lab anyway. If I may be so bold as to ask everyone to return to our conference room, we'll continue this discussion after lunch."

The somber mood set the pace for the walk back up. Few people talked, and even fewer smiled as they entered the engineering room. Colton, Jackson, and Adkins blankly trudged up the corridor to the briefing room. They thought they knew where this was going, but now they were considering the revelations of the past few minutes. For McCallister, this wasn't just business: This was visibly personal.

When they reached the conference room, the smell of Peruvian food overtook their senses. As excellent as their prepared dishes were, it was hard to get their mind around what they had already heard.

CHAPTER 7

SHOW TIME

Two Years Earlier - 2033

W e're at station zero, boss." Cody looked at Kelly as the ship gracefully slowed to a stop. One of the factors motivating TxC to use this class of ship for the *Kronos* was its precise maneuverability and familiarity with the fleet.

"Okay, inform the crew to set up for the jump." Kelly's voice drifted a little as she looked out the window. Kelly always orientated the ship to face Earth for the jump. To her, this view made it worth dealing with anything else.

TxC meticulously planned some of the preparations, while others evolved from trial and error. The ship's ID beacon became an issue on the first flight of the Kronos. While in the testing phase with an unmanned crew, the station's defense system nearly destroyed the Kronos on its maiden jump. Two instances of the Kronos appeared for five minutes until the Kronos made its initial jump into the past. The doublet sent the nearby space station into high alert— and for good reason. During the war in 2028 with China, the Chinese had developed a type of stealth technology to steal a ship's ID beacons and then use a cloaking device, making them look like the ship whose ID they had just taken.

As the second *Kronos* ship appeared out of nowhere, the defense system began arming its countermeasures and was preparing to fire on the new entry. Fortunately, the team contacted the base and gave a plausible explanation of what had just happened. Moving forward, the Kronos carried two IDs: one for coming and one for going. All stations were made aware of the circumstances and given a credible reason why the double ID occurred. While some commanders were wary of the explanation, none made an issue.

"You're on, Brandon!" Kelly called over the intercom.

Brandon unbuckled himself and went to the Temporal Rift Computer (TRC) to build the time gate. He looked at the expected time: thirty minutes.

"CHAMP, can you verify the software version currently in the TRC?" Brandon asked, since verification always kicked off the first step of the jumping protocol.

CHAMP quickly responded, "Yes, Brandon, this version was uploaded by Dr. Wallace one hundred and sixty-two minutes ago. It is version five-point-one-two-four, and I've verified the CRC against the CRC in the version control database."

"Thank you, CHAMP." Brandon returned to his tasks.

The interface glowingly responded, "My pleasure, Brandon."

Brandon smiled at the reply. One ongoing joke very few people got was CHAMP's voice. Brandon derived the voice module from HAL's voice, a self-aware computer in the movie 2001: A Space Odyssey. Brandon smirked whenever CHAMP said, "I can't do that…" One time, David Carter was on the ship when CHAMP responded, "Sorry, I can't do that, Dave." Brandon couldn't stop laughing for five minutes.

With a couple of presses on the touch panel, TRC ran the solving matrix to make the jump portal. The COM came alive with Brandon's voice. "I've started shutting down all of the external sensors and communication systems for the jump, and TRC is working on the solution. We're trying a thirty-minute jump today! The longest one yet.

"You have about thirty seconds. It's time to turn the ship over to the TRC." Brandon sat back down. Once active, the ship had approximately sixty seconds to go through the portal before it collapsed.

Kelly pushed the "TRC AP" button on her flight panel to put the ship in autopilot mode. The TRC would create the portal and then launch the ship as fast as possible to fly through it, at which point it would change the ship's ID. All of this happened in a fraction of a second. It was faster than a human could react, requiring CHAMP to fly the craft.

Cody looked over at Kelly and said, "So you know every one of these jumps is shortening our life by that jump time, right?" He always had a unique way of looking at things. "When we get back, I think we should get this control column looked at. The slop is getting pretty bad."

Kelly shifted the controls slightly. Sure enough, the column had a fair amount of play in it. "We'll get Wilson to look at it when we get back." Kelly returned to focusing on her duties when the ship's radar alert began blinking wildly. The reflections from the constructed gateway looked similar to a solid wall on the radar, and the ship was warned of an imminent collision. Then she heard the engines spinning up. "Here we go!"

Brandon chimed in on the intercom, "Hey, Kelly, has anyone heard about the doublet?"

Looking over her console, she noticed a blinking COM light on Cody's side. "Cody, you got a message."

Cody checked the console and pressed the message button:

NO SECOND SHIP PRESENT. ABORT MISSION.

"Abort! Abort! Abort!!" Cody yelled and reached down to press the 'TRC AP' button to give control back to the pilot, but it wouldn't disengage. Cody knew that there would be no turning back once the engines started. He pressed it again just to make sure. "Too late! We're in for the ride! Nothing we can do. Be prepared for emergency maneuvers on the other side, Kelly!"

Kelly immediately placed her hands and feet on the flight controls. Her heart fluttered with anticipation of the unknown. She looked at the control panel for any indication of a problem, but the board revealed nothing. She pressed the "Master Caution" button to stop the radar alarm from complaining about the imminent collision. The cockpit remained eerily normal: no strange noises, nothing out of place. Everything looked acceptable. The ship's nose had already crossed the gate. In a fraction of a second, the jump would be over.

CHAPTER 8

THE CONUNDRUM

Chantilly - Fall - 2035

McCallister regained his composure, but the expression of grief remained in his eyes and forehead. "I apologize for my 'lapse' back there. I consider all of these projects my family, and I take them all very personally. Dr. Adkins, I'm sure you can see where this is going at this point.""I've got a question," Colton said. "Does the government know about this?"

McCallister cleared his throat. "The short answer to your question is no. But NASA and the Office of Space Affairs have sent us some queries." McCallister liked the question because it cut to the chase. Governments swooping in and taking control of projects like this were a common trope in movies and literature. Like Colton, the idea of whether the government should know about projects like this had crossed his mind many times before. "Other than the team from Helsinki and some borrowed scientists and engineers from a close sister company, no non-TxC employee even knows about the existence of these devices. You three are joining a small list of people. There was an incident that raised the attention of the military concerning having the Kronos appear twice on their tracking systems.

"We convinced them this was new stealth technology, and the proof was that one of the ships disappeared after a short time. Other than this little snafu, this project remained black to all but those working directly on it.

"I know you all have more questions, so don't worry. We'll answer all we can, but if you allow me, I'll continue." He looked again at the three, and all of them nodded. Pausing momentarily to recollect where he stopped, his features soured. "The project was failing, and lower-tier managers realized it was only time before funding would be cut off. Survival instincts must have been kicking in. They began to press the science team for more 'impressive' results.

"By this time, human trials were already underway for the Kronos, and everything was working pretty well. We had done six manned missions when the science team started adjusting the equations in what we called the 'Temporal Rift Computer' or TRC for short. The team successfully expanded the time from fifteen to twenty-five minutes. That said, there were some anomalies in the equations. For instance, on the thirty-seventh mission, the craft's position drifted about five kilometers. The position was okay on the subsequent two missions, but the time jump was off by about five minutes.

"It seemed each iteration or change in the TRC calculations brought new instabilities. The TxC management team watched each of these jumps closely at this point. When jump number thirty-nine resulted in more erratic behavior with time, our board made the difficult decision to cut the program and destroy most of its technology. Just like you, we were concerned this could get into the wrong hands and be a vehicle for weaponization. We've already had enough deaths this century. So, taking this out of the equation seemed like the right thing to do. I had the termination papers on my desk, ready to sign. One more thing bothered us. As far as we knew, and as strange as this might sound, no one from the future had come to warn us that our project was either helpful or dangerous. We concluded that this meant there was no future for the project. No pun intended."

He spoke with an unexpected passion as his temples pulsated more with each passing comment. "Three more jumps were already planned, and we felt it better to allow them without informing anyone on the team. This was the end, and we planned to reassign the team to other projects.

"The week following mission number thirty-nine, two scientists approached management to discuss a significant improvement that might be possible in time control. They analyzed the jumps, looking for the source of the anomalies. They found inversions in one of the fundamental calculation matrixes. The error was present since the start of the *Kronos*, not just on the last three missions. The equations were correct in the code used for *Kairos-IV* but somehow got changed in *Kronos*. "The scientists believed the anomaly explained why *Kronos* worked well in short jumps but grew unstable in longer ones. "Despite this revelation, the project was still dead. We believe someone in management got wind of the approaching termination. We don't know who or how this information leaked, but we know managers began pressing their team for more results. Mission number forty was the first mission in Kronos with the corrected matrix. The science team tried to push the time gap further to keep up with the past missions. In this case, they were aiming for a thirty-minute jump. It was ambitious but not impossible. Because of the mathematical error, the science team brought in four 'observers' from Chellos, a company we often use to validate findings. TxC vetted these four, and we'd worked with them before. Our group knew of their excellent work and high integrity." He paused again, looking down at the floor, then sipped some water.

Colton's teeth clenched as his attention became laser-focussed. "On June third, at eight forty-seven AM EST, the Kronos departed from one of our space stations. It took the ship forty-five minutes to fly to the staging point for the jump.

"Because of this technology's security, we informed the space station that this ship was performing cloaking tests, which would explain why two instances of the same ship might appear in a sector. Getting a report from the station saying they could track both ships was customary. The young officer on duty with this responsibility didn't realize the importance of relaying this information. "The control station was our last safety check."

McCallister carefully stopped his train of thought to explain his last statement. "Imagine you were taking a test, and the professor administering the test could tell you whether the answer you were about to give was right or wrong... even before you answered the question. Would this help? If it were a molecular biology exam, it might only help marginally, but if it were a true/false test, it would result in a perfect score. The message was that they saw the two ships, giving independent verification of the test even before completion.

"So, the Kronos arrived at the launching point at nine thirty-five AM EST. The station would have relayed the message that two ships were in the area. No one explained to the young officer at the control station that relaying a single-tracked ship was more important. The message arrived late to the Kronos at about nine thirty-six. We suspect they were already into the jump sequence when they got it. "According to the station, they received an acknowledgment message. By nine thirty-eight, there weren't any ships to track at the jump location." He surveyed the people in the room.

Adkins, Jackson, and Colton listened intently. They could envision the tragedy playing out before them, knowing the inevitable ending and hoping for a different one. Adkins grimaced at parts of McCallister's story. Young Jackson stayed very still and quiet. Colton was finding it even easier to fit their piece into this puzzle.

"We've been in scramble mode for the past two years on this. One of the main scientists was on the crew, while the other was in the lab. We've looked for the Kronos.

"We've tried running models based on the algorithm to determine where the Kronos went in time. The models all indicate they should still be with us right now. It wasn't until you contacted us that we had any idea where, or more correctly, 'when' they were." McCallister looked at Adkins with an expression of gratitude laced with resignation.

"There had to be a plausible cover for the loss of so many lives. We already had much of that story worked out. All the men and women on the Kronos knew the risks. Family attachments became a factor in choosing our crew. "We put extensive insurance policies on each of them, for what it's worth, and they were given the choice of where the money should go in the event of their death. We, as a group, quietly mourned their passing. We flew six pastors and about twenty surviving family members to the moon base to have them pray over the staged crash site. No one could see there weren't any bodies in the ship because we'd opened a tiny nuclear waste canister, preventing anyone from getting too close.

"Gentlemen, I assure you I take no pleasure in the fact that we had to cover up these deaths, and I find no solace in it either. I've stayed awake at night, trying to figure out what we could've done differently to prevent all this. If I had a time machine, I'd have returned and prevented us from starting this project. I wanted to show you one more thing. It shouldn't be of any particular surprise to you."

Reaching into his sports coat pocket, he pulled out a box that looked like a case for a pair of glasses. Slowly, he opened the case to reveal what was inside. "Colton, this key module is an uncorroded version of the one you found in the strongbox." His hands shook as he lifted it out of the case, handing it to Colton. "A key like this controlled the *Kronos'* computer system."

McCallister looked at Adkins. Adkins' eyes showed that he felt the sincerity and gravity in McCallister's remorse. All he could do was nod slowly in acknowledgment of his pain. His body language conveyed the completion of his story, but this meeting wasn't over yet.

Colton studied Erin, who had avoided making eye contact with him the whole afternoon. Based on her response, he suspected she wasn't aware of the entire sequence of events. She seemed as shocked at the story as him and his two friends.

After Gell tended to McCallister, he continued speaking. "I hope you can see the predicament we've been struggling to solve. We've spent considerable resources in an attempt to find them and try to rescue the crew. Until your visit last week, we'd assumed the worst, that they'd died. I want to convey to you something, though. Since last week, we've talked at length with our team. "Knowing the approximate jump date may help them pinpoint what went wrong with the Kronos." Theseus stopped and checked on McCallister. He seemed to be more relaxed now as he listened to Gell's words.

"Unfortunately, I think you could surmise that the time machine design is strictly a one-way trip. With the technology we possess, we can't save the crew in the sense of bringing the Kronos back to 2035. But that doesn't mean we can't possibly communicate with or help them. We have some thoughts on this that we can discuss later." Theseus turned to Adkins and waited until he believed he had undivided attention.

"I don't know what you think about me, and honestly, I don't care. I know the kind of reputation men like me have. If you must know something about me, I don't abandon my faithful. I'm asking for your help. I'm offering you all jobs here at TxC. We'll pay you generously, and you'll have our considerable resources at your disposal.

"I'd like for us to discover the rest of their story. I believe it'd honor the crew to see their impact on our history, if any. We don't have the capabilities to do that in-house, but I believe your group does. I hope you can track their path and bring clarity and closure to this issue. You won't be supervised or second-guessed, but I believe you can help us do what's right for this crew. Please help us and our friends." He was about to end when another thought came to mind.

"Oh, and if you don't want your reputation associated with corporate attachment, we could arrange to hire your company as consultants. All of these same resources would still be available to you. I'm not trying to bribe you here. I'd fully understand if you said no and walked away." Colton evaluated Gell's words and body language. The visionary wasn't negotiating, nor was he manipulating. The request was a call for any aid he could find, and he believed Adkins could provide benefit and insight.

CHAPTER 9

HONEY, I'M HOME

Late Summer of 1530 - Day 1

Jumping always gave Kelly an uneasy feeling. For a heartbeat, complete disorientation reigned, and all her senses canceled. Then everything normalized, and her awareness reset and carried on. That said, she was anything but relaxed. She gripped the controls so tightly that her knuckles blanched white. Drops of sweat trickled down, and her heart throttled in her chest.

She looked down at the control panel to see if something had failed. The 'TRC AP' button flashed amber, which generally occurred after the jump sequence completion. All the controls behaved, though some warning lights changed from amber to red.

There were multiple red flashing warnings now: **GPS SIGNAL LOST, SATELLITE COMM LOST, TRACKING REFERENCE LOST.**

Kelly studied her display, trying to make sense of it. She found her voice to prompt Cody, "We must've broken our antenna array. Let's bring the ship to a complete stop until we can sort this out." Her mind spun as she considered what was happening. *Maybe this is why the ship never showed up, and they couldn't transmit.*

"Wilson, Alex, I need you up front, pronto!"

Kelly barked over the intercom just as Cody poked her arm. "What, Cody?" Kelly continued to look down at the blinking lights when Cody poked her again. This time, she looked over at him.

He was calmly looking out the window and pointing to Earth. She looked outside. Slightly off-center but in full view was her home. "Yeah, that's Earth, Cody. So what?" She came off irritated because she was. *We've got misbehaving screens and all sorts of other mayhem, and this guy just wants to stare out a window.*

"There are no lights," he said.

"No lights where? Are the external lights out, too?" She tried to get a handle on Cody's cryptic comment.

"No lights on Earth." His very matter-of-fact reply suffered from any indication of emotion.

Kelly looked out the window at the planet again. Even though it was nighttime in this hemisphere, there were identifiable natural landmarks, such as peninsulas like Italy and Florida. What was missing were artificial lights. The sun lit up Asia, but the land didn't radiate with man-made light. It was as if the entire planet was suffering from a blackout.

"What in the world?" Kelly said. Just then, Wilson and Alex joined them. "Wilson, what do you see out there?"

"Earth!" Wilson answered sarcastically. The comment came off funnier in his head than when he said it. He leaned over and squinted, thinking he was supposed to be looking for something near their ship. Then Earth caught his eye again. Something was different, and it took him a moment to figure it out. "No lights!"

"No lights," Cody repeated.

"What does that mean?" Kelly was trying to make sense of what they were seeing. *Why would there be no lights on Earth?* she pondered. *Maybe a nuclear bomb was set off?*

Wilson scratched his head. "Got me, boss. Did you call us up here for something?"

"We've lost all communication. Can we check to see if our antenna array has been damaged?"

Kelly went on trying to solve what she could. "Give me five. We can check it from cargo bay two," Wilson said as he and Alex headed aft.

"Wilson, check the ship for any other damage while you're at it," she shouted down the hall as the two darted off.

Brandon showed up next. "Hey, what's going on? It feels like we've stopped moving."

"Yeah, we're looking into things right now," Kelly said. "We've lost all communication. Satellites, the moon bases, and Earth are all dead. Go tell CHAMP to look around and see if he can find something." "Where are the lights?" Brandon looked out the window at the dim Earth.

"There are no lights," Cody said.

"We don't know where the lights are. Let's just solve one thing at a time." Kelly got on the intercom. "Ladies and gentlemen, we're experiencing technical difficulties, including lost communication with home base. There's no need to worry. We have plenty of fuel, food, and oxygen. As far as we know, the ship is still flying fine. You're welcome to get up and move around. We're hoping this won't be too long." After switching off the intercom, she asked, "Hey, could our shield be filtering the light from Earth?"

"Yeah, possibly," Cody said. He was the only one left in the room.

The intercom came to life with Wilson's voice. "Hey, boss, the antennas are good, and the ship looks fine."

That made no sense at all. Kelly unbuckled and headed to the general hall where Brandon's workstation resided. "Brandon, I can't figure out what's going on." She had an edge of concern in her voice.

Brandon stared ahead in disbelief but was able to say, "CHAMP, can you tell Kelly what you just told me?"

"Certainly, Brandon! Other than natural phenomena such as radio frequencies, I can detect no intelligent RF anywhere. I started a visual analysis of the planet using the front cameras. I don't have the resolution to pinpoint the exact date, but I'd estimate this is Earth in the mid-1500s.

"I've based this on a few man-made landmarks found in Europe. Notre Dame, for instance, is present, but the Arc de Triomphe isn't, nor is the palace at Versailles. I've located about twenty-two other castles and can't locate another six. The progression of castles leads me to conclude somewhere near AD 1525 to 1535. I'm sorry, but I started in France because this is where the camera happens to be pointing. If you would like, I can expand my analysis beyond this."

"Umm… Err. Yeah, CHAMP, see if you can narrow it down some." Kelly's head was spinning with CHAMP's information.

"Kelly, you don't look good. Would you like me to provide you with some water and an aspirin?" CHAMP asked.

"No, CHAMP, thank you." Kelly sat down next to Brandon, thinking about what this meant. Her eyes widened with the revelation. "Brandon, I think we're trapped."

CHAPTER 10
IF YOU CAN'T BEAT EM...

Chantilly - Fall - 2035

"Theseus, this is a lot to digest," Adkins ventured. The situation both overwhelmed and intrigued him. The request for his team's assistance made sense. Before all these revelations, Adkins had already discussed different possibilities or scenarios with Colton and Jackson. But hearing these words coming from Gell himself was unexpected.

"You're asking us to drop our current endeavors to find these few individuals. Also, what do you think we can do? We're not physicists or mathematicians. I'm an engineer, but we're academic historians."

"Exactly!" Gell said. "What if history was speaking to us? You found this strongbox, and now a whole new world of possibilities has been opened to you. Could this team have wanted someone to find the strongbox? What if they left clues through time, allowing us to track them and their effect on history?" Gell impassioned them.

"What good would that do?" Colton interjected. The situation seemed pretty hopeless. "Mr. Gell, you didn't lie when you reported their deaths. They are dead now, and this is our reality.

"I'm thankful they didn't die on the date you reported, but our discovery makes them no more alive today."

Gell frowned. Though Colton was right, he wasn't looking at the whole picture. "I'd like to find out how they survived their predicament. Did they live full lives? Was their knowledge of technology put to use? If they thought to leave this box, isn't it possible that they might have left more for us to discover? Did they affect history? "I think we need to track them and find their 'artifacts' before others do.

"If it makes sense to you, maybe we can learn more about the two orders mentioned in the document. Then we might understand better what's going on. Are the names unaccounted for part of the other order? I can't imagine why they'd be at odds with each other, but it would help if we knew more, don't you think?" Gell had mastered the art of rewarding a person's ego and having them believe that, somehow, his vision came from them. In truth, it always partly came from them, but Gell was helping it come to the surface. He wanted Colton to believe in the value of this endeavor.

Colton put up no resistance and nodded, which relieved Gell.

"I don't know about you guys, but I'm in," Jackson quipped, unable to contain his zeal. "Time travel, history, advanced technology, secret orders, spy stuff, and some detective work. Sounds like one sweet adventure."

Adkins looked at his men and gave Colton a smile that conveyed he understood that they all wanted to help. "I believe we want to help you, but it would be wrong of us not to take some time to ponder what this looks like for us and our work. Beyond us, we have six more on our full team. I'd like to include them. It's Thursday. Can I meet with our team tomorrow to discuss options? At the onset, I think it would be easier for you to hire us, but honestly, to keep secrets of this magnitude, it would make more sense for you to make a historical department in TxC and hire us to man it."

Gell's excitement grew at the response and possibilities.

"Thank you for being so understanding. Take some time. We'll talk more next week."

"I have one more question before we go." Colton looked at McCallister and Gell. They projected confidence regardless of the curveballs thrown at them. "So we know that two ships would appear when the Kronos jumped back in small increments. How do we know this is the first or only time this five-hundred-year jump has been made? Is this a one-time thing, or has this happened repeatedly?"

No one knew this answer, but it made for a good place to end the discussion. Each group committed to deliberate this more. Anton appeared to escort them out of the building.

Colton left the meeting physically drained. By now, his tie was off and in his pocket. He didn't remember doing that! They rode in the limousine to the hotel for the night. About ten minutes into the ride, Colton realized he hadn't talked with Erin before leaving. Mad at himself, he sat quietly, looking out the window.

"Any of you up for dinner tonight?" Jackson asked.

"I could eat. I know of a great steakhouse near here. My wife and I used to go there before…" Adkins's voice wandered off. Cancer is a cruel opponent, and Carol Adkins succumbed to her long fight three years earlier.

Colton looked over at his friend, thinking of the ordeal Percy endured. "Carol was an amazing woman, Perceval. I think she would love for us to eat there, even if it's just to honor her memory. I miss her too."

Adkins smiled, overwhelmed with emotion. He did his best to suppress the tears—not sharing with the others that he hadn't returned to their favorite restaurant since Carol died.

"So, it's settled? What time, guys?" Jackson asked.

"Six thirty. I'll call and make the reservations," Adkins quickly added.

With the time settled, Colton went back to staring out the window. Lost in his thoughts, he was startled when his phone vibrated. It was a number he didn't recognize. *It's probably some scammer, but whatever.*

"Hello?"

"Colton? This is Erin Warmouth."

Colton looked over at Adkins and Jackson. Should I be talking to her? He decided to take the chance.

"Hello. We didn't get a chance to talk today," Colton said in a lower voice, hoping the other occupants wouldn't figure out who was on the other line.

"No, I'm sorry about today… well… all of this. I was wondering if you'd like to join me for dinner. I promise not to dwell too much on this, but I wanted to say a few things."

"I'd like that," Colton said. "But we just made dinner plans. Could I interest you in breakfast in the morning?" Disappointment overtook him, but he didn't want to back out of dining with Adkins.

"No, I'm leaving tonight. But that's okay. When we get back to Boston, we can try at another time." Erin was also disappointed but not surprised. Such a late invitation was a bit of a long shot. They both hung up, and Colton quietly looked out the window again, but this time with a bit of a smile.

"Why don't you invite her to dinner with us, Colton?" Adkins sprouted a grin.

Colton looked a little stunned. "What? You think we wouldn't notice?" Adkins said.

"We're detectives at heart, son. Call her back and invite her."

"Umm, okay." He picked up the phone and called Erin.

"Hey, Erin. I was wondering if you would like to join us for dinner. We're eating at one of Percy's favorite restaurants, and you'd be a welcome addition."

"Really? I wouldn't be intruding, would I?" Her voice couldn't mask her excitement about the prospect.

"Are you kidding? We've all heard each other's stories a million times over. It'll be nice to have someone else tell some new stories or endure some old ones." His smile came across the phone. "We're meeting at six o'clock in the hotel lobby to travel over if you want to join us," he added, hopefully.

"I'll be there. Casually dressed?" He caught the little joke in her honest question.

"Most definitely. I need to get out of this suit, pronto!" Chuckling, he said goodbye and hung up.

Adkins and Jackson sat watching Colton, smiling and saying nothing.

"What?" Colton's mien was that of a young teen caught sneaking out of the house at night.

"You have great taste, son." Adkins smiled, then went back to reading the newspaper from the door pocket of the limousine. Colton smiled and then made sure to add Erin's name to his phone contacts.

"I wonder if she has a sister?" Jackson stated plainly.

Colton was about to place his phone back in his pocket when it vibrated. He quickly pulled it out and looked at the notifications. His shoulders slumped in irritation as he read the text.

Hey Colton, this is Trevor Mills again. I just wanted to connect and remind you that I'm here if you want to get your side of the story out. You're free to text me at this number.

Colton quietly cursed as he set his phone to block this number. This bastard is a real ballbuster. The irritation lingered for a few minutes but slowly dissipated as thoughts of dinner with Erin overtook his mood.

CHAPTER 11
THE WAITING GAME

Late Summer of 1530 - Day 1

ow in the heck is that possible?" Quinton Riggs shouted from the back of the room as Kelly did her best to contextualize their situation.

Riggs was a bit of a wildcard in Chellos Corporation. Wildly brilliant but equally prone to fits of rage, Chellos had promoted him twice into upper management, only to demote him back to engineering in a few short weeks because of confrontations with the people under him. Yet he was too valuable to let go. In fact, in the last demotion, they chose to keep his salary and benefits at the upper management level in hopes he wouldn't leave. The extra money suited Riggs just fine, and he continued to work in their R&D department.

With all sixteen crew members, the large cargo bay seemed very small. The tension building in the conversation reached a disconcerting level. In the background was the soft purr of the stabilizing engines and the environmental regulators. Typically, this sound comforted the crew, but today, it heightened the friction created by their predicament.

"Quin, I'm no happier about this than you are," Kelly said. "CHAMP is pretty certain we're stuck in the sixteenth century, around the year 1530. And, when I say stuck, I mean stuck.

"We all know that our time device can only go backward. There's no possibility of moving ahead using this device. Athera, is that true or not?" Dr. Wallace studied the people around her. They were looking for hope, but her words would not provide such sustenance. "You're correct, Kelly. If we wanted to, we could try jumping further back in time. I estimate we could possibly make two more jumps with our current power, but since our last jump was supposed to be only thirty minutes, I'd be hesitant even to try."

Kelly quickly retook the conversation. "So, we're pretty much stuck in the sixteenth century. Welcome to our new reality, so denying or complaining about it isn't helpful. We must develop a plan soon because this cargo ship has limited supplies. We have a couple of problems that we'll have to address."

Kelly was unafraid to push back against Quinton. They'd had their share of run-ins, but she knew he would listen, even when he was angry. "We have no home base to go to, which isn't a big deal because we can land wherever we want. The problem is we don't have land-directed control bringing us in. Translation? CHAMP will have to fly us in without positional reference, and Cody and I can only watch.

"Brandon believes CHAMP can do it, but entry without external navigational references hasn't been done in over ten years… um… You know what I mean. It'll be rough, so we'll need to do some things to protect the ship during reentry. This process includes removing the antenna array and locking down the blast windows. We'll have to fly without visuals until we land."

Kelly kept her delivery unemotional, but the looks of hopelessness from the group dismayed her even as they reflected her internal feelings.

"The next issue is that, much like our jumps are one-way trips, the trip down is also one way. Once we commit to going, we're stuck in the sixteenth century… probably forever." The last word resonated uneasily.

"This is why we need to protect the antenna array.

"If TxC manages some sort of rescue attempt, we'll need to contact the rescuing party. According to CHAMP, our SOS beacon can keep transmitting for at most seven years. So, I don't know everybody's background here, but does anyone here have significant historical knowledge?"

One of the Chellos employees raised her hand. "I've got a minor in European history." "What is your name?" Kelly felt embarrassed that she only knew Quin's name from their team.

"Aecha Kyong." Aecha Kyong was a Korean national. She survived the first wave of Chinese aggression that pushed American forces off the Korean Peninsula. Escaping in the middle of the night in an abandoned fishing boat, her family fled to Okinawa, Japan, where the Navy base collected Korean refugees. One of six children, Aecha eventually came to the United States and studied as a physicist. Her hobbies always drew her to reading about history and playing strategy games. She ended up with a minor in history as a result.

"Aecha? Yes. We'll need help understanding some things beyond what CHAMP can tell us about this era. Is there anyone else who can help?" Kelly knew enough to realize the more information they had before landing, the better.

Wilson reluctantly lifted his hand. "I know a good bit about the Reformation. My parents were church history professors at a few different Bible colleges."

"Wilson. Good! Anyone else?" Kelly scanned the room, looking for any more hands. Sadly, no one else spoke up. "Well, I'm sure we all know bits and pieces to contribute to decision-making."

The room remained somber, as Kelly kept talking. "So, this is a fun fact. We carry viruses that can potentially kill off large portions of the population. How can we solve this problem, or are we doomed to keep to ourselves for the rest of our lives? CHAMP, do you have any thoughts on this?"

CHAMP was quick to respond. "Yes, Kelly, I do. I think it'll be okay. Modern immunization methods address what made explorers from this time contagious, so my references say that we won't spread sickness to the people we're in contact with.

"To be safe, the team should be re-immunized with our onboard synthetics. We'll need to gather resources to generate other immunizations. That will take time, but it isn't imperative to have them soon. TxC required immunization in order for the crew to be allowed on the space station. I also think our interactions will be challenging. Humans have become accustomed to very clean foods in our time, and foods here will carry much more disease. After two weeks of quarantine, the crew should be safe to interact with others from this era. In that sense, we're far more susceptible to getting sick than spreading sickness."

"Well, that's good to know. Okay, how many sci-fi people do we have here?" Kelly looked around the room, and about three-quarters of the hands were raised.

"Yeah, I pretty much figured this. So, we're in uncharted water here, but I figure this subject has come up many times in the sci-fi world. What does everyone think about interaction with people? For instance, I remember the prime directive in Star Trek, but that's probably a lame example. What are some of your thoughts?"

"Well, what effect will we have on what we knew to be true?" Dr. Wallace chimed in. "Based on our collection of time jumps, we know time is just like a thread that keeps going. So, has our presence here affected history as we know it?"

A few murmurs from the others filled the silence.

Wallace continued, "We all know and have read about the butterfly effect. Suppose we rely on CHAMP for information and make minor changes to the course of history. In that case, as precise as it was on our timeline, all of CHAMP's historical knowledge will become increasingly inaccurate as the moments tick by."

"Maybe we're part of this history and always have been," Quin interjected. "In which case, CHAMP's accounts will remain accurate. We don't know, and I don't know what we can do to prove or disprove any of this because we, too, are trapped in history now."

"You bring up great points, Quin. What if history has already accounted for our presence here?" Dr. Aurum said. "Maybe our insertion here was always part of history." Kelly realized the conversation had become theoretical rather than practical. "Everyone, these are all great ideas and questions. I think we can figure some of this out when we get down there. At some point, I think we'll have to destroy the ship and say goodbye to the twenty-first century. We can't just hide it. Can you imagine the alien visitation theories if they came across this ship in the twentieth century? You'd have people with tin-foil hats coming out to contact the mother ship."

Kelly's joking put them at ease. But it was only a brief diversion. "Sorry to get back to the matters at hand. Based partly on what you all seem to know and the availability of some amenities, I think we should find some remote place in Europe or possibly a remote place in Wales or Scotland to hide. We speak a form of English, so landing in Britain could lessen the learning curve. We could build a small community and stay somewhat self-sufficient and isolated. Most of us could blend in, and the rest we could protect. I'd love to hear some other thoughts."

Voices erupted around the room.

"Australia or New Zealand would be my picks, but you make a lot of good points for Europe. I'm good in Europe, too."

"They didn't speak English until the 1700s!" someone else countered.

"America is out unless we went to the west coast, and even then, it would be pretty rough living."

"Asia is ruthless at this time, so I'd agree about Europe. The Scots and Welsh know their land too well for us to just hide, so I'm reasonably sure continental Europe is our best choice."

"Hawaii or Fiji would be awesome for a time, but I don't think we would enjoy the hurricanes, volcanic activity, or tsunamis. I'm good with Europe."

"I think we need to be, more specifically, in northeast Europe, northwest Poland, or northeast Germany.

"The weather is unpleasant, but there are forests, mountains, rivers, game, and some distance from the more heated wars of this time."

The chatter continued for ten minutes, but almost everyone agreed northern Europe would be the best bet.

"Well, it sounds like we're booking a flight to Europe," Kelly said. "I wonder if CHAMP can figure out an ideal place for us to set up base."

"Okay, Kelly, northern Europe is the best choice. I've three possible sites that I'd be happy to tell you about," CHAMP said, listening and ready to comply quickly.

It's too bad that CHAMP is a computer, Kelly thought. He seems like a nice guy.

"Thanks, CHAMP. We'll get back to you on that," Kelly said.

"We have much more to figure out, but this is enough for now," she continued. "We should stay up here a couple more days just in case they try to rescue us. We have some work to do to configure the ship for reentry, then we can head down to our new life. This sucks, but we have to make the most of it. We're not the victims here; we're the overcomers, which means we deal with everything thrown at us with poise and control. While we're up here the next few days, we'll have to get a little creative with sleeping arrangements, but foodwise and everything else, we should be good." Kelly did what commanders do but knew this was just the honeymoon. While challenging work instills unity, it can only last so long. Someone will inevitably think, Yeah, fine, but I could have done it better. She concluded that the group could form a non-totalitarian government later because they had plenty of candidates for the positions. For now, this responsibility fell on Kelly.

The group dispersed with a combination of angst, fear, curiosity, and even some optimism. Kelly sat quietly and pondered the conversation for a few moments. Not too bad for having your entire universe rocked in just a few hours. She sighed and returned to the cockpit.

CHAPTER 12
OLD STORIES

Chantilly - Fall - 2035

olton was the first to enter the lobby. "Okay, guys, I'll see you here around six. Percy, are you going to contact RoboRide?"

"No need, Colton, TxC has already given us a vehicle. It's in the parking garage here. You're welcome to it if you have any errands to run before dinner. We have three hours." Adkins pulled the key fob from his pocket. "It's a nice car too. So very different from the pieces of junk we usually get. McCallister gave me the keys when we were walking out."

Colton looked at Jackson, and they both shook their heads. "I think we're good. See you both in three hours."

Colton immediately walked into the lobby, checked in, and headed to his room. He happily shed the suit, replacing it with a stylish silk button-down shirt and slacks after a long hot shower. The day wasn't hard work, but it was grueling nonetheless. Mentally weary, he sat on the sofa and listened to some music. Quietly relaxing as he contemplated what they had learned today, it rejuvenated him.

None of the men could mentally escape the information presented to them. It was right out of a novel, and its surrealism was vexing.

As he relaxed, his mind turned to the text they'd found in the strongbox. He wondered who had written it and what the point of putting it in the box was. He also thought about what happened to the other crew members. But the Latin text drew him. His mind kept going back to the translation of the words. There was a single phrase he was unable to shake:

praetorium temporis

The phrase translates to "the hall of time." The team had assumed the inserted text was a poetic metaphor, but now it didn't seem like a literary device. In the context of today, it meant so much more. Colton focused on what he could remember from the writing. He went to reach for his laptop, but the charger was still in his luggage bag, and he knew his battery was low. Rather than get up, he chose to rest and collect his thoughts. *What if this message wasn't a message of affiliation but rather a message to us for today?* The wheels in his head spun rapidly until his alarm cheerily chirped at him. His phone showed that it was five fifty. Time for him to meet up with everyone.

He arrived first in the lobby and searched the area for Erin. To his disappointment, but not unsurprisingly, Adkins walked in first. He nodded to Colton, looking pleasant but distracted.

"*Praetorium temporis?*" Colton blurted out hesitantly, yet loud enough for Adkins to hear.

Immediately, Adkins looked up, his eyes widening with surprise. "Yes! I see you were thinking the same way I was." He looked relieved to not be alone.

"The phrase kept sticking in my mind," Colton said rather abruptly. "When we get back to the office, I think we need to scrutinize the text."

Adkins' face beamed and his shoulders broadened as if expressing that he couldn't agree more.

Colton turned to see Erin walking through the hotel's front doors. He admired her modest outfit: a knee-length jade-colored dress, tasteful pearl necklace, and matching earrings.

Colton considered her attire the perfect fit for the occasion. He took a deep breath at seeing her, and the noise caught Adkins' attention. The young man mustered a grin and turned to approach her. *I wonder if I even have a chance with her. Colton, she's so out of your league.* His thoughts weren't comforting, and it showed in his demeanor.

Adkins subtly gripped Colton's arm. "Wait for her to come over here, Colton. You don't want to scare her off."

"Okay, point taken… DAD!" Colton said with a smile that Adkins reciprocated.

There was a double ding from the elevators. Jackson eagerly stepped out, looking around the expansive lobby. Colton waved him over as Erin approached.

"You are most brave to join us, Dr. Warmouth. Thank you for accepting Colton's invitation," Adkins said, warmly welcoming her.

Colton took mental notes. In another life, Adkins could have been a U.S. ambassador. He always seemed to know what to say.

"You all were quite chivalrous to allow me to join you. And please, call me Erin. Whenever I hear 'Dr. Warmouth,' I want to look around for my dad."

Everyone laughed.

"Did you drive here, or did you get a ride?" Adkins asked.

"No, I drove one of the company vehicles."

"Oh! Well, I've got a request. I made reservations for the four of us at six thirty. I looked at our car, and I think the backseat is somewhat cramped. Erin, I wondered if you wouldn't mind driving to the restaurant? Jackson and I'll drive together, and Colton could tag along with you?"

Colton watched as Adkins offered the suggestion. To his recollection, the car Adkins told them about wasn't small. Then he understood what his friend was doing. *This guy is one smooth operator!*

"Yes, I'd be happy to drive. Can you give me the address or the restaurant name?" Erin turned to Colton, both sharing a smile.

"It's called The Ferris. It's a steakhouse with excellent seafood, though my wife preferred their lamb. The place is maybe twenty minutes from here. I hope this choice is okay with you." "The Ferris. Got it. And yes, it sounds wonderful." Erin entered the restaurant's name into her phone. "Okay, I found it! I think we're ready to go."

As they left the lobby, Adkins winked at Colton, who couldn't help but give an audible snort, making Adkins laugh.

CHAPTER 13

THE WAITING GAME

Late Summer of 1530 - Day 3

"CHAMP, what about something like a compost toilet?" Wilson queried.

"That's a possibility and an excellent short-term solution, but a drain field is a better overall answer. It won't be as hard to make as it sounds."

"Okay, can you print out some plans and procedures?"

"With pleasure, Wilson."

The Kronos remained in orbit for three more days as the crew made two spacewalks to remove the antenna array and secure the windows.

As Kelly walked through the ship, she noticed groups huddling and making plans. Despite the initial shock of what occurred, the entire crew was engaged.

Cody walked up to Kelly and nodded in the direction of three scientists. "Take a gander at the Triumvir over there. It looks like they've laid out an entire strategy, complete with illustrations. Maybe they're planning a hostile takeover for world domination."

Kelly pushed back. "Cut it out. They are friendly people if you get to know them."

Cody's lips puckered as he shook his head.

"Lisa and Brett are for sure, but Rand only talks to smart people. I need not apply."

Dr. Rand Aurum, the team's head mathematician, was charismatic, calculating, and rarely wrong. The lack of emotion hid an incredible love of music and his ability to play many conventional instruments. Rand insisted that any trips outside his office included the Jadec siblings, Brett and Lisa. Brett was a brilliant mathematician/physicist, and his younger sister was an equally brilliant astrophysicist. Kelly affectionately referred to these three as 'The Triumvir,' and they grew to like it. There were also rumors that Lisa and Rand were dating.

CHAMP hailed her. "Kelly, I've considered every factor you've given me and believe I've found a suitable spot in eastern Germany to set up our base."

Kelly cleaned her hands as she listened. "Great, CHAMP. Can you tell me about it?"

The computer gracefully replied, "I'd be happy to tell you. The location is southeast of the modern 2033-era Brandenburg Air Force base. There's an uninhabited castle that should work for short-term housing. The location is deep in the forest, and a moderate-sized river runs nearby. From observing the activity around the location for the past two days, no human life is within four miles of the target area. There's a small village, Gamburg, of about twelve hundred people situated five miles south of the camp, but there's a bog between Gamburg and our target. It's unlikely they will expand in this direction. The land is currently part of the Holy Roman Empire, and I see a very low probability of habitation in the next fifty years. The density of the forest will make the main potential prospects to finding us hunters or the occasional fisherman. I believe it meets all of your criteria."

Kelly thought about the information and asked, "What sort of government will we expect to deal with around there?"

CHAMP took a moment to reply. "That has a multifaceted answer.

"If you're found squatting on the king's land, you would be, at best, banished, but more likely put to death. Eventually, you'll have to figure out how to acquire land legally from the kingdom. The king is Charles the Fifth, and you would have to deal with Henry the Fifth, the Duke of Mecklenburgh."

Kelly pumped her fist at the news. "Well done, CHAMP."

CHAMP glowingly responded, "I think so."

Kelly could hear Brandon chuckling at CHAMP's smugness from the other room.

CHAMP also provided information regarding survival in the area that needed to be shared with the crew. Aecha was tasked with this job, and she took it seriously. "We'll have to learn a few languages in this region. Low German will be a priority, as will Latin."

"What about all of our tech? Are we just going to abandon it?"

"Well, getting a signal for our phones will be hard." Aecha's comment brought a communal laugh. "I think, over time, we'll have to remove technology from our camp, but initially, we can use it to set things up. We don't have much time until winter, so it only makes sense to take advantage of our knowledge to get things running."

Brandon spoke up. "I think we'll have to abandon a lot of the gadgety tech we've grown accustomed to, though there are a couple of items we need to mark 'essential' as exceptions to this rule. CHAMP will be invaluable to us for getting us situated. I know how to move him off the ship." Bandon knew there had never been a time that the crew needed CHAMP more than now.

"Wilson could do something similar with the communication array. He can keep CHAMP and the radios running for a long time using a combination of solar and hydroelectric power. We could also use some of the other computers for spare components, storing the parts in dry, sealed boxes that are in the cargo bay."

Wilson nodded in acceptance of Brandon's assessment.

"Okay, everyone, I think it's time for us to commit to going down. Sadly, no rescue team has come for us, so we must make it to the ground and survive. Are we ready?" Kelly looked around at the group. Most of them acknowledged they were ready. A few stared blankly.

"Well, our friend CHAMP has found a good location. This area has an abandoned castle, but don't get your hopes up. "It's just a three-floor building with some potential gardens within a wall. It'll be nothing like what you see in movies, but it'll do for an initial coverage of the weather and will give us a good starting point. There's a stream with fresh water and ample game for us to hunt and eat. No one has lived there for a considerable time. It'll be in serious disrepair, but we should be able to get it up and going rapidly because we're motivated.

"We're going to have a large learning curve, doing a lot of things that, up until now, were taken care of for us. The start isn't going to be easy, but I know we can do it. Fate gave us a life sentence, not a death sentence. Let's make the most of it, okay?" The speech was Kelly's pep talk to herself as much as the crew. She knew she would need many more of these in the future.

"Now for the bad news," she continued. As if everything isn't bad news right now. "I'm not going to lie. The ride down is going to be rough. We must secure everyone in their seats with extra harnesses for safety. Everyone will need to get up and move when we land, so I want you all prepared. We'll open the back cargo bay door and exit the vehicle. When we exit the ship, we'll gather to assess what needs to be done next."

It was very fortunate that the Kronos was a converted cargo/personnel transport. All vehicles traveling to the moon base required four essential parts: a solar power collector, a hydroelectric power collector, an air/water purifier system, and a well-stocked medical deck. The cargo bay contained a myriad of harnesses, tarps, winches, and pulleys.

All of these parts would become essential elements in their initial survival. "As you know, CHAMP will do the honors of bringing us in. I don't like to admit it, but he flies better than Cody and me combined."

"Thank you, Kelly." CHAMP was always listening.

"You're welcome, CHAMP. By the way, CHAMP, are there any last-minute instructions from you?" Kelly always thought it was weird to talk to a computer like it was a person. Still, Brandon had done a fantastic job giving CHAMP a great conversation and dynamic social algorithm

"No, not really. Everyone, I'll do my best to land us. I'm very confident it can be done." CHAMP ended his comments, and she broke up the meeting with a prayer. Some people smirked, but even the most agnostic in the room agreed they needed a greater power more than ever.

The crew assembled at their stations as Alex and Wilson helped secure the passengers for reentry. Kelly and Cody prepared the main cabin door in the cockpit and then strapped themselves into the pilot and copilot seats.

With everyone secure, Kelly spoke one last time over the intercom. "Okay, everyone, we're ready to go. I'll turn the helm over to CHAMP, and we'll be on our way!" Knowing the trek ahead was dangerous, she looked at her copilot. "Cody, you're a great friend. Thanks for everything."

"Aw shucks, Kelly, you're gonna make me blush." He grinned, and she wasted no time smacking him in the back of his head. Cody was like a sibling to her, and the sentiment was mutual. They both played their parts well.

With the front windows completely covered, the cockpit felt even more confining. Kelly made every effort to ignore her discomfort. "CHAMP, it's time for you to take us in." She timidly took her hands off the flight controls.

"Okay, Kelly. Thank you. I'll call out where we are in the process as we go along."

The control panel lit up with activity almost immediately, and the ship began the smooth transition forward.

"Kelly and Cody, I know you'll want to put your hands on the controls during this process. Please refrain from doing so. The margins for error are microscopic," CHAMP said with a hint of humor in his voice.

She looked at her copilot and nodded. At this point, the two were mere spectators on a harrowing ride.

"We'll enter the earth's atmosphere at Mach 25 and seventeen thousand knots. When this occurs, the ship is going to experience some violent vibration. "We'll be covered with positively charged plasma created by air molecules breaking apart from the heat surrounding our ship. Don't worry. Our shields will protect us both physically and thermally." CHAMP explained this so matter-of-factly that it helped put Kelly at ease.

"People, brace yourself. Here's where it gets bumpy," Kelly announced over the intercom. She looked down at her control panel, and the main display changed to a simplified screen with the words Manual Reentry flashing in red. Her heart raced, and her neck felt tighter in her flight jacket. Was this supposed to happen?

CHAMP responded, "Kelly, your control panel changed to the Manual Reentry display. The flight computer automatically does this, but I'm still flying." Her calmness returned.

The ship's nose lifted moments later, and the Kronos began to shake violently. The vibration's magnitude caused a shelf of technical pamphlets, user manuals, and logging charts behind the copilot seat to break and spill it's contents over the floor. All they could do was watch and brace themselves for the rapid deceleration.

As the shaking continued, the Kronos audibly complained through creaks and groans over the tasks CHAMP asked it to perform. Tiny cracks of light appeared through the front window. Kelly and Cody scrutinized them, worrying if this would grow larger with the heat.

Small items were falling and rattling around the interior down the hall from the cockpit.

A metal box of locking bolts fell on Wilson, and he spewed out a choice string of cuss words to commemorate the occasion.

Kelly looked down. The left hydraulic pump had a warning light illuminated in amber. "CHAMP, do you see the warning light?"

CHAMP responded immediately. "I do, Kelly, and I'm trying to address it as we speak."

The few seconds of no response were killing Kelly. Then, the amber caution light transitioned to a red warning light. Before Kelly could speak, CHAMP said, "Kelly, I'm going to need you to do something." Kelly was all ears. "What can I do?"

"I believe the hydraulic pump is overheating because of the thermals coming through the environmental regulator. We need to close that port so that the pump can cool down. We don't have much time, so you must manually crank the wheel to the left of the circuit breaker panel. Have you located it?"

Kelly looked and found the wheel. "Yes. So I need to crank it clockwise?"

CHAMP answered, "Yes. All it should take is about two turns."

The request would be simple under normal flight conditions, but with the violent shaking, reaching the wheel and turning it didn't prove easy. Kelly tried to move, but the accelerations held her in her seat. She finally reached the wheel, only for it not to budge as she tried to turn it.

CHAMP noticed it hadn't moved. "Kelly, I need you to turn that wheel immediately."

Kelly screamed, "I'm working on it!" She grabbed the wheel with both hands and twisted it with all her might. To her relief, the wheel broke free and turned.

CHAMP noticed the change. "Excellent job, Kelly. I can take it from here."

It only took a few seconds before the panel indicator turned from red back down to amber.

Kelly asked the million-dollar question, "Are we good, CHAMP?"

CHAMP remained silent longer than Kelly expected. "Yes, Kelly. You saved the day. The pump will remain amber, but the redundant system will cover the shortfall. In the meantime, the shaking is about to increase in amplitude."

As predicted, the shaking increased in the deceleration. CHAMP spoke again. "We're going to be doing some maneuvers to slow us down. They will produce side forces moving you around in your seat. Hold on tightly and don't worry."

The Kronos began performing S-turns, slamming the occupants left and right in their seats. Then the nose turned up rapidly, pushing them forward and down deep into their padded chairs.

The rest of the crew held their composure during all of this. An occasional scream erupted, but the team sat in silence for the most part with each bump, shudder, and turn. Some closed their eyes, some sat praying, and all waited for the violent actions to subside.

This collection of maneuvers seemed to take an eternity for the crew. Eventually, the shaking dissipated as Kronos leveled out. They were now flying at two hundred and fifty knots, well under Mach 1. There were no sonic booms to draw attention to the ship at the current speed. This silence was necessary because the Kronos flew low enough to be visible to the naked eye. The crew discussed this and concluded that it was unlikely the Kronos would ever fly again unless a rescue team showed up in the next six months. Whoever saw this object flying very high in the sky would have discounted it as a shooting star or just some kind of high-flying bird. The crew wasn't concerned.

"We have about an hour until we reach the target site. We won't have visuals, so I must fly to our landing point. I'll need you to re-open that port again, Kelly, or this cockpit will get very cold," CHAMP explained, to which Kelly quickly complied.

"Understood, CHAMP. I'm glad you were flying and not me."

"Thank you, Kelly. I am too."

"Okay, folks, we're through the worst of it," Kelly said over the intercom. "If you want to unbuckle yourselves and walk around, I think it would be safe to do so. We have about an hour until we land." Crew members began clapping and cheering.

Kelly looked down the hallway as she marveled at the ship's ability to survive entering the atmosphere. Her mind drifted back to her first few weeks of flight training and how the excitement of the moment overtook her sense of fear. Remembering one of her fellow cadets vomiting as they practiced emergency reentry drills, stiffened her. At the time, it brought giggles, but now she realized that his dreams were shattered that day, bringing her heaviness. The following day, he applied for and was granted a transfer to a ground unit. Well, Kelly, there is no way to transfer out of this job. Grimaces followed as her mind continued to wander.

"There's no feeling like being a copilot of a copilot. Do I get any credit for this landing? No matter, I don't think we'll need recurrent classes to keep our pilot's licenses this year."

Kelly retorted, "Well, Cody, now that I think of it, I guess I'm getting a permanent transfer to the ground. I just didn't request it." The two pilots laughed wryly as they realized they were saying goodbye to their careers.

CHAPTER 14

THE BOARDROOM

Chantilly - Fall - 2035

Theseus Gell sat at the head of the boardroom table. The circle of men and women around him ran TxC. Looking down at the agenda, all items were completed. Scanning the room, he said, "Ladies and gentlemen, that was the last issue. It's a pretty short docket tonight if you ask me. Are there any ad hoc items that anyone would like to add?"

Kevin Anderson could barely wait until Gell finished to interject. "I want to discuss this Adkins' Historic Preservation Company."

Gell dryly responded, "Yes. Dr. Adkins and his team found an artifact that belonged to the Kronos team."

Kevin looked down at his notes. "I heard about their meeting. There were some interesting fireworks there. Have you found a way to silence them?"

Gell looked confused. "Silence them? Do you mean to sign an NDA? Yes, I've got them signed and in hand. If that's not what you meant, would you care to elaborate?"

Kevin removed his glasses and looked at Gell squarely. "That's not what I meant, but at least you have that in place.

"This room isn't the place to elaborate on such things, but we can't have it become public knowledge that we rigged a ship on the moon and faked the deaths of sixteen people. Wouldn't you agree?"

Gell shifted forward in his chair. "What are you suggesting we do?"

Kevin looked at the other board members, who remained non-committal on the subject. After a brief pause, Candice Deckert chimed in, "Theseus, if you don't find a way to squelch this, it could cost our company billions of dollars."

Kevin continued, "Also, I'm looking, and I see that we're in the process of dismantling the technology for the Kronos. Shouldn't that have come across the board's plate?"

Gell tilted his head. "How so?"

Kevin looked slightly irritated. "I mean, couldn't we use that technology on other projects? You arbitrarily chose to shut it down without our consent. Do you realize how many billions of dollars we've committed to making that work? Also, we've spent hundreds of millions trying to determine what went wrong with the Kronos, and now you just want to tear it down. Oh, and you're perfectly fine with entertaining these archeologists and their new discovery? Am I missing something here?"

"This technology was cataclysmically dangerous," Gell responded. "We've already lost sixteen people as a result of its uncertainty. There's no way we wanted that technology to leave this company and be used for someone else's plans. It's the right call, and I stand by it. As to the archeologists, they came to us, not the other way around, so get off my case, Kevin."

"Is that your call to make?" Kevin retorted.

Gell paused momentarily before answering. "The Nobel Prize was created because the inventor of dynamite didn't want that to be the first thing people thought of when his name was mentioned. The technology in the Kronos has the potential to be far more devastating for our company and for humanity.

"It's too dangerous to pursue, and my first allegiance is to keep our company safe. Yes, I made that call, and you would have, too, if you were in my shoes."

"Theseus, we probably would have agreed, but you didn't even give us a chance. I find that disappointing," Candice said. "You're right about it, though; that is your call to make. However, I think you have a board like us for a reason. Wouldn't you agree?"

Gell nodded in acknowledgement. "I see your point. I'm sorry if this made you uncomfortable. I'll try to consider that in the future."

Candice looked surprised at Gell's admission. "It's not like you to just acquiesce without a fight."

"This isn't a fight. I value all of your input. I want to switch gears slightly. I'd like to discuss Liam."

"What has he done now?" Kevin replied.

Gell shook his head and said, "Nothing at all. I'm worried about the strain of the Kronos event on his mental well-being. Since the disappearance, he hasn't been the same, but these meetings with Adkins' team have bolstered his morale. If for no other reason than helping him out, please humor me and allow me to do what I think is best here. I think the results will help TxC and Liam."

The members looked at each other. Most nodded in support of Gell, but Kevin remained reticent. "I'm okay with this, but I'll closely monitor where this is going. I don't think I need to remind you that if they chose to divulge our secret, it might be a mortal wound to TxC. It would be up to you to explain to Chellos what we did with their four missing engineers. You understand that, right, Theseus?"

Gell looked down at the table before answering. "Kevin, if you met Dr. Adkins, you wouldn't worry about such things. He's a good man, and so are his people. They'll help us, and in doing so, they'll help Liam."

"That may be true, but know that you have a short leash on all of this. For the time being, I want this added to our agenda.

"Any information or updates should be passed on to the board. Is that reasonable?"

Gell studied Kevin for a beat longer than expected before he replied. "I'll add that to the agenda, Kevin, and I'll pass along more information. Is that satisfactory?"

Kevin nodded, but his grim expression told Gell more. "That is adequate."

Gell tried to calm his irritation and decided he couldn't let that comment slide. "Do you have any more suggestions to make it more than adequate?"

Kevin leaned back in his chair with a satisfied look on his face. "No, what you have proposed is sufficient for me. Is everyone else good with this?" He scanned the other members, who seemed to be trying to stay out of the firing lines between these heavyweights. The room remained silent.

Watching Kevin's reactions, Gell was convinced he enjoyed getting under his skin. Gell resisted the urge to bite back. "Well, with no further discussions, I think we should move to adjourn the meeting." The ensuing look of disappointment on Kevin's face brought Gell some comfort.

CHAPTER 15

NEW DIGS

Northern Germania - Summer of 1530 - Day 3

anding in three minutes," CHAMP called out.

"Okay, everyone, take your seats and buckle in. Our final landing is coming up." Kelly said over the intercom. *Three minutes until we begin our new lives*, she mused. Using its hovering thrusters, the Kronos touched down in a small clearing in the middle of the forest. It sank slightly into the ground and rested nearly level.

"Open the bay doors, CHAMP," Kelly said.

"Sorry, but I can't do that, Kelly."

A laugh drifted from Brandon's general area. Kelly glanced over, wondering what was so funny.

"Why not, CHAMP?" Maybe something broke during entry… though Brandon wouldn't laugh about that.

"Wilson secured the latch, so he must manually open it before I can bring the cargo bay doors down."

"Right." Kelly chided herself for not remembering the obvious.

"Already on it, boss." Wilson jumped up and headed to Bay Area One.

"Okay. Great. Thanks, Wilson!" Kelly assessed the ship's condition. Regardless of anything else, CHAMP once again came through, landing them perfectly where they'd planned.

The few hills near the landing point offered themselves as repurposed dirt. Though it was late summer, the fresh water still flowed with ample strength to support the generator.

Kelly thought opening those bay doors symbolized the start of their new life. It was as exciting as it was scary. Fittingly, the sun crested the hills when they opened the doors to their "new" world, greeting them with a bright red sky.

"CHAMP, that was an excellent example of flying! Thank you! Unfortunately, this will be your last spaceflight as well." If she sounded overly appreciative, it accurately conveyed how she felt.

"Thank you, Kelly. It was a pleasure, and I guess we'll all need to find new jobs."

The doors slowly opened. Wilson walked out first to assess the situation. The woods surrounding them reminded him of his childhood home in New York. In the distance, deer cautiously drank at the stream. He noticed a few fish jumping as well. He inhaled the first taste of fresh sixteenth-century air.

Later, he confided in Kelly that the opportunity to see the stars at night excited him the most among the things he thought about with their new life. The light pollution had tainted the wonder of lying down and looking up at the heavens everywhere he'd lived on Earth. The space station offered unparalleled views, but you could only see them through protective glass. This unfiltered view exhilarated him and he exhaled slowly.

"I don't see any evidence of humans, and I don't see any predators," he declared, easing down the ramp.

The crew started trickling out. Shock turned into smiles for many as they emerged on a lovely, peaceful summer morning. The forest was a hearty green. The air felt cool on their skin, and the chatter of small animals and insects tickled their ears. The cloudless sky and mountains rising beyond the forest cried for a great photo opportunity, yet none of those things mattered any longer.

The group walked out, untethered by technology and enjoyed the planet's natural beauty.

"Okay, this has been quite a couple of days," Kelly said. "We have a lot to do, but I think we should enjoy the morning before we go too hard at it. Well, except for the antenna array and the S.O.S. beacon. Can we get those up as soon as possible?" Kelly looked at Alex and Wilson.

"We're on it! The rest of you enjoy your morning," Alex said, half-joking.

"Thank you. And sorry," Kelly replied with an apologetic smile.

"Wait for me. I'll help," Vercelli said. He joined his friends with collecting tools and the antenna array.

The trio completed their initial tasks in less than an hour. Wilson also unsecured the blast doors on the ship's front, just in case they needed to move the Kronos again.

"Kelly, we've only got about twelve weeks until the cold begins," Cody said. Growing up in the northwest, he knew about the realities of frigid winters.

"Yeah, and we have a lot to do. At least we can leverage some of the tech in the Kronos to speed all of this up." She was worried but determined not only to survive but also to thrive. In her heart, she wanted to ensure they gave every effort to carry on with excellence.

At noon, the group gathered for tasks. The commander wanted to delegate more responsibilities quickly so every decision didn't fall on her. For the short term, she saw them living in a situation where food and fortune were communal, and labor division fell upon people's specialties. Their government would be a council with some sort of rotation. But until it was all organized, she would have to be the icon out front.

"Okay, we have a fascinating problem here. Most of us are on this ship because, in some capacity, we're leaders in our fields of expertise. For this reason, we have the potential to have too many cooks in the kitchen.

"I neither think I'm the best leader nor think less of any of you. I've been taking charge on account of I was the ship's commander, but I don't think having this in the long run is healthy.

"We're off the ship now, and I'd like us to consider how we want to run things. For now, I'll keep us focused, but once we have our basic needs taken care of, I'd like us to begin to set up some form of government. So, I ask, can everyone live with this arrangement for a while?"

She scanned the crowd. Most heads were nodding. With the consensus of affirmation, she continued, "Well, okay. I'll do my best not to screw this up too much.

"I think housing and bedding should be today's priority. We need to start doing a couple of other things, like getting with CHAMP and determining the best place to make a refuse repository. We must also find the easiest way to gather food and collect fresh water."

"For tonight, we can eat fish," Cody said. "I can catch enough for everyone." He grew up in the woods. Watching the fish jump assured him he could probably catch ten or so without equipment.

"Really? That sounds great."

"Can I join you?" Gretta, the fish farm advocate, stepped forward. Though she was thirty, her childlike face and petite figure got her carded every time she tried to order a drink. The corners of her eyes squinted when she talked, which made her endearing to almost everyone. She also sported a nimble intelligence in engineering. Her specialty was modeling the physical phenomena in closed-loop systems. At heart, she was still a bit of a tomboy and loved doing the same things her older brothers did. "I had a stream like this by my house growing up. I can help."

"I'm Cody," he reminded her as he reached out to shake her hand.

"Gretta's the name. It's nice to meet you, Cody, officially." She shook his hand. The two walked back into the ship to get a cargo net, twine, and a cooler.

The two strolled out a few minutes later and headed to the inviting stream. Both Wilson and Kelly observed their progress and were content with the prospect of discovering new friends.

"Wilson, you want to take someone and check out the castle? It's about three hundred feet that way." Kelly pointed over one of the mounds.

Wilson evaluated the situation. "I can do that. Jason, why don't you come with me so we can examine it together.?" He figured removing one problem was a massive favor to Kelly, and he could put up with the project manager for a few hours.

Jason's eyes lit up at the idea of not having to do manual labor. "Sure. What do I need to bring?"

"Nothing, really. I just want to ensure I have someone slower than me in case a bear is hiding there." Wilson looked at Kelly knowingly. It was all she could do not to burst out laughing.

"Umm... you don't think there are bears, do you?" The manager looked a little worried and couldn't tell whether Wilson was teasing or being truthful.

"We had lots of bears in Kazakhstan," Alex said. "They'd go into smaller villages and take people. They can smell fear; it drives them into furious rages."

"Guys, this isn't funny. Now, are there bears or not?" Jason asked.

"Yeah, but they probably won't bother us. Just in case, here's a knife you can carry." Wilson gave him his pocketknife. It had a six-inch blade and a comfortable grip. "You know how to use one of these?"

"I'll manage, thanks." Jason grabbed it and clenched it in his fist.

"I want it back, Jason! That's my favorite... no, wait... that's my only knife." The realization struck Wilson hard enough that he paused momentarily to consider the loss. *My drawer of over thirty knives, and now this is it. There's no chance of turning back, even if I wanted to. This whole thing sucks in so many ways.*

The thoughts stiffened Wilson's lips as he worked through them in his mind.

"I'll take good care of it, Wilson."

"Okay, let's go." Wilson started walking. Jason clumsily followed behind him. On his way out, Wilson high-fived Alex for piling on to his bear story. It was the most entertainment he'd had in a week.

CHAPTER 16
DINNER WITH FRIENDS

Chantilly - Fall - 2035

Oh yes, that 600-class Mercedes looks *very* cramped in the back." Erin watched Adkins pull out of the parking garage, and she smiled. Colton's face flushed slightly, but he wasn't sorry.

Her utilitarian Honda Civic was still comfortable. "I bet we could fit this whole car in the back seat," he added with a laugh. An empty fast-food bag and water bottle lay on the floor in the back. Erin realized where Colton was looking.

"I ate that this morning. Not quite what you guys had on the plane ride, right? My car back home is filled with Kranstan's breakfast sandwich boxes. Unfortunately, I love them way too much. That bagel was a disappointing replacement."

Colton smiled, happy to have something to talk about. "I love Kranstan's. The closest one is about five miles from my house. I don't get there enough because it isn't on my way to work."

They both sat quietly for a little while. Suddenly, her happiness receded, replaced by seriousness. "I want you to know that we've invested millions of dollars trying to figure out what happened with the Kronos.

"I've spent countless hours scouring algorithms and code to determine what caused this catastrophe. We did our best to help bring closure to these families and honor our colleagues. Your team has been our most promising lead yet. I'd love to say I didn't know about the cover-up, but it seemed like the best way to keep this quiet at the time while we sleuthed what happened. I'm sorry things came out this way, but I believe we acted in good faith to our friends. If I didn't, Gell would have already had my letter of resignation."

He put his hand on her shoulder to stop her from beating herself up. "I believe you. I don't think you would have come if you weren't sorry. Now, you promised me not to talk about business. I'm just hanging out with my friends tonight in a new city. I'd like to have a quiet evening, a nice conversation, and hear some good stories. How does that sound to you?"

"Quite lovely." Her entire body loosened, and her smile returned.

They arrived at The Ferris and parked two cars down from Adkins and Jackson. As they caught up with the others in the restaurant's entryway, they could see the chef had come out from the back and hugged Adkins. Colton admired Adkins' effect on those who knew him. Adkins garnered love and respect from everyone he met.

"I guess he does know this place," Erin observed.

"Yes, it was a favorite of Percy's and his wife's. She passed from cancer a few years ago," he said quietly.

Her face showed great empathy. "I'm so sorry to hear it. I'm glad we were able to make it here tonight." He appreciated her sincere sentiment.

"Colton? Erin? I'd like you to meet someone. This is Renaldo. He's the chef and owner here."

Renaldo enthusiastically welcomed the group. "It's a pleasure to meet you all. When I heard my friend Percy was coming, I took the liberty of preparing some items. I hope you don't mind. We reserved your favorite table, Percy, and Nathan is still here, so he'll be your attendant. Everything is on us tonight, so please be my guests. I hope you'll enjoy it."

"Renaldo?! Absolutely not. I insist on picking up this bill," Adkins said. "No way! Kathleen has already spoken. She also told me I better make you happy, or she would kill me." Renaldo's wife was a close friend of Adkins' wife, which is why they'd tried out the restaurant in the first place. When Renaldo told her Percy was coming by, she burst into tears. She wanted to ensure Renaldo treated her former best friend's husband like a king tonight. Of course, this was an unnecessary request for Renaldo.

Adkins graciously acquiesced, saying, "Well, thank you so much, Renaldo,"

"But of course! I'm so glad to see you. If it's okay, Kathleen may stop by a little later." It would have been okay for Percy to decline the request, but it was obvious Renaldo wanted him to visit with her. Kathleen probably took her death almost as hard as Percy did.

"I'd love to see her!" The warmth of Renaldo and Kathleen's love made Colton wonder why Adkins had stayed away so long.

"May I get you all some wine? A nice Merlot or perhaps a chilled Chardonnay?"

"I'll have my usual," Adkins requested. Colton knew he fancied a glass of a Bordeaux, though Colton could never recall the name of it.

"I'd love a glass of Riesling if you have it?" Erin ventured pleasantly.

"Merlot, please?" Jackson asked.

"How about just a glass of sweet tea with lemon?" Colton asked, craving his childhood favorite. You can take the boy out of the South, but you can't take the South out of the boy.

Renaldo's eyebrows raised as he escorted them to the table. Their server already awaited them.

"Nathan, I'm so glad to see you," Adkins greeted the waiter.

"Dr. Adkins, I was so happy to hear you were in town. It's wonderful to see you as well." The server was a tall man in his late thirties.

His hair and clothes showed his attention to detail, and if one looked closely, they would see a tattoo adorned his forearm, indicating he'd been a U.S. Marine at some point in his life.

"Well, everyone, our chef has already prepared appetizers for you, some of which we already know Percy will love and others we hope you'll enjoy. Your drink orders are on the way," Nathan said with a side step to make room.

Four attendants placed on the table some of the most memorable dishes Colton had ever seen or tasted. When the attendants left, Nathan told them he would return shortly to get their main dish orders.

Each of the appetizers was uniquely delicious, which made conversation much easier. Stories started rolling off their tongues. Adkins told stories about a tribal chief offering his daughter as a wife and how Adkins could respectfully decline and not lose face with the chief or tribe. He also told the story about watching tanks roll through the town square with him caught on the top floor of a Prague castle.

Colton followed Adkins' tale with his own. Each of the guests had their own stories to tell, and their audience was captivated.

The steaks and seafood did not disappoint them. The chef prepared the meal perfectly, and the flavors mixed well. Each bite, story, and laugh made the night wonderfully unforgettable.

Right around the time dessert came, Kathleen showed up. A taller, mildly overweight woman with bold, hazel eyes welcomed them with her smile. Her unmistakable voice boomed larger than life. Kathleen naturally attracted attention but didn't care, nor was her ego affected by it.

Renaldo came out with her, and they stayed for a while and talked as everyone enjoyed a delicious dessert Renaldo proudly said Kathleen had invented. The conversation continued, and Kathleen fit right in.

A while later, Erin looked at her watch and realized the time had slipped by too quickly.

"I'm so sorry, but as lovely as all of this is, I've got a plane I must catch. Dr. Adkins, thank you for this night. I needed this more than you know. Thank you also, Renaldo and Kathleen. I can't think of a better meal I've ever had." Erin placed her hand on Adkins'. "Thank you for allowing me to be family tonight."

"I should be the one thanking you. It was so nice to have you with us. And Erin, it's Percy. When someone says 'Dr. Adkins,' I think, 'Man, am I old.'" They all laughed.

"You're not old, Percy. And besides, you're still very handsome and charming." Kathleen frowned a little as she looked at Adkins, putting her hand on his other hand as if he needed moral support. No one spoke poorly of her friends, not even if it was an act of self-deprecation.

Colton stood as well. "Well, this is my ride. I'll see you all in the morning?"

"Yes, Colton, the flight leaves at nine, so let's meet in the lobby at eight?" Adkins said, to which Colton agreed with a nod.

Once Colton and Erin walked out, Renaldo sat beside his wife and the remaining guests. "Those are two amazing people, Percy. They make a lovely couple."

Adkins shook his head and smiled. "Would you believe that they just recently met?"

"Well, Lord willing, I think there's a wonderful possibility there."

"I think I'd like that very much," Adkins said. "A toast to newfound love and a life of bliss." The four raised their glasses and swallowed down the lovely beverage.

The parking lot was well-lit, but the gravel was uneven as Colton and Erin made their way out to her car. The uncertainty of the ground made the walk a little longer, but neither seemed to mind. "You know you could have stayed, Colton. I'm sure they could have found room for you in their vehicle."

"I like my choice a whole lot better." He looked at Erin and smiled.

The comfort with which the two of them could talk warmed him. He enjoyed sharing his stories with her and couldn't wait to hear more of hers.

They both got into the car, and she drove him back to the hotel as they shared a few more stories. When they arrived, sadness overtook him as he realized the evening had to end. "I can't think of a better night. Thank you for accepting my invitation. I wish it didn't have to end. "I know you have to go, but would you be up to having dinner with me back in Boston?"

A coy grin overtook her face. "Do you think you can top the food we had tonight?"

Colton outright laughed. "Highly unlikely, but I'm game to try if you have some ideas."

"Let's talk some more this weekend, okay?" She needed to leave to catch her plane, and he didn't want a bad mark on his record. He decided to seize the opportunity and leaned over to hug her. It was awkward, but it beat a handshake by a long shot. Plus, he could write it off as a Southern thing. He quickly hopped out of the car, shut the door, and waved to her.

CHAPTER 17

THE CASTLE

Northern Germania - Summer of 1530 - Day 3

Wilson walked quickly toward the castle, forcing Jason to keep up. Even though Jason was pretty sure the bear threat was exaggerated, he'd feel like an absolute idiot if a bear did show up.

When they arrived at the castle grounds, Wilson looked for signs of recent habitation around the walkway. So far, only smaller wildlife had left any evidence. He was already on the hunt for a solid bow and hunting materials.

The walls and overrun gardens reflected years of neglect, but the underlying structures stood firm. The two men jumped the stone wall to enter the interior of the castle grounds. Vegetation from the gardens covered the pathway, but it was easy to kick aside. They eventually arrived at two large doors at the base of the castle. One door had lost its top hinge, and the bottom one hung by a single flange. The other door seemed rotted, though still attached.

Wilson pushed on the dilapidated door, causing it to fall to the ground. The sound frightened the birds in the surrounding trees. He looked around to identify if something else was made aware of their presence. Off in the distance, bushes rustled. Wilson stood still momentarily, holding his hand in the air as he watched to ensure the coast was clear.

After a long pause, he continued surveying the grounds.

He stepped over the door into a large, unlit room with ample external lighting, He evaluated the room and put away his flashlight. The chamber smelled musty and uninhabited. Jason put his hands over his nose and peered in behind Wilson, who turned on his flashlight and looked around the chamber. He saw broken swords and a few shattered arrow shafts on the ground without their tips. In one corner lay two skeletal bodies in armor. Animals had picked the bodies clean a long time ago.

Jason gasped when he saw the bodies.

"Don't worry, they're long dead, and this isn't a horror movie," Wilson said in the cold, half-joking manner of a professional soldier.

The words only slightly lessened Jason's hesitation. He avoided even looking in the corner for the rest of their exploration.

In the far corner, was a narrow set of steps. Carefully ascending to the second floor, they discovered a room illuminated with natural light entering from very narrow windows. Jason ambled over to the large banquet table in the middle of the room. Benches sandwiched both sides of the rough-hewn table, and he sat on one for a moment to rest after having rigorously dusted off a space.

"See those slots where the light is coming into the room? Those are narrow, so the people here could shoot arrows at unwelcome visitors." Wilson used the light from the openings to evaluate the room. "This could easily and comfortably seat all of us."

Wilson examined the multiple shelves secured to one of the walls. Little value remained, but the shelves' robust design testified to excellent craftsmanship. Scattered satchels and some broken pottery littered the dusty floor. Certainly, the many visitors to this place had cleaned out anything that was still useful many years ago.

The stairs on the front wall of this room led to the third and final floor.

Wilson moved over to climb them, and another dead soldier greeted him, blocking his passage forward.

Wilson cautiously moved the body with his foot so he and Jason could continue walking. The third floor was empty. Wilson surmised this to be a sleeping chamber. There were hooks on the sides of the walls for hanging clothes and weapons. The multiple slits on every wall allowed natural light into the room. There was a large amount of dust, but everything seemed habitable.

"Okay, we've seen what we need to." Wilson was about to turn and leave when he noticed something in the corner. "Well, what do we have here?" He turned on his flashlight again to get a better glimpse. A pair of traditional Turkish composite bows lay in the corner. They were missing bowstrings but looked otherwise unbroken.

"What are bows going to do for us?" Jason's eyebrows furrowed in confusion and modest irritation.

Wilson continued to examine the bows with amazement. He thought the workmanship would humble anything he had seen in modern times. The intricacies and inlay alone must have taken months to create.

"Maybe get us dinner? We can make the strings ourselves." His reply had an edge that the manager didn't notice or perhaps chose to overlook. Wilson didn't care either way.

Wilson believed the bows weren't typical for this area. Most European bows would be straight when unstrung and have a graduated curve when bent. Turkish horsemen traditionally used the doubly curved bow, but it would be no surprise for someone to consider them worthless and leave them behind if you didn't know how to take advantage of their design.

"Look around. We might find something else," Wilson said.

Despite not wanting to touch anything, Jason began searching, and in one of the other corners, there were a couple of dusty tarps that looked like tattered bedsheets or tablecloths.

Though they exhibited some disrepair, they could be repurposed into clothing and other necessary items in the near future. Wilson looked at Jason and told him to pick some of them up. Jason ungraciously complied. As he lifted one of the tarps, a rat ran across the floor, causing Jason to jump and scream. Wilson laughed but then tried to muffle it when Jason fixed his gaze on him. They left the castle and returned to camp with a few items to show for their trip. By the time they arrived, multiple projects were underway.

"Kelly!" Wilson saw her helping pull tarps out of the cargo bay for some makeshift tents. The Kronos was big enough for most of the crew to sleep but not all, so some would need to.

"Hey, Wilson, what's it look like?" she queried.

"About that…" He grinned. "The building hasn't been used for a long time. It's hard to say, but based on the dead bodies we found, I'd guess it's been at least fifteen years. Don't worry, they were just skeletons, but I'd say we need to dig them graves out of respect." He shared information with her like they were both back in the service.

"So, the building itself is in good shape?" she asked.

"Well, mostly. It's a keep, not a castle, but that's no biggie. The doors are non-functional, and looters cleared out anything of value."

Kelly stopped him for a moment. "Sorry for my ignorance, but what's the difference between a keep and a castle?"

"Well, I'm glad you asked. A keep is the building that is considered the stronghold. A castle is the entire walled area, including the keep. There are walls around this building, but they are in no way capable of holding out an enemy. Hence, we just have a keep."

"You learn something new every day! As a former Marine, you would think I might have known that."

Wilson chuckled and continued with his assessment, "There are three floors. The middle floor has a huge dinner table with solid benches and shelving for storage, and there were weapons on the first floor we may be able to repurpose.

"All the tapestries are gone, but overall, we have a building with good bones needing some love. Within the walls were areas for gardens, and based on the vegetation around there, we should look at them first for potential vegetables to eat. Both the walls and gardens need significant tending to be made useful."

"I see you found a couple of other things." She inspected the bows and the cloth.

"Yeah, these are exquisite. I'll be able to use them for hunting And I figured the cloth might be handy for clothing or other things. There were a few more of those linens in there. We just brought one."

"I think we could turn this into our short-term home and long term, our assembly hall. It needs some work, but it would be easier than starting from scratch." There was the reason Kelly sent Wilson on this scout trip: Wilson instinctively understood what needed to happen to move things forward. "Thanks, Wilson... and Jason. Great work! This is excellent news!"

Alex walked up as they finished. "Did you guys see any bears?"

Jason looked at him, unamused. Wilson held back his laugh as Jason turned and glared at him, then handed back Wilson's pocketknife before storming off into the camp.

"Did you see any *bears*?"

Wilson nodded affirmatively and, to Alex's delight, mouthed, Oh yeah.

CHAPTER 18
SECRET SECRETS

Chantilly - Fall - 2035

C olton couldn't wait to get down for breakfast in the morning. Arriving early, he stood in the entryway of the hotel restaurant, anxiously waiting for Adkins to show up so they could talk.

When Adkins appeared in the lobby, Colton called out, "Percy! How are you?"

Adkins turned towards the sound of his name, surprised to find Colton there so early. "Is something wrong, Colton?" Adkins studied his employee with curiosity.

"No, not at all. I've something to share with you. I think it's a big deal."

"You're not eloping, are you?" Adkins looked at him with a twinkle in his eye.

"What? No! This is serious." Colton faked being slightly offended. In truth, he rather fancied the notion.

Adkins wasn't buying it for a second. "Okay, what's so important that you show up to something before me?"

"I found a code in the text." His face was a mix of pride and excitement.

"A code?" Adkins tried to sort out what Colton was saying.

"Yeah. Last night, I got to the room after Erin dropped me off.

"I was full of energy, so I opened my laptop and started looking at the texts from the strongbox. The phrase praetorium temporis appeared multiple times in the document. I figured it had to be significant. Even you latched on to the same thing."

"Of course. No one includes a phrase that redundantly without reason."

"We scanned the original document to turn it into a digital one, allowing us to add spaces and translate on the fly. I studied the digital documents for a while, but something kept pulling me back to the original texts. I went over them a million times and thought I was getting nowhere, but then I saw it. It was something that should have been more obvious. The calligraphy was beautifully done, but whoever wrote it seemed inconsistent with the use of serifs. Only occasionally would letters have a different type of font. At first, I figured it was sloppy, but it bothered me how meticulous everything else had been in this document. It didn't seem logical its creator would just allow these errors through the whole thing."

The pieces started coming together.

Upon seeing realization dawn on Adkins' face, Colton continued. "I was looking down a line of the text with five of these mistakes. Up until now, I hadn't seen a succession like this. So, I was mentally noting the letters. The letters were 'l,' 'o,' 'c,' 'a,' and 't.' I kept going, and two lines down, there were three more letters: 'i,' 'o,' and 'n.' So, they spelled 'location.' This string went far beyond any coincidence. I returned to the beginning of the document, and the authors had a complete message in the text. I also realized our repeating phrase was a period for their sentences." He momentarily paused as he saw Jackson come in.

Adkins looked at Colton. "Oh my goodness, Colton, you're brilliant. Jackson, you're missing it. Colton is telling me how he found a secret code. You can't just leave me hanging here, Colton. What did it say?"

Jackson's eyes immediately focused, going into concentration mode. Colton pulled out a sheet of paper. "Here, read this." The message captured their attention.

"Would you look at that!" Adkins' eyes widened. "This is enormous! We need to contact TxC immediately. They will want to hear this."

"Let's wait to get back to Boston and enjoy our weekend. If you tell them today, they might want us to stay longer. But for now, breakfast, anyone?"

Chapter 19

I'm the Boss

Northern Germania - Late Fall - 1530 - Day 135

leeping in the keep made for better slumber than tents on the ground. No doubt the castaways would have slept well anywhere, given the backbreaking tasks and sheer manual labor required to ensure their survival. Based on the images from space that CHAMP provided, the team had located an ideal spot to begin their camp. The location accessed high ground, eliminating flooding concerns from the bog to the southeast or the riverbanks.

Clearing the areas tested their stamina, even when utilizing re-purposed tools from Kronos. CHAMP laid out a plan that allowed most of the trees to remain intact. Still, many trees had to be taken down for lumber; they left in place the ones growing along the perimeter to keep the camp hidden.

Kelly and Wilson took a moment to assess the progress. She shook her head. "I cannot believe how fast we're setting these things up."

Wilson looked across the camp. Rather than concentrating on the positives, he focused on what remained undone. "Yeah, but we have a long way to go, and the days are already getting cool. I hope we can make it more functional before winter."

Kelly put her hand on Wilson's back. "Look, we'll have at least four cabins completely done by then, and we can put four people in each cabin. Maybe we should ensure that these four over here are ready for winter? We'll still finish all the cabins at our current pace, but maybe we won't have them completely winter-proof. What do you think?"

"I know we've mentioned this before, but right now, that feels like the best plan forward. Let me get with CHAMP and see if we can modify some priorities." Without another word, Wilson was off to discuss things with the ship's AI.

Jason walked out of one of the nearly finished cabins, rubbing his eyes and stretching. Out of his peripheral, he saw Kelly approaching. Looking around, he saw Vercelli working on one of the doors. "I thought you said you'd be done with that door yesterday."

Vercelli looked up to see Jason glaring at him. "Why is that your business? You aren't my boss. Go away and let me work."

Jason's eyes narrowed. "I've been your boss the entire time you've worked at TxC."

Vercelli returned to working on the door. "We aren't TxC employees anymore, and I sure as hell am not going to put up with you telling me what to do, especially when you sleep half the daylight away! Go bother someone who gives a crap about you."

Kelly couldn't help but laugh at the retort. Jason turned and glowered at her. Kelly's eyes grew fiery. Taking an aggressive step forward and clenching her fists, she said, "You got a problem, Jason? We can settle this like real adults if you want. Would you like to set me straight?"

Vercelli broke out laughing. "That would be the saddest ten seconds of his entire life."

Jason's eyes darted wildly, and he stuttered, "I'm... You... I mean, I wouldn't waste my time with you, Kelly. You're an ignorant grunt. I went to Harvard University. Where did you go?"

Kelly took two steps closer to him. As she did, his head pulled back.

She, in turn, cocked her head as she said, "Yeah? I went and defended our country from the Chinese while you sat in your preppy, foo-foo classes and contemplated the fragility of daisies. I've got a bachelor's in Astrophysics from Texler Virtual, but that degree is now five hundred-plus years away. Here's the thing, Jason. What is that diploma doing for you right now? I can wield a hammer and work on construction. I can scale a ten-foot wall and run a five-minute mile. In case you were wondering, I can also kill you with my bare hands. I have skills that work to help us right where we are… in the 1500s. What about you? All you seem to be able to do is yell at people and sneak naps in the cabins you did little to help build. The next time you snap at me, you better be prepared to back those words with hardware because I'll humble you and your fancy degree. Do you follow?"

"Yes," Jason hissed.

Kelly got even closer to his face. "I'm sorry, what did you say?"

Jason's eyebrows dropped while his nose wrinkled. "Yes, sir!"

"Okay, now you're getting it. Go to Alex and ask him what job needs to be done. If you want, maybe you could show him your diploma to figure out which broom would fit the duties for which you're qualified. And Jason? Don't ever pull that crap with me again. Are we clear?"

Jason's hands trembled as he stood uncertainly.

Kelly calmly repeated herself, "Are we clear, Jason?"

"Yes, we're clear."

"Good. Now go find Alex." Kelly pointed to the north of the camp, and Jason walked away with his face beet red and his lips tightened.

Vercelli came up to her. "Kelly, I've known you for ten years, and I've never seen you talk to anyone like that."

Kelly looked down to the ground, and her cheeks flushed. "I just channeled my dad. That punk probably didn't deserve both barrels, but he's pompous and lazy. He walks around this camp like a manager who never does anything.

"When he called me a grunt, I was about to murder him. I didn't like hearing myself speak."

Vercelli put his fist out. "That was great, Kelly, and I loved every minute of it." Kelly reluctantly reciprocated the fist bump. He briefly studied her face. "Kelly, listen to me. Without politics and prejudices, leadership isn't given; it's earned. Like it or not, you've earned this spot, and I feel way safer with you in it."

Kelly felt the tension in her chest ease up. She put her arms around Vercelli and hugged him, then looked around. "I'm going to go find Athera. Thanks, amigo. I needed that boost."

Vercelli bumped his chest twice and pointed at her. "I think Athera is in the Kronos."

Kelly gave him a thumbs up and headed in that direction.

As she walked, she passed Jason again, holding a rake and heading to the gardens. He quietly sneered at her when she didn't look at him directly. Though Kelly's anger lingered, she felt compelled to say something. "Look, man, you just need to find something that you're good at here. We're all sacrificing, so sacrifice with us. You know?"

"That's easy for you to say. Everyone loves you."

"Maybe so," Kelly answered, "but you make it pretty hard for someone to even like you. Lose the attitude, and it'll make your life way better. I promise. Here's the thing: Do you want to lead? Great! Then serve the people around you. You don't just get a badge and get to tell people what to do. That's the reason you perceive people don't like you."

Jason frowned as he listened to her speak, and as soon as she finished, he walked on to do his menial chore without saying another word.

Kelly watched him the whole way. Even his response to Kelly's apology irritated her. She felt sorry for him for a moment, but things needed to be done, and her list grew by the minute as she stood there. Winter was fast approaching, so they needed to be prepared. She turned and quickly headed to the Kronos.

CHAPTER 20

SECRET SECRETS

Northern Germania - Winter of 1531 - Day 155

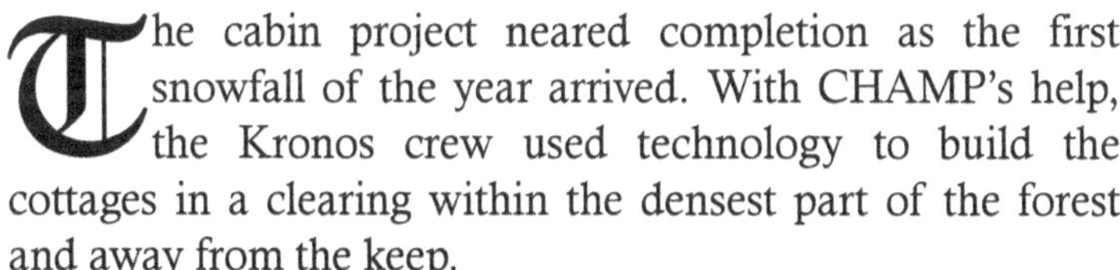

The cabin project neared completion as the first snowfall of the year arrived. With CHAMP's help, the Kronos crew used technology to build the cottages in a clearing within the densest part of the forest and away from the keep.

"I think the modifications we made on the final three are significant," CHAMP happily declared.

"I agree. Great job, CHAMP," Wilson said.

"Thank you, Wilson. It has been a pleasure working with you on this."

Wilson watched with contentment as the finishing touches put an end to the construction phase on the last few homes. He grinned and declared, "Finished."

"It's hard to believe we could do all this so quickly." Kelly joined him as they admired the crew's handiwork.

"I know! It hasn't even been six months yet." Wilson surveyed each step of the process. To his delight, the team performed well above expectations. CHAMP's ability to make recommendations to their plans had benefited them greatly.

Each house had an efficient kitchen area, including room for eating.

A stove/fireplace and a washtub rounded out the kitchen. The cottage contained two bedrooms at opposite ends of the house, with the potential for a third bedroom if needed. The wood used on the floors became problematic because of the process that they used to cut and prepare the lumber. When wet, the planks became more slippery than expected. This minor setback was solved by using sand to score the wood. Overall, the house design performed admirably.

The original plan included breaking the crew into groups of two for each home. Of course, this opened a whole can of worms. The original intent consisted of building eight similar two-occupant dwellings, which worked out well because of the breakup of ten men and six women. In practice, pairing the rooms became contentious. Three of the eight floor plans became three-occupant dwellings. Quin preferred to live by himself, which enhanced some of the growing tensions in the group, since it seemed like he was getting special attention.

None of the cottages took advantage of modern technology beyond clever and efficient designs. The crew did their best to make the latches on the doors, the roofing, and the walls to period. Most occupants had small items they scavenged from the Kronos, like flashlights, tools, and personal effects. Other than the tools, most of these items wouldn't stand the test of time, so there was little worry about them appearing in a modern-day documentary. The dwellings also contained a small compartment in the floor where they could hide these modern amenities, should anyone come over.

Kelly looked around. "Hey, have you checked on Emma? Bless her heart. She's pretty embarrassed about the accident."

Another of the Chellos engineers, Emma, had the distinction of being the worst injured in the construction of the cabins. One of the support beams fell on her and caused a break in her left arm, but CHAMP created a cast that allowed it to heal correctly. Her injury slowed her ability to make clothes for the camp, but she continued trying.

"No," Wilson answered, "but I think I saw her with Aecha about an hour ago. Did you know that she was one of three twin siblings?" Kelly's eyes widened. "Really? Dang. Bless her parents' hearts."

Wilson burst out laughing. "For sure! Sorry to switch gears, but I heard you talking to Cody about the last flight of the Kronos. You know, I didn't think you would be that broken up about it."

Kelly's cheerful exuberance lessened as she adjusted one of the locks of hair off of her forehead and looked at the ground. "I know, me either, but it hit me hard. It felt like walking a horse into its grave. I might have shed a tear as we did it. When I look in the cave, she's so torn apart now. It's hard to believe that she ever flew."

Wilson put his arm around Kelly with a rueful smile. "It'll be okay."

"Hush, you!" Kelly pushed him away and chuckled.

Taking one last flight, the team had hid the Kronos in a massive cave discovered in one of the hills. The shelter also included a metalworking shop with a high-grade furnace. They removed and stored two of the four engines. Brandon repurposed one engine as an efficient blowtorch to help deconstruct the ship. The ship's scuttling marked the finality of their predicament. Still, the alloys taken from the ship ended up in many of their other projects, like making hinges and locks for the doors. Gretta excelled in metalworking as did one of the other project managers named Gerry. As a former mechanical engineer, Gerry enjoyed using his hands again, and it brought him great personal pleasure. They both created most of the designs used in the camp.

"I'm just glad we don't have to sleep in the castle anymore," Kelly said enthusiastically.

"Yeah, you snore a lot," Wilson jested, though it earned him a swift punch.

"I do not!"

"Oh, yeah... you do."

"You have no room to talk," Kelly said.

"You sound like a freight train when you're deep in sleep."

"I've heard that a lot in my life." Wilson smirked as if this was an accomplishment that made him proud.

It had been a few months since anyone else had slept in the keep, but these were the last two who waited to give themselves cabins until everyone else had settled into homes. The past six months had taken their toll on the crew's weary bodies.

With the completion of the cottages, the crew used the Keep as their assembly hall. The Keep's roof had the solar collector, beacon, and communication array scuttled from the Kronos. A secret door led to the roof, where there was a self-destruct device Wilson believed would shatter any component on the roof beyond recognition should it be needed. They covered the gardens with removable planks to grow some winter vegetables. Another major project had them revitalize the water well in the middle of the Keep's grounds, including a hand pump (which, although not found in this time period, was made with period components).

Wilson and Alex even designed and built two outhouses. Their rudimentary, gravity-fed plumbing system went to a septic drain field. They weren't entirely fresh, but they were better than anything else used in the world at that time.

Cody walked over to Kelly. "Hey, I'll be down at the mill if you need me. I think I'm close to having a better fish farm tank." At the moment, his biggest passion was for the mill and raising quality fish to eat.

Kelly patted his back and said, "Okay, Cody. I'll be down to help in a few minutes."

The mill sat beside the stream, hiding the hydroelectric generator under the water wheel. The power from this device ran to a secret room found under Brandon and Vercelli's cottage. This basement also stored the extra electronic components and was physically more extensive than the cottage above it. CHAMP was the main power draw and was still alive and well in its new dwelling.

140

One of CHAMP's tasks was to scour historical databases for any reference indicating their presence already in history. So far, the searches hadn't come up with anything conclusive. Whenever Brandon conjured new queries, CHAMP would happily comply.

When taking CHAMP out of the Kronos, Brandon discovered the source of the lines that showed up on his display immediately prior to the jump that placed them in the sixteenth century. Brandon began cussing and couldn't stop himself for over two minutes.

Kelly heard him. "What's wrong, Brandon? Did you cut yourself?"

Brandon shouted out of the front deck of the ship. "Kelly? I've got something to show you."

Kelly walked over, and Brandon explained the problem. "It appears someone intentionally scored the wires on the power line so they'd eventually have burned out both CHAMP and the TRC. RF interference generated from the opened cables produced interference on the display. Strangely, it looks like someone else tried repairing the wires using electrical 'tape' and paint."

"Holy crap! That sure looks like some form of internal espionage issue to me."

"Me too! Hey, CHAMP? Was anyone on the ship messing with you before our last jump?"

CHAMP quickly replied, "I'm sorry, Brandon, but I can't answer that question."

Brandon looked slightly insulted. "Can't? Can you show me video footage from the hours before our last jump?"

CHAMP cheerily answered, "I can't do that, Brandon. Those files have been redacted."

"What?" Brandon rubbed his chin. "CHAMP, I created you. Override the redaction."

CHAMP responded, "You can't, Brandon. You don't have a high enough security clearance."

"What the heck?" Brandon's face turned slightly red.

Kelly interjected, "CHAMP, as captain, I order you to open those files."

"I'm so sorry, Kelly, but you also don't have a high enough security clearance for that."

Brandon jumped back in to ask, "Who has this sort of clearance?"

"Brandon, you know I can't answer that question."

Kelly and Brandon stared at each other for a few seconds. Finally, Kelly asked one last question, "CHAMP, is there anything you can tell us about the few hours before our launch?"

CHAMP happily replied, "I'm again sorry, Kelly. I'm not at liberty to discuss that with you."

Kelly's reply was classic Kelly. "Well, it's too late for this to matter, isn't it?"

Brandon reluctantly nodded. "Do you think anyone on our crew might have done this?"

Kelly considered the question. "I'm going to say that's unlikely. First of all, they'd be sending themselves back in time. It'd be like volunteering for a death sentence. Secondly, I don't know anyone on this ship with a high enough clearance to block our access. Rand and Quin are probably smart enough to hack it, but I can't see either of them damning themselves to this outcome. Someone in the company with big purse strings and large influence had to do something like this."

Brandon slowly shook his head, taking in Kelly's speculation. "That sounds pretty lousy. If we were home, I'd find that bastard and pay them a nasty visit."

Kelly's head bobbed. "Yeah, you and me both."

Brandon rigged CHAMP's secret room with a self-destruct mechanism. Because there were too many parts to destroy everything, CHAMP designed large tanks to hold two inert fluids. The tanks would open after the explosion and immerse the room. The combined fluids created a potent acid capable of destroying most of the evidence of their existence and then rapidly breaking down so as not to be toxic to the land or people around it.

Most of the team worked relentlessly to get them to this point of self-sufficiency. The ability to produce without the amenities of their former lives caused the most stress. Cody, Kelly, Wilson, Alex, and Aecha worked with great focus and determination. Others, like Jason and Quin, spent more time complaining and questioning Kelly's decisions. Kelly knew the time had arrived for her to change how the camp functioned. She had no intention of leading this long, but the immediacy of their needs took precedence over any interruption of unclear vision. With the camp situated, a decent food supply available, and the Kronos hidden, it was appropriate to allow a transfer of power to the group.

Many discussions resulted in the determination that Kelly would step away, and they'd elect three others to a governing council. Every two years, one council member would rotate off while another was voted in from the group. The crew chose their top three selections by private ballot. The top four vote-getters would then participate in another vote to determine the first council of three, designating the fourth as an alternate.

Kelly received the most votes but re-explained that she didn't consider herself suitable for this role. "Maybe when one of the three rotated off in two years, but not now." She said, "The following four people were at the top in the running: Wilson, Aecha, Brandon, and Athera. In the second round, Brandon ended up the alternate. The second largest vote count went to CHAMP, but Kelly didn't see the need to mention this.

After the vote, Jason immediately questioned the process, demanding to see the ballots. Kelly handed them to Jason, who announced that CHAMP was better than any of them (other than Kelly). He quickly put down the papers when he realized his only vote was written by himself.

"You obviously don't need me around here, so I might be considering leaving our commune and pursuing a life down at Gamburg to the south of us in the near future," Jason said rather pompously to the laugh and mocking of the few listening.

"Good luck with that, Jason!" Gretta said plainly to him. "*Wie geht es deinem Neidrigdeutschen?*" The phrase translated to 'How's your Low German coming along?' Low German was the dialect of the small village located near the camp. The region was a relatively unoccupied part of the Holy Roman Empire.

Jason's eyes squinted, and his jaw stiffened. "Oh, I don't know what you said, but I've some idea. I could survive and learn the language if I needed to."

Gretta turned and dismissed his comment. "You just don't get it. Do you understand that you wouldn't have survived at all if it weren't for us? We've been working our butts off to get everything running, and you've just complained a lot. Earth to Jason! We don't need a manager here, especially a non-technical one like you. We need hands and feet, not a belligerent mouth."

Jason's chest heaved and his face grew redder as he wilted at the reality of her comment. CHAMP taught lessons daily to most of the team, but Jason had rarely joined. His refusal to learn was already problematic, but now it was an even bigger issue. Jason figured he'd better start learning the language.

"Should I just shoot him and stuff him somewhere?" Wilson whispered over to Kelly, who laughed out loud at the prospect but then frowned at the ramifications of his sentiment.

Wilson's idea was funny but also scary. Up until now, the group had lived with a self-governed moral compass. The crew disagreed on formal rules, but wisdom handled most disputes. Kelly, for one, saw this as dangerous. In her mind, she couldn't help but remember reading Lord of the Flies in high school. The prophetic wisdom this book provided now flashed warning signs in her head.

Jason's threat exposed another delicate problem that was waiting to happen. Kelly knew that amicably or not, people were going to part ways at some point. It was unlikely that this team of sixteen would stay together until the end of their lives.

CHAPTER 21

FIRST CONTACT

Northern Germania - Summer of 1531 - Day 325

re you sure that you're up to this?" Wilson asked. "As up as I'll ever be! But I'm glad that you and Alex will be joining me," Gretta responded honestly, though her breath fluttered as she said the words.

The camp had slowly morphed into home and routine. Some local supplies would help the process significantly as reality dictated the inevitability of interaction with the local village. The council had determined that Gretta was the best choice for this first step. Since her parents were German immigrants to the United States, she already spoke well enough to get by. Though the dialect of the time differed from the German of her childhood, Gretta quickly adapted. She had the smallest learning curve in the group.

"It's time to go. Good luck, guys!" Kelly waved to the band travelling with Gretta as they headed to the small village.

The council decided they would go to Gamburg just over five miles from their camp. The need for materials to make clothing and metals necessitated the interaction. Cody and Wilson had prepared some pelts for trading and a few other small trinkets of interest.

Wilson and Alex escorted Gretta down to do the transactions. Alex knew German, and Wilson's stationing in Berlin for a few years aided in understanding a fair bit and speaking some. They made up a story to tell if questioned, giving them some cover.

The incoming road trickled with tradesmen and peddlers. Gretta realized that their plans might go better than expected. She could feel her heart racing as she approached the outermost vendor.

"Good morning, fraulein." The older man standing in front of his cart offered a variety of fruits and vegetables. His German sounded different from what she had learned, but she could compensate after a few exchanges.

At first, she kept her answers very simple. Little by little, she became more adventurous and improved with each interaction. Occasionally, words would catch her by surprise, but the merchants focused on the opportunity for sales, and in a few hours, she became comfortable conversing.

Gretta rejoined Wilson, Alex, and their wares. "Okay, I think I might have found the best candidate for selling our pelts. At least he seems honest in his dealings."

The road going into Gamburg opened into a large courtyard, and today, at least twenty carts circled the marketplace. Wilson and Alex walked into the village for the first time and, like Gretta before them, felt overwhelmed by the experience.

Historical depictions of homes and buildings with dirty beige and brown fascias were inaccurate. Most buildings sported a vibrant blue or green exterior with yellow and white accents. The thatch roofs of meticulous design crowned the homes, and the general attitude offered a cheerful welcome to all visitors. Flowers flourished, and the smell of fresh bread and pastries exhilarated their senses.

It would have been easy to overlook certain parts of Gamburg with all this welcoming beauty. Wilson observed two classes of a small town when it came to the children. Gamburg's younger demographic didn't surprise him.

Despite the difference of five hundred years, the patterns remained similar.

Much like the children, horrible dwelling places lurked in the shadows. Nicer homes were intentionally placed to distract from these terrible domiciles, but the downtrodden were easy to find if you knew what to look for. For now, Wilson's focus returned to the youth.

The well-tended-to children were healthy looking and didn't particularly care about the passing visitors. They sat comfortably with hearty grins and were engrossed in play. The poorer ones huddled in the darker corners of walkways, watching everyone who passed and noticing every stranger. Occasionally, one would smile despite their almost feral observation of the marketplace, constantly on the lookout to ensure their safety.

Wilson observed a pair of boys with ragged clothes and matted hair that bespoke their dismal station in the town. Following them stealthily across the courtyard, he noticed a man drop a piece of his apple as he walked. One of the boys darted over and grabbed it so quickly that the man hadn't noticed the missing piece yet. While the boy devoured the tiny sliver, a merchant yelled at him and chased the urchin into a small alleyway.

Wilson stopped Gretta for a moment. He reached into his bag, pulled out two fresh apples, and walked to the alleyway where the young boy had escaped. Immediately, he saw the two boys sitting in some shade. When Wilson looked closer, he realized that they were probably brothers. The two youths prepared to run away at eye contact, but Wilson quickly kneeled, holding out the fruit offering.

At first, the two boys just studied Wilson, neither moving away nor closer. Finally, the smaller one carefully walked up to him. Wilson extended one of the apples and smiled. The young boy quickly grabbed the apple, shouted *"Danke,"* and ran off.

The second young man slowly approached as Wilson extended the apple to him.

Realizing there were no strings attached, the boy reached for the fruit. He looked Wilson in the eye and said, "*Danke.*"

Wilson smiled and replied, "*Gern geschehen.*" He watched the younger boy take a large bite of the fresh apple. Gretta reached over and hugged Wilson. Her arms couldn't reach entirely around his frame, but she squeezed.

Wilson cautiously embraced back. "We'll have to make more visits like this. So, Gretta, you said the merchant is close to here?"

Gretta pointed to a man about sixty feet from their position before leading Wilson to him. The merchant displayed an extensive array of pelts while a young man, presumably his son, minded the stock.

Gretta began speaking with him and pointing to some of the pelts her companions carried. Within a few minutes, the man purchased everything they had brought into the village.

The pelts and trinkets rendered some silver thaler, the coin of choice for the Holy Roman Empire. Gretta then turned around and spent most of their earnings on textiles, leather, threads, metal scraps, and twine.

With the little they had left, she found a merchant selling baked goods and purchased some fresh loaves of bread and a few pastries for their trip back. The three returned victoriously to the camp, much to the delight of the team. Unfortunately, the pastries caused some stomach issues for the three of them. Much as CHAMP predicted, they weren't prepared for the uncleanliness of the food from this era. By the time they arrived back at the camp, the trio had to run to take advantage of the primitive toilets in the camp, and they were ever thankful for them.

CHAPTER 22

DANGER

Northern Germania - Summer of 1531 - Day 355

The success of their first venture to town ensured many more trips over the coming months. Regular contact with the villagers brought the team an ever-increasing awareness of life's many plights and extreme hardships in the Middle Ages.

One morning, Gretta and Cody headed to town to get their usual food items. As they walked towards Gamburg, Cody noticed something unnerving. "Wow, I haven't seen that since my tour in the Congo." He pointed to a pile on the village's south side.

Gretta cocked her head and squinted in the direction he motioned. "Cody, I see what you're pointing at, but I don't know what that is. It looks like a pile of wood."

Cody looked down to the ground and took a deep breath, unable to speak momentarily. "No. Those are dead bodies. They cover them because they think it'll stop whatever they were spreading."

Just then, Gretta swatted a mosquito on her neck. "Ouch. That thing bit hard."

A week earlier, it had rained for four days. The riverbanks had swelled so much that Cody had to make an extra ramp to enter the mill.

Sweltering heat had followed once the rain subsided, and the bog produced mosquitoes at a feverish pace

Cody continued with his proverbial knowledge. "Did you know, in our time, that mosquitoes were the deadliest killer of humans in the entire world?"

Gretta smiled while she rubbed her wound. "Really? I'd have never guessed."

Cody rapidly nodded. "Yeah, they kill about three million people yearly."

Gretta expressed a questioning smirk. "How do you know all of this?"

"It was part of our scare training before we were stationed in the Congo." Cody got even closer to Gretta as he spoke. "We were given government-issued mosquito repellent that we were to apply generously. The stuff stunk, but it worked well. I wish we had some now!" He vigorously slapped at the annoying biters. "One guy in our group refused to use it. You know what happened to him?"

"He died?"

"No. But he did catch malaria."

"That's terrible."

"Oh yeah. The poor schmuck thought he was dying, but with treatment, he recovered." Cody stopped and looked up in the air as if he recalled something else. "You know, when you get malaria, you have it the rest of your life."

"I've heard that too." Gretta put her hands on Cody's arms. "Okay, focus, Cody. You said those are dead bodies over there?"

Cody took a second look. "Oh, yeah. Without a doubt."

Gretta began wringing her hands. "Do you think it's some form of the plague?"

"No idea, but based on what I've seen, they're going to dig trenches and burn those bodies."

Gretta stared in horror. "Burn them? Why?"

"They're trying to protect the village from catching what killed them."

Gretta stopped walking. "Cody, we should just turn around. We don't want to get what's going around."

Cody hesitated before he said, "That's a good point. I think you're right."

The two turned and headed back to the camp. About an hour into the two-hour walk, Cody noticed that Gretta had trouble keeping up. "Hey, are you feeling all right?"

"I'm fine. I just feel a little tired."

Cody stopped walking. "Do you need to rest?"

Gretta straightened up and rubbed her neck. "Nah, let's just get back to the camp."

"Okay, let me know if you need to rest." Cody looked concerned but turned and kept walking.

CHAPTER 23

PESTILENCE

Northern Germania - Summer of 1531 - Day 359

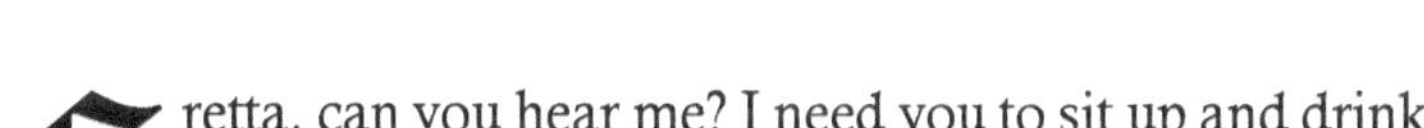

"Gretta, can you hear me? I need you to sit up and drink this water." Kelly leaned over and propped up her friend.

Gretta looked around and squinted her eyes. "What? What's going on? Oh, wow! This is one hell of a headache." She rubbed her head and tried to lick her lips, to no avail.

When Kelly touched Gretta's arm, she could feel the radiated heat. Gretta rubbed her neck, and Kelly saw a red rash draping down her back. "Hey, just stay right here. I'm gonna find Cody and get you to CHAMP."

Gretta closed her eyes and nodded as Kelly quickly turned, heading for the cabin door.

In less than ten minutes, Kelly returned with the cart and Cody. Gretta heard them approaching, and she tried to raise her arms. She settled for raising a single hand.

"Gretta, we're here. We're going to lift you into the cart. You don't need to move. We'll do the moving for you," Kelly said.

Gretta barely nodded her head. Cody gracefully lifted Gretta. Kelly kept the door open as Cody carried the passenger. As they transported her, Kelly tried to hold Gretta's head to avoid any more injury.

Doing so, Kelly felt a large bump on the back of her neck. "Cody, I need to look at something when we get her in the cabin." Cody nodded as Brandon helplessly watched them carry Gretta into the room. Carefully, they laid her on the examination table.

"No, that would be nearly impossible. But placing these devices around our camp and the bog should significantly reduce the chance of being bitten until cooler weather arrives."

"What about making this same device for Gamburg?"

"Gretta, do you know what this large bump is from?" Kelly asked.

Gretta struggled to speak. "No. What bump?"

Kelly carefully moved her hand over the swollen area. "This one right here."

"Oww!" Gretta winced at the pain of the touch.

Kelly's hand jumped off quickly as she said, "So sorry, dear."

Cody looked at the bump. "I think she got bit by a mosquito there a couple of days ago. You know, when we were near the village."

Gretta started crying. "Am I going to die like those other people?"

Kelly instinctively put her arms around Gretta and held her. "We're on this, girl. CHAMP will solve it, and I'm right here."

Brandon stepped in. "CHAMP, can you examine this wound? Could she be allergic to the bite?"

One of CHAMP's robotic arms quickly came up to Gretta's neck. A light came on as the area was scanned. It responded in his unsettling, cheery voice. "Gretta, I'm going to need to draw some blood. This will hurt a little, but it'll only be for a moment."

Gretta mustered enough energy to respond, "I understand, CHAMP."

A second arm raced toward her, carrying a syringe with a needle. "Okay, Gretta, brace yourself.

"I'm sorry that this will be uncomfortable." The robotic arm gracefully placed the syringe point into the swollen bump on her neck. Gretta gritted her teeth but said nothing.

The mechanical arm removed the needle, extracted the blood, and returned it to the medical analysis subsystem. CHAMP explained the process, "Gretta, I apologize for the discomfort. This is going to take at least ten minutes for the system to examine your sample. In the meantime, we need to bring down your fever. We don't have a modern way to do this, but the river water should be about sixteen degrees Celsius. Would it be possible to get a bath of that water? It'll help."

Cody jumped up. "I'm on it, CHAMP." "Gretta, I noticed that the mosquito's proboscis is still in your wound. Can I try to extract it?" CHAMP asked.

Gretta grimaced, but then she took a deep breath and said, "Okay."

"This shouldn't hurt."

Quickly, a robotic arm approached Gretta with an appendage resembling a tweezer set. The probing arm's light turned on, quickly removing the object from her neck.

A noise came from the front door of Brandon's cabin. Moments later, Cody entered with one of the metal bathing tubs. "I'm going to get a bucket so we can fill this."

"Gretta, it appears you've contracted an aggressive form of encephalitis," CHAMP said. "Usually, ticks would carry this, so I don't have historical data to ascertain the problem. I can't determine the exact strain, and we don't have the materials to make a perfect antidote, so it'll take a series of shots to cure you. For now, let me give you a shot that will ease all your symptoms. This medicine will also put you to sleep. I'm also sorry–The injection will help, but a cold-water bath is still necessary."

"I'm on the water." Cody quickly turned, adding, "I've some more to tell you, but first, let me get this water going." He moved so rapidly that he accidentally hit the doorframe on his way out.

The impact caused him to stumble back slightly, but with determination, he continued his mission.

Once again, one of CHAMP's appendages inserted a needle in Gretta. The young woman limply lay on the table without immediate change. With a barely audible grimace, she waited for her misery to subside as her eyelids grew heavy.

CHAPTER 24

A CALL TO ACTION

Northern Germania - Summer of 1531 - Day 373

retta stayed in bed for the next twelve days. She began moving slowly on day thirteen, and by the fourteenth day, she cheerfully reentered life. That morning, she walked over to Cody's place at the mill.

The noise in the mill forced Gretta to shout, "Cody, are you in here?"

Gretta giggled as she heard a loud clunking noise, then a string of cuss words. She called out, "Are you okay?"

Cody quickly popped up from the lower deck. "Gretta! You're alive."

Gretta giggled. "Yes, thanks, in part, to you."

Cody pointed to himself with his thumbs. "Me? What did I do? CHAMP is the one to thank."

"The last thing I remember is you running like a bat out of hell away from me to get a cart. I just wanted to thank you." She had a basket full of pastries and bread that she handed to him. "I made this for you last night."

Cody's mouth watered at the smell of the fresh raspberry strudel pastries. "Well, you're welcome, and I'm so glad you're better. I was worried. But you didn't need to do this." Cody took the package from her. He had his eye on one of the berry pastries.

"No, I think I did." She leaned over and hugged him. She tried to kiss him on the cheek, but her height only afforded her a peck on the shoulder. "I've got to run, but thank you."

Cody watched the little sprite of a woman cheerily walk off. He smiled as he returned to his work.

Gretta's brush with death prompted an emergency council meeting in CHAMP's room, as the computer's input was vital.

"CHAMP, what can you tell us about this mosquito/ encephalitis situation?" Brandon asked.

CHAMP came to life. "We've had an unusually humid and hot summer. The combination of heat and precipitation is the ideal breeding ground for mosquitoes like this. I suspect the real problem is the bogs between Klugstadt and Gamburg." CHAMP's positivity made the group uncomfortable as they paired the provided information with the image of the piled bodies that Cody had mentioned.

"CHAMP, can we do something to protect the camp?"

"I'm glad you brought that up, Brandon," CHAMP responded. "I've already made two extra sets of the antidote to have readily available. Cody is storing them in a container in the mill. This will ensure that they stay cool. I also have a two-part solution for Klugstadt."

"What do we need to do, CHAMP?" Wilson asked.

"Well, I'm printing out a recipe for a natural mosquito repellant that we should distribute among our crew. The ingredients should be readily available down in the village."

Brandon said, "Okay, that's the first part. What's the second part?"

"I've found a bait/trap mechanism in the database that I believe we can make to thin the population. We're nearing the end of summer, so I suspect we need about a month of protection, and then the mosquitoes will naturally die down."

"How does this mechanism work?" Wilson wondered.

"I determined that we could use some pipes from the Kronos to accommodate this plan.

"We'll bait the mosquitoes with a warm hyper-CO2 generator through a perforated pipe. Then we'll put an agent in the CO2 to kill them almost immediately. We'll use baking powder, vinegar, and brewer's yeast to generate the attractional CO2 and a pair of inert chemicals to kill the mosquitoes."

"So, will this kill all mosquitoes?" Wilson inquired.

"No, that would be nearly impossible. But placing these devices around our camp and the bog should significantly reduce the chance of being bitten until cooler weather arrives."

"What about making this same device for Gamburg?"

Immediately, Aecha stared at Wilson. Before CHAMP could reply, she interjected, "Wilson, we can't do that."

Wilson crossed his arms. "Why not?"

Aecha gasped. "You know why. It would interfere with history."

Wilson snickered. "Maybe you didn't notice, if we implement what CHAMP is proposing, we're already going to reduce the chance of ALL people getting bitten, right? Not just our camp."

Aecha stayed quiet for a moment, considering Wilson's observation. "Yeah, that's kind of true."

Wilson grinned. "I know. So, we might as well go all the way."

"This is uncomfortable for me," Brandon thought aloud.

"Me too," Aecha said.

"Listen to me on this. We need that village. In many ways, we're helping ourselves. Also, Aecha, how could you look those villagers in the eye and say, 'I'm sorry for your loss' when you know that you just allowed their loved ones to die unnecessarily?"

Aecha looked down and rubbed her hands on her dress. "That's not a fair argument, Wilson, but you make a good point."

Wilson clapped his hands together. "So… are we in agreement on this?"

The group agreed, and the meeting adjourned. When the council announced the new plan to the rest of the team, Kelly stared at Wilson, shaking her head.

Later that day, she found him. "Hey, can I talk to you?"

Wilson calmly replied, "Sure, Kelly. What's on your mind?"

"You know exactly what's on my mind."

Wilson looked at her coldly. "So, you don't want to help these people with a problem that they won't be able to solve?"

Kelly clenched her jaw. "That isn't the point. We're affecting the natural path of history."

"So what?"

"You think it's yours to change?" Kelly's arms were now folded.

"Well, how's that different from thinking it's not yours to change? We can legitimately help these people not die terrible deaths. You don't think that's a good thing?"

"What I think is that we need to ensure we don't screw up history. Don't you think we have some responsibility to preserve the natural progression of events? Where does this lead? Now, it's just preventing a mosquito infestation. What about giving them a cure for the plague? I'm not a history buff, but even I know it was the Black Death that allowed the rise of the middle class in European society. Without it, the world would still be rulers and peasants. We're playing with fire, and I don't want to mess things up, nor do I want to get burned."

"This is going nowhere. I'm going to implement what CHAMP recommended. You think about this for a couple of days and get back to me. In the meantime, we could use your help."

Wilson walked away, shaking his head. Kelly watched him, staring incredulously.

CHAMP's plan worked well. To their knowledge, only one more villager passed away. Some in the camp, like Gretta, took this as a great win, but Wilson and Kelly weren't the only ones having heated discussions on the matter.

CHAPTER 25

HOLY UNION

Northern Germania - Fall of 1531 - Day 415

Wilson caught up with Lisa. He laughed as he said, "Are we officially naming ourselves 'Klugstadt'? It's not like it rolls off your tongue." The name meant 'clever town,' and he preferred over 'the camp' or 'the base.'

Lisa smiled at him as she replied. "It's better than the absolutely nothing we've used for the past year." Looking up made his stature even larger and more intimidating. She realized how grateful she was that he was her friend.

"True! So, are you certain about this? Are you ready?" He looked at her, dressed in a white gown, and took a deep breath in admiration. To the people of the sixteenth century, this would have been an odd dress color for a marriage, but Lisa still had her modern proclivities, which influenced her choices.

"Yes! We had already been dating before all of this. Rand is a good man, and now the roughest time is over, I'd like to do this." Lisa looked determined and excited. Wilson grinned, happy for her and her soon-to-be husband.

"Brett? It's time. I'm heading up front, so are you ready to walk your sister down?" Wilson leaned down and kissed Lisa's forehead.

Brett nervously smiled and nodded. Lisa squeezed her brother's hand a little tighter. Brett loved his sister and Rand, for that matter, and couldn't be happier; they were finally going to get married. His thoughts turned to their parents and what they were missing.

Wilson left the two of them and went into the assembly hall. The Klugstadt community had prepared the gathering place with flowers and fresh food for the wedding feast. Everyone gathered for the momentous occasion.

However, the joyous wedding celebration couldn't quell the growing tension in Klugstadt. Cliques formed at the reception. Quiet whispering and subtle stares became more and more overt. But none of that mattered for today. Lisa and Rand's wedding took center stage, and everyone tried to put aside these issues to ensure this was the happiest day possible.

Cody and Wilson designed and built a new cottage for the newlyweds. It sat slightly apart from the rest of the homes for a little more privacy. The layout benefitted from the first eight cottages' mistakes, fixing many minor issues. They also built a new storehouse to keep grains and other foods safe from the environment.

Wilson looked down to ensure his clothes were still clean, as dirt and stains had a way of finding him. Today, he felt quite civilized between the clothes, a fresh bath, and a clean shave. Though awkward, he liked it enough to smile.

Aecha passed him and stopped in her tracks. "Whoa! Wilson, you look twenty years younger."

Wilson blushed at the compliment. "Thanks. Hey, look, Alex made it. I was beginning to worry, but now I'm good."

Alex had gone down to Gamburg and procured a few barrels of excellent stout and wine from a pub he and Cody frequented. On returning, he was all smiles with his mission accomplished.

"Had me worried, sir," Wilson said.

"Come on, I made it with time to spare."

"Not much time."

Wilson gave him a knowing grin that Alex chose to ignore.

"Are you ready to officiate?"

Wilson sighed. "I think so. I'm ready as I'll ever be."

"You're going to do fine," Aecha said. "By the way, here are the rings." She handed Wilson the icons.

Wilson admired the handiwork. "Aecha, these are really amazing."

She straightened up at the compliment. "Why, thank you. I'm pleased with them, but more importantly, so are the bride and groom." Aecha had forged both alloy wedding bands, which were simple but tastefully elegant. The design pleased Rand, and Aecha witnessed a rare display of Rand's emotion when she presented the final product to him.

Wilson went over some last-minute mental notes. Finally, he blurted out, "Well, I think everything is in place, and it's time to start."

Aecha's eyes brightened as she patted Wilson on the back.

The hulking man walked in to officiate. To no one's surprise, his simple officiation came off flawlessly. Patrons marveled at his eloquent stories and traditional vows.

The wedding clicked on every level. The beauty and practicality allowed a pleasant escape from the rising tension in Klugstadt. For the day, all bickering subsided. Even Jason stopped sulking and joked with the group. The food had continued to improve. Though no one complained about meals, today, everything just seemed better.

Lisa received many gifts. Athera penned a book of poetry with exquisite and touching prose. Her love of people only bettered Athera's command of English. As the oldest person in the group, this year had been extremely difficult for her, yet she handled it with grace and optimism.

Wilson and Vercelli had traveled to Frankfurt to acquire a hand-painted picture depicting the Triumvir. The Italians thwarted the Ottoman Empire's expansion at Vienna only a year or two earlier, so travel to the south remained hazardous.

Though not huge, Frankfurt contained enough resources to get what they needed. They borrowed a farmer's cart and a horse for the journey and promised to bring back supplies in exchange. The farmer happily accepted their offer, and three days later, they returned with supplies for the farmer and some much-needed goods for Klugstadt.

These episodes of mixing with the locals were getting increasingly common but also more troublesome. There continued to be the fear that the locals may follow them and find their hidden village. The five miles between Klugstadt and Gamburg gave some comfort, but it remained on the minds of anyone who returned.

By now, the local parasites of this area that affected them earlier had run their course. Food from Gamburg became more common, and the wedding feast reflected that. The celebration took advantage of the Keep, using its courtyard to house the food and dining tables.

As the wedding couple entered the courtyard to the cheers of the entire town, Lisa began to cry. The setup, tapestries, food preparation, and decorations had been put in place without her knowledge.

Brett came over to put his arm around his sister, but Rand's arm had already taken up that space. Awkwardly, he stepped back and asked, "Are you all right?"

Lisa gleamed. "This is the most wonderful day of my life. I can't believe all the work that everybody did to make this so lovely."

Kelly heard the comment, and more tears flowed. She took a deep breath before she spoke. "Lisa, it was an honor to do it. You deserve a day like this."

Lisa left Rand's side and reached out to hug Kelly. Not to be left out, Rand hugged her too and said, "Thank you for everything, Kelly."

Kelly hugged them back. "Everyone chipped in here. That's why Klugstadt works. Everyone contributes."

That night, after the group consumed the last of the stout, Wilson sat quietly in his room, and the happiness couldn't overcome the growing conviction. The philosophical clash over history wore on him. Windows of opportunity were everywhere, while people like Kelly saw traps to destroy history. He considered the options and what must change to bring personal peace. The possibilities started to entrench his heart. What was tolerable, and worthy of making a stand in the community? He also considered possible bridges to burn.

CHAPTER 26
CRACKS IN THE FOUNDATION

Northern Germania - Fall of 1531 - Day 440

Very little evidence of the Kronos remained, save for some select parts in Brandon's basement. Even the engines and blow torch had to be destroyed. The only things using power in the camp were the beacons, radio, and CHAMP. A hailstorm damaged one of the solar panels beyond repair, but the two remaining panels kept things running adequately.

Life in Klugstadt moved beyond just surviving, and the inhabitants started to thrive. Some might have even admitted they began to like their new-life and were thankful for this strange twist. But beneath the surface, philosophical strains were eating at the group's unity.

As Alex walked out of his cabin, he saw Wilson walking down the main street. "I'm going on clean-up duty. You want to join?" he hollered.

The task of walking and erasing tracks going into the camp and along the Keep's perimeter was assigned to Alex and Vercelli. Shrubs and trees hid the pathways and evidence of the village. Over time, the task grew in complexity as the foot trails got more defined.

Wilson heard his friend and took a deep breath. "Sure, let me go grab my knife."

Alex waited as Wilson made the short run to his cabin. He promptly returned, then they headed out.

The paths to Klugstadt remained well hidden, with the mill being the only landmark visible from the water. Cody had chosen to move in and live away from everyone else. If someone showed up there, he could insist he was alone, seeking a private life.

Nestled in the forest, the Keep kept the deception going. From the outside, the ancient building looked abandoned. In the year or so of the residence, few visitors had stumbled on Klugstadt. The council developed stories to explain their presence there as well as a nuclear plan to destroy all evidence of themselves.

"So, you have a council meeting tonight?" Alex asked.

"Yep. I almost forgot. I'm glad you reminded me."

"How's that been going?" Alex grabbed a small apple out of his pocket and took a crunchy bite of it.

Wilson tipped his head left and right several times but never answered the question.

Alex chuckled at his friend's response. "That good, huh?"

"It's okay, but let's just say it isn't that fun. There's a division, and I'm on the minority side."

Meetings were becoming more and more contentious. Four months ago, when Rand proposed to Lisa, the discussions among the council became lively. Rand's proposal was neither surprising nor caused any problems, but it brought some hypothetical situations into question.

First, should the team refrain from procreation? The three talked for hours and hours on this simple subject. The council's final discussion concluded that they had no business forbidding it.

They next addressed the issue of whether Klugstadt citizens should take spouses from this period. Again, the answer came back to the belief that they had no right to forbid it.

The heart of these issues centered around integration, assimilation, or isolation.

Wilson seemed to find himself on the wrong side in most of these, causing tension in the council.

Wilson already knew tonight's meeting would have some flammability, and he dreaded being the one who lit the match.

Hours later, as they completed their circuit of the camp's secluded perimeter, Wilson turned to his friend and said, "Alex, I'm about to start a war in the council."

Alex scrutinized Wilson. "Are you right?"

"Umm, yes. I think so."

"Then it's worth the war."

"Really?" Wilson tried not to sound skeptical.

"Ruffle the feathers and get over it," Alex said. "At least, that's what I'd do."

Wilson ran his hand through his hair. "I don't know. I agree with you, but I hate the idea that I could make enemies tonight."

Alex put his hand on Wilson's shoulder. "Look, the bottom line is that you see people in need and know we can do something about it. They see rules that can't be broken. They need to open their eyes and change. We both know it."

"I think you're right. Hey, man, I gotta leave you and make it to the meeting. Thanks for your support. We'll talk about this later."

Alex waved as Wilson ran off.

Wilson, Brandon, and Aecha met at Brandon's place. As usual, Brandon provided some cheese and wine for the discussions. The initial conversations were light and superficial.

Tonight, Aecha overflowed with her desire to talk. "I'm still giddy thinking about the wedding. Everyone did such a wonderful job. I don't know how we could ever top that."

Brandon eagerly chimed in. "Wilson, you rocked as the officiant. When I got married, our pastor stuttered and messed up about every other line of the vows. A holy nightmare! He was the nicest guy, and no one cared, but I think his nerves got the best of him."

"Thank you. I was nervous, too, but Lisa's serenity floored me."

Putting her hand on Wilson's arm, Aecha exclaimed, "Yes! She was serene. I wouldn't want to face her in a poker match."

The group laughed, unwilling to leave the pleasant occasion behind and face their differences.

Finally, Brandon looked down at his notes. "Well, we don't have any new business to discuss. We've made it through most of the pressing matters, but Wilson, you told me you wanted to bring up some old business?"

Wilson looked down at the table for a moment and exhaled. "Sorry, but I feel we need to discuss this more. We don't have closure on so many issues, and we need to come to some sort of agreement." The atmosphere at the table tensed, but Wilson persisted. "Should Klugstadt start working to help the people around us? We could better their lives in so many ways. Just look around our camp. We could help them farm better, teach them about fish farms, improve their medicine, and even educate them. It's hard for me to go into the village and not want to fix a lot of their problems." The room suffered a stony silence as Wilson dropped this open-ended question into their lap.

After a long moment, Aecha said, "You know how we feel about this. This statement isn't a question but more of a constant sticking point with you. When you say we need to agree, you're really saying 'I don't like the current agreement.' We believe that the history we already know should be protected, limiting what we can do. I'm sorry. I struggle with this too, but I think we're right to limit our exposure to this period." Aecha's compassion was reflected in her word choice, but the ongoing nagging wore on her.

Wilson sat quietly as Aecha spoke. When she finished, he tried a new tactic. "If you had the opportunity to go back, or ahead in our case, in time and kill Adolf Hitler, would you do it?" He crossed his arms after presenting the argument.

"The question is unfair, but your idea isn't.

"Would the world without Hitler be better? Maybe, but let me ask you these two questions. Would there be an Israel without Hitler? Can you guarantee another monster wouldn't rise to replace him? You know the history, and anti-Semitism wasn't exclusive to Hitler. History… um… our history is a result of both the good and evil that occurred."

"Tell that to the millions put to death and heinously tortured under his Nazi flag. Tell that to the destroyed infrastructures and shattered families." Wilson's temples pulsated as his eyes blazed with passion.

"So, you can guarantee that wouldn't have occurred without Hitler?" Brandon interjected.

"No, but I feel like we must do something. To sit back and do nothing when you know you can help is tremendously callous of us, don't you think?"

"It's terrible for sure," Brandon said. "I don't disagree with you one bit on that. But there are more issues that you're just choosing to overlook. What person can judge these actions? You're judging them through the lens of an American. What if I were from Japan and saw America dropping an atomic bomb on Hiroshima as evil? Should I assassinate Dr. Oppenheimer? Who started the Crusades? Was it the Moorish invasion or the Christian one? History, as we know it, is tainted by our centric perspective."

Brandon finished and took a deep breath. He couldn't look Wilson or Aecha in the eye, so he sat clenching his teeth.

"Brandon, I think we can find needs, and I believe we can help. If that messes with some history, so be it!"

The group left the meeting weary and without resolution, except for Wilson's heart, which became more resolved to his view with each interaction.

Wilson continued to go down to Gamburg and see preventable illnesses, which sickened him. Simple advancements in technology would improve everyone's quality of life. Modern society would never tolerate the depravity he often observed in the village.

Klugstadt could help these people, and it didn't sit well with Wilson that they weren't.

CHAPTER 27

PHONE HOME

Boston - Fall - 2035

Rather than going to TxC's facility, Adkins chose to bring Gell's team to their office this time. Though not particularly large, priceless artifacts adorned the walls, and the period furniture impressed visitors.

Colton considered asking the team to surrender all their electronic devices before entering the conference room, but he realized his own pettiness. He looked down at his watch as his foot nervously tapped.

Adkins leaned over to Colton. "Did you talk to Erin about your discovery?"

"Umm, no. We barely talked at all. Erin dealt with a work emergency that took most of her weekend. I'll be surprised if we see her here today," he said with a bit of disappointment.

"Gell said she would be here, and I'm glad. I like her, and I think you two have… chemistry." Adkins being older than Colton made him sound more like a dad than a friend.

"I like her, too. She may be the most amazing person I've ever met." Colton's painfully honest reply surprised him as he said it, but he knew Adkins' ears remained safe for such commentary.

"You mean next to Theseus Gell, right?" Both men looked at each other and burst out laughing.

"I'm so glad we're here and not having to endure those speeches at their lobby," Colton said. "Still, the man is way nicer than I expected. I'd say I kind of like him, but I don't totally trust him." Colton stared out the window and watched Erin get out of her car. He smiled and took a deep breath.

"Agreed." Adkins looked up to see the TxC team in the parking lot, approaching the entryway. He quickly walked forward to meet their guests with his hand extended. "Theseus, I'm glad you could make time to join us. We have something of tremendous importance to share."

The TxC entourage arrived promptly at eight AM. Gell, McCallister, and Erin all walked through the door.

"I hope it isn't as shocking as our previous meeting," Gell said.

"I think it'll be exciting for both of us," he calmly replied, though, in his heart, he was very anxious to share what Colton had discovered.

"Well, we have everyone here if you're ready," McCallister said with a smile.

"Of course. Let's begin." Adkins motioned for everyone to enter the conference room. The group shuffled in and saw a table lined with coffee, water, juice, and light refreshments on the left.

Colton waited to greet Erin. Her lilac perfume trumpeted her arrival. She smiled as she stopped to talk to him. "Hey, you! You look excited about this meeting."

Colton nodded with an almost juvenile excitement. It caught her off guard. "I think you're going to enjoy it, too. Hopefully, it's a little better than your weekend sounded. Are you up for dinner tonight?" *Where did that come from?* Colton thought.

"Sounds amazing. Call me." She smiled, then turned to greet Jackson.

Well, that's a great way to start the meeting, he mused while entering the room with a spring in his step.

"Hello again, everyone," Adkins opened. "Thank you for joining us. I don't want to take too much of your time beating around the bush, so I'll ask Colton to come up here and share what he discovered."

Smiling, Adkins pointed to Colton.

Colton awkwardly smiled back and stood. Before he started, he leaned down and took a drink of water. "Sorry for that. My parched throat screamed for refreshment. I do wish it were sweet tea, though. Thank you, Percy, for giving me the floor here. I know there are many things to cover, but this information is important. We discovered it this weekend." He pressed a button, on the controller, and the room darkened. A monitor came to life with the Adkins company logo displayed. Pressing a second button caused the display to show one of the artifacts they found in Germany.

"I'm sure by now you all recognize this. It's the strongbox we found in our last excavation. In it, we found two artifacts." He clicked a button and the familiar key was displayed on a large projector. "One, as you recall, is an object that you identified as a key or module from the computer system on the Kronos. I also presented this text." The screen changed, showing the document. "We translated this and found familiar names on the bottom of it. If you look at the rest of the text, you'll find a repeated phrase." Colton showed a slide highlighting the occurrence of the phrase in the document.

praetorium temporis

"This phrase translates to 'the hall of time.' It kept sticking in my head on our tour of your facility in Chantilly. After dinner, I wasn't sleepy and had some energy to burn off, so I stayed up and studied the text." He glanced over at Erin at this point. She obliged his look with a smile.

"One thing I thought about was if I were stuck in the past, how could I talk to my friends in the future? Well, one way would be to include a coded message. I began to scrutinize the text with this theory in mind."

Gell and McCallister leaned forward, fully engaged.

"Nothing in the text caught my eye, but I looked at the OCR version of the document again. We took pictures of the document and then used software to convert all the letters into digital ones.

The process allows me to do things like add spaces and punctuation or do a lexical search of the body, all of which are necessary for me to translate what I'm reading properly." He showed a slide of the digital output to clarify what he had explained.

"But I wasn't getting anywhere with the digital version. So, I started wondering about the possibility of something being hidden in the literal transcripts. I started to look more closely at them." The slide showed a blown-up image of a few lines from the document. "Looking at these lines, I wanted to show you some things I noticed. First of all, you see our common phrase 'praetorium temporis' on the right side of that third line." Using his laser pointer, he highlighted the phrase.

"When I started looking at the lines, I noticed something that originally didn't catch my eye. "Before I show it, I need to familiarize you with a term most of you have heard but probably don't know the meaning of. The term is 'serif.' A serif is a small mark at the end of a letter. So, for instance, Times Roman font has them." A slide showed text with Times Roman letters, and he pointed to the serif on the characters. "While the Arial font is what we call 'sans-serif,' meaning it has no serif marks." The slide advanced, showing an example of an Arial font. He then returned to the lines from the text in question.

"The author wrote this meticulously by hand, with excellent penmanship, but I saw something important. I noticed inconsistencies with the calligraphy because some letters were made with serifs while others weren't." He used his laser pointer to show some of these letters with the extra mark. "If you collect the letters with serifs, it'll read 'crew is safe.' This phrase 'praetorium temporis' acted as a period for the sentences." He then presented a slide showing all the characters found in the document.

He quickly changed to the slide revealing the entire astonishing message:

The Kronos crew is safe. Scuttled ship in 1532. Some records are hidden at location sixty-two-point-one latitude and ten-point-three longitude – just south of Lake Haustsjoen.

"I added the hyphens." Colton proudly gleamed. He looked over at Erin, whose mouth hung open and eyes sparkled with astonishment. I think she's impressed. Good one.

Gell exclaimed a breathless "Whoa!"

"Do we have a GPS coordinate of that location?" McCallister asked.

"I searched for it," Colton said. "It's a good bit north of Germany in Norway. Haustsjoen is a lake in the middle of nowhere. The location of the land in question is accessible but on the uninhabited side of the lake. I think the authors of this letter knew this area would be unsearched, whereas everything in Germany would have been scoured and scrutinized."

"When can we get there and find these records?" Gell said.

"Well, we can't just show up and start looking, if that's what you're thinking," Adkins chimed in. He loved Gell's enthusiasm, but experience made him painfully aware of the bureaucracy required to do such searches.

"Maybe, if someone else owns it," Gell said. "But what if I just purchase the land in question?" The way Gell spoke of freely spending such money captured Colton's attention. "We have multiple companies in Norway already. What if I have one of the resource companies buy this land as a potential site for research? Could you then look around to ensure we aren't destroying ancient relics before we clear the land to make a facility?"

Gell understood how governments made simple tasks difficult and quickly figured out ways to circumvent the systems. He realized that if a local company made the purchase, the issue would be moot, and TxC had the money and resources to make it happen.

"I suppose it could solve the question of why we're excavating without going through the normal channels," Adkins said.

"If I hire your company to oversee this, would you be able to work with our Norwegian team to find these records?" Gell looked right at Adkins. He didn't know what Adkins had told his staff, so this statement gave him every opportunity to break the news rather than have it sprung on them.

Unlike most supervisors, Adkins kept little from his team. Having already briefed them, he replied quickly, "This is definitely in our wheelhouse, Theseus. We're in."

"Good. Then, if it's okay with you, I'd like to hire you exclusively for the next year, with the option to continue this agreement for at least the next few years. I'd like to send a team over to Adkins' to negotiate the details as soon as possible. We'll also attempt to acquire this land as soon as possible."

"We have some smaller jobs that we're committed to that are scattered over the next year. If we can see those sites properly finished, this sounds like a workable plan," Adkins said.

Gell stood up and addressed the room. "Ladies and gentlemen, I want to make this clear–We're truly indebted to your team, Percy. And these discoveries… Colton, that's a hell of a find! I don't know how you even saw it! I'll spare no expense to ensure our trapped friends are heard and honored. I know they are the right group to bring closure to this. Now, I must talk about another job we need to hire you for related to the Kronos project." Gell looked at Adkins and Colton who patiently awaited his proposition.

"Armed with your additional knowledge, we've had lengthy discussions over the past few days. We've decided it would be worth our time to see if we can 'track' our friends through the sixteenth century. "We would also like to hire your team to search for more artifacts with the Kronos team's fingerprint on them.

"We don't care if you want to divulge this to the historical community, though we would prefer you didn't. You now have an idea of what to look for in history. Possibly, what we find in Norway will help this even further. One thing we would like to know is what happened to the other eight members."

"I can't speak for our team, but I think we'd be interested in investigating their whereabouts as well," Adkins confirmed.

"I hoped you would say that, Percy. You'll know how to handle this. Whatever your team needs, we can make it happen. I want it clear that your decisions are the final word. We won't stand in your way. If, at some point, you believe we've crossed an ethical boundary, I expect you to let me know, and we'll put an end to our actions at once. Your 'no' means no, and though I might ask questions, I'll not try to coerce you to go beyond your limitations." All Gell's excitement left as he said this. The entire room stilled as they contemplated what this expedition meant to Gell.

"I appreciate that, Theseus, and I hope you'll get the relief you're looking for through our efforts" Adkins said.

The next half-hour was taken up with discussing logistical matters and some legal understanding of their agreement on the job, then the meeting concluded.

Erin immediately went up to Adkins after it ended. "I didn't get to say hello coming in, Percy."

Adkins' face warmed as he turned to her. "Thank you for your card the other day, Erin. You must have written it on the plane that night so I could get it on Saturday. That made my weekend."

"It was an amazing night, and I wanted you to know how much I loved and appreciated it."

"I didn't get a thank you card," Colton said, feigning offense.

"How do you know? Maybe it got stuck in the mail." A devilish smile played across her face.

Colton thought that the smile made her look even more attractive. "Hmm. Maybe," he said.

"So, rather than competing with the amazing meal in Virginia, what would you say to us having pizza? I go to a place near here that I think has the best pizza on the planet."

"That sounds wonderful," she said. "I must warn you, though, I've got a strong opinion on what's best, and I haven't found anything close here in Boston to what I used to get in Philly. I'm really curious to see what you think is good."

"Great! Would you mind if I picked you up at six? Maybe we could go down to the pier and walk around afterward if it isn't too late. It's about a three-block walk from the restaurant." He couldn't hide his enthusiasm at this prospect.

"I'll text you my address. See you at six," she said, grinning. And without another word, Erin walked over to McCallister.

"Did you ask her out?" Jackson tapped Colton on the shoulder.

"Um, what?" Colton had been too busy watching Erin walk away.

"Yo? Earth to Colton! Did you ask her out on a date?" Jackson looked again, anxiously waiting for a reply.

"Yep! And she said yes."

"So, are you taking her somewhere nice? I've some recommendations if you want."

"We're going to Poppa Antonio's for pizza."

Jackson's eyes popped open as he did a double-take. "You go there all the time. The pizza there is great, don't get me wrong. But why would you take Erin there?" The young intern looked seriously confused.

"The pizza is magical, and let me give you an important tip, my friend. Dating isn't just about getting to know the person; it's also about the person getting to know you. Do things so that they can see the real you, or at some point, the real you will catch them off guard." Jackson nodded as he pondered the words of wisdom. Colton walked on to talk with Adkins.

"I asked her out tonight," Colton told Adkins.

"Well done! I hope you have a wonderful time."

"Me too. I'm nervous."

"Just be you. Who couldn't like that?" Adkins chuckled, patting Colton on the back.

"Thanks, Percy. You know how to make me feel more comfortable."

"That's why I'm paid the big bucks. Speaking of pay, I've given you and Jackson big raises. TxC said they're hiring us, so I don't want them to get away with junior numbers on my two stars in the company. Don't be shocked by your next paycheck, but please keep it quiet from the rest of the staff. I've raised their pay, but nothing like you or Jackson."

Colton couldn't help himself and hugged Adkins. The action caught Percy by surprise as he returned the gesture of gratitude. Nothing else was said as Colton turned and walked away.

The young doctor went to his office, sat alone at his desk for a few minutes, and considered the day's events. *I asked a girl out on a date, and she said 'yes'; I impressed not only my boss but one of the most influential men in the world; and I got a big raise,* Colton mused. *I don't think the day could go much better, and there's still potential with Erin's date tonight.* He laughed at himself and decided to leave early from work to prepare for the evening's activities. *I hope Sudsie's can make my car look good enough for the date.* He grabbed his keys and headed to the car wash; they would need all the time he could give them.

CHAPTER 28

THE END IS NIGH

Northern Germania - Spring of 1532 - Day 525

Winter of 1531 wasn't kind. The snow and bitter cold exposed some design flaws in the roofs of the cabins. Though they could structurally hold the snow's weight, the imperfections in learning how thatching worked caused some of the cabins to be briefly uninhabitable until the team could repair the water pouring into them. As a result, one cabin required a large part of the floor to be replaced.

Other innovations worked but brought more challenges. The baffled chimneys with a filtration system helped hide the smoke from their fireplaces, but they couldn't entirely remove the trails in the cold of winter. Because of this, more patrols were necessary to ensure a hunter didn't follow the smoke into the village.

As the promise of spring finally turned the white landscape green, Klugstadt witnessed its second marriage. Aecha and Vercelli celebrated their happy union with a simple celebration. The two of them took over one of the two-room cottages without needing to build another home.

As another couple united, the rift between Wilson and Kelly grew.

Their contention dumbfounded the group because everything indicated they respected and liked each other. The two fought a philosophical war, and their arguments compelled others to take sides. Quin and Athera often argued the same issues.

"So, are we going to stand here and ignore all the cries for help from the folks we encounter?" Quin asked, purposefully stirring up the hornet's nest as he waited for a reply.

"We all know what a moral and righteous man you are. Would you like to declare yourself the sovereign and just guidance for all mankind?" Athera snapped with biting sarcasm.

"Oh yes, because it's moral to stand and do nothing. I don't claim to be a guru. I just want to ease people's suffering. But I guess you would stay silent and let Hitler, Stalin, or Mao do their worst."

The piety in his voice was answered by the disgusted look on Athera's face. "Oh, here we go again! You're taking the most extreme case and claiming it as the standard!"

"Well, give me an example of not interjecting being the right thing to do," he barked back, his temples pulsating as he waited for her reply.

"Sir Alexander Fleming and penicillin," she responded.

"Oh, come on! Who would have stopped Fleming from leaving the petri dish unclean while on vacation? Who?"

"You would have if you didn't know the whole story or chose to ignore parts of it. You don't know the whole story here, but you're all gung ho to render judgment based on your limited knowledge of the situation."

"This is hopeless." Quin waved his hands in the air and stormed out of the room, exasperated.

Cody spent more time in the pub down in Gamburg. Though his German wasn't robust, it improved dramatically as he flirted weekly with the pub owner's daughter. Cody couldn't resist Gisela's allure. A bright, happy, beautiful girl with straight blond hair, blue eyes, and a curvy figure, she garnered the attention of many suitors.

Her boisterous voice and laugh attracted Cody even more.

Locals considered it quite off that Gisela remained unmarried at twenty-one. Most blamed her father for watching young men like a hawk and scaring away all but the bravest. Perhaps Cody's awkwardness with the language or simple pity compelled her father to like Cody. Gisela and Cody clumsily communicated as they grew closer over time. Cody wanted more than Klugstadt could offer him, and his frustration with the secret aspects of their lives multiplied. He wanted to introduce Gisela to his friends but didn't know how the camp would react. Timidly, he approached Wilson. "Hey, man. Can we talk?"

"Yeah. Did you break something in the mill?" Wilson laughed at his own comment.

"No, not this time. It's about Gisela."

"Oh, you want to bring her around, don't you?"

"Yeah, I do. Do you think that would be a problem?" As he said this, his body language told Wilson that this wasn't just a request but more of a pleading.

"Let me talk to the council and see what we can do. Your situation has already come up in our discussions, so I don't think it'll shock anyone."

"Okay. Thanks, man."

"You bet!"

The subject came up in the next meeting, and the other two members disagreed with Wilson on allowing Gisela access to their village. Brandon and Aecha worried that locals would overrun Klugstadt once visitors were allowed, and there might even be legal repercussions if the Mecklenburgh Guards discovered their location.

Aecha suggested they help Cody rent a parcel of land down by Gamburg from one of the local nobles, and Cody could come to Klugstadt to work. They could visit him and meet Gisela while keeping their camp location a secret.

Brandon weighed in and agreed with Aecha.

"I don't think we've made good enough ground rules yet for handling these interactions with the locals. Perhaps someday we'll be ready, but that isn't today."

The response infuriated Wilson. "It's been more than a year, Brandon. We should have established ground rules for these kinds of interactions long ago. And how long? How long do you think we can keep this place hidden? It's only a matter of time now before someone stumbles on us and tells. We've been lucky so far, but sometime soon, that luck will run out." He stormed out of the meeting and went to the water to think. Kelly caught up with him.

"Wilson? Hey, slow down!" she shouted to him.

"Oh, Kelly! I guess you've come to mock me?"

Neither Wilson's tone nor his demeanor was pleasant, and a frustrated Kelly took offense, saying, "What the heck, Wilson? When have I ever mocked you?" She paused before adding, "Grow up!" She was frustrated and disappointed. He was behaving like a child, and she wouldn't let it slide.

"You've twisted the minds of the other council members. "They won't even listen to reason. I'm pretty tired of all of this." It was evident to Kelly that the weight of leading was pressing on Wilson.

"I haven't 'twisted' anyone, Wilson. I know we don't agree on some things, but I also know you're a good man. Please, let's talk and work some stuff out." Her calmly delivered words did nothing to balance Wilson's vexation.

"Kelly, the shackles I'm wearing right now with our restrictions are killing me. I don't like the man I'm becoming. We can do so much to help, but we choose not to." He then explained Cody's situation and the inequity in allowing people to marry in the camp but not offering Cody the same opportunity with Gisela.

She considered the problem and his perspective. "Does Cody want to get married?" she asked.

"Well... I don't know if he does or not." This revelation caused him to consider that he may have overstated his case.

"You don't seem very happy here, either. Why don't you and Cody just buy a property outside Klugstadt and move there? I don't think anyone would mind. We would much rather you be happy and see you less than have you miserable all the time."

"That's not the point, Kelly! I want to help people, and you're binding my hands." His observation cut straight to her heart. She wanted to help people, but felt compelled to choose restraint with what was known by the crew out of respect for the future. "So, if it's not Gisela, who will it be? You know, we'll be found out at some point, and then what? I seriously think it might be time for us to all part ways. If I'm not allowed to use technology to help others, why should I be allowed to use it to help myself?"

"Because what we're using is from our world, not theirs. You must see the difference." Kelly saw the merit in his argument but couldn't back off from what she believed. "We can't run from this unfortunate responsibility put on our shoulders. I lay awake many nights, worrying if we've already affected this period too much. It would be easier to ignore the future we know and try to fix their problems, but would it be the right thing to do? I don't think it would."

"I understand your position. I just don't agree with it." Wilson huffed showing his impatience of the redundant argument. "Can we talk about this some other time? I don't think we're going to resolve anything tonight." He tried to smile, but it came across more like a grimace.

"Of course. Sorry to have bothered you." She knew full well that this conversation wasn't satisfying to him, and sooner or later, incidents like this would result in bigger problems.

A few hours later, Cody found Wilson and received the bad news. Cody's anger grew.

"I might take them up on the property idea," he said matter-of-factly.

"It's not right." Wilson hurt for his friend and wanted to give him more options.

"Says you. But you know, and I know we can't speak for everyone. Bringing Gisela here has risks of exposure they aren't willing to take right now. So, if I can't bring her here, I want to bring her somewhere I can say is my own." Cody admired his friend's tenacity in standing up for what was right.

Wilson reluctantly accepted this answer, but it stung. "Okay, well, only the king owns land here, so what we would have to do is rent land from one of the nobles. Maybe we can forge some papers giving you a position of importance in a distant land, and all you would ask is for a plot of field you would personally hold and tend to in return for a monthly payment. The story would also give you cover for your crappy German." Wilson had used CHAMP to read up on how things worked in this era.

"Wow, this has some serious potential. Can I sleep on it, and we can talk more later?" They agreed and exchanged farewells.

As Cody walked away, Wilson decided to sit a while longer on the side of the stream. The peaceful water helped soothe his spirit, which was heavily weighed down by the decisions being rendered and the lack of agreement with the council. An hour later, he decided it was time for him to take significant action. In this case, action included making more visits to CHAMP and taking meticulous notes for later use. With only Brandon in the cabin since Vercelli's marriage, it would be much easier to sneak information out of the basement.

The next day, Wilson went down to Gamburg and procured some blank notebooks from the local bookbinder, a transaction that would become commonplace for him over the next year. His plan would take many months, but he could finally part ways with Klugstadt when it was completed. Wilson never wanted to do anything to hurt his friends, but that didn't mean stay here and watch people suffer when he could help.

CHAPTER 29

THE DATE

Boston - Fall - 2035

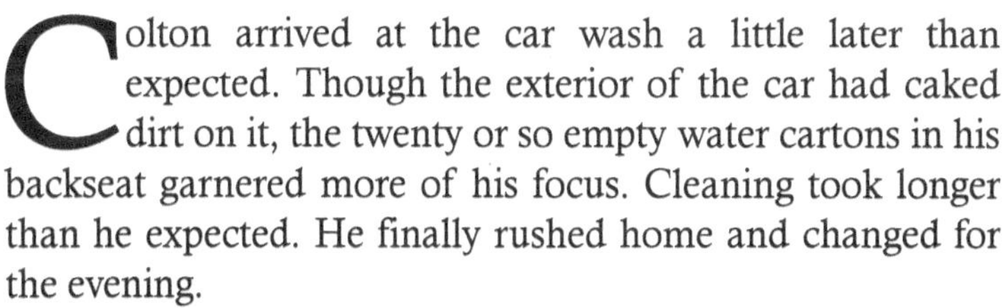

Colton arrived at the car wash a little later than expected. Though the exterior of the car had caked dirt on it, the twenty or so empty water cartons in his backseat garnered more of his focus. Cleaning took longer than he expected. He finally rushed home and changed for the evening.

He got back into his clean now-car and texted Erin about heading her way, arriving at her condominium complex at 5:58. He thought to himself, *Two minutes to spare! I'm just in time.* He planned on pulling in and parking until he saw her standing at the lobby entrance, dressed in jeans and an attractive top. He zipped over and rolled down the passenger window. "Need a lift?" The comment came off corny but cute, at least he hoped. *Kind of like the bad dad jokes Percy recites on occasion. Maybe I'm slowly becoming Percy.* He snickered to himself. *Well, there are much worse things to become.*

"Why, yes, but I don't normally take rides from strangers," she retorted with a daring smile as she opened the door and hopped right in. "Nice. Piña colada is one of my favorite scents."

"Oh, I got the car cleaned before I came here. I didn't want you thinking I was a total slob."

"Let me know where you get your car cleaned. It looks like they do a great job. "And I was so glad you offered to drive because my backseat is currently a repository for water cartons and coffee cups."

Much like Adkins, Erin put Colton at ease with effortless honesty and a few kind words. Her casual comfort in conversation made her already-pleasant temperament even more engaging.

"Full of cartons? How about that! I hope you're up for some pizza!" The grin never left his face as he started driving.

"You bet! I'm starving." She wasn't kidding. Over the lunch break of the morning meeting, she ended up trying to address a few problems on another TxC project and hadn't eaten anything all day.

"Thankfully, we're only about ten minutes away." Colton steered onto the main highway. "So, those are nice condominiums. Have you been here long?"

"About two years. I like them, but I don't love them. I grew up with a yard, and it's tough for me to get used to condo life." Her smile left momentarily.

"I know what you mean. I think I told you I grew up on a farm, right? I miss waking up in the morning to the sounds of birds and the wind blowing through our gardens."

She imagined that and liked the thought. "How in the world did two rural folks end up in Boston?"

They both chuckled.

"I think, like you, this is just a place to rest. I end up all over the place. Adkins keeps me busy on-site, which is something I like."

"You're right. There's no way I could get to do the stuff I do now back in Indiana. I love all the work and even like working here at TxC, but when we talk about hearing birds and walking in a field, a part of me wishes for the simplicity of my day-to-day."

Colton nodded in complete agreement and understanding.

Erin paused like she was looking for the best way to articulate her thoughts. "It's like this constant fight between what we like, need, and want. I think we're all just figuring out the balance between them."

Colton kept driving, but his mind and heart rallied around this statement. He wanted to shout 'Amen' but figured it wouldn't go over well.

"Wow! I sure am cheery company!" She almost seemed embarrassed that the dialogue had waxed so somber and philosophical in such a short time.

"I love this. You can only have so much conversation about the weather, scenery, and changing times. I'm really with you on the struggle." His words put her at ease, which showed in her countenance.

"Well, look at that!" As the car turned into the restaurant's full parking lot, another car pulled out, giving them a spot directly in front. "I think things are working out well!" He grinned and slipped into the empty slot in front of Poppa Antonio's Trattoria.

Quickly, he jumped out and came around to open her door. The pair entered the bustling restaurant, where a hostess in a short black dress welcomed them and then stepped out to guide them to their table. She smiled as she spoke. "Dr. Shaw, you're right on time! Right this way, please. We have your table waiting."

The hostess walked them through two dining rooms to a set of stairs that led to the second floor. Upstairs, the noise level dropped significantly. Mediterranean archways were the only thing impeding the harbor's lovely view, and traditional Italian music played lightly in the background. The Tuscan-themed floor ratcheted up the class from the first floor.

Colton had never been up on this floor before. The more formal setting misrepresented what he portrayed to his date. Typically, Jackson and one or two other friends would sit at the café tables in the first dining room at lunch. It wasn't classy or glitzy, but they loved the pizza, and the atmosphere remained lively.

"Wow, look at this view!" Erin stopped for a moment to admire a spectacular sight of the bay.

He breathed a quiet sigh of relief, enjoying the venue's unanticipated twist. "This is wonderful!" Unfortunately, he couldn't turn off the historian in his mind. The decor around the room clashed with cultures and times. While some placements were tasteful choices, others shouted "inexpensive" to the trained eye. The German word 'kitsch' could describe much of what he was seeing. Still, the room's coziness invited them to peruse, and he loved discovering it with her.

The attendant turned and directed them to a lovely table marred by the dull metal pizza tray stand. "Can I start you with something to drink? Perhaps our Italian sangria?"

"I'd love to try the sangria. Is it good?" Erin said, pursing her lips in curiosity.

"Yes! It's my favorite drink in the city. Watch out, though—it's potent."

"I'll take a glass, please, and I'll be careful," she replied, thanking the hostess for her advice.

"Could I just have a glass of sweet tea with lemon?" Colton asked.

"Dr. Shaw? You're off work! Do you drink sweet tea all the time?"

His smile covered his embarrassment. "What can I say? I love sweet tea. But the sangria does sound tempting."

The hostess graciously smiled. "You should try it sometime. I think you'll like it. I'll have those drinks out momentarily." She turned and went to a station to put in their drink order.

The menus were already on the table. They both looked down at the impressive selection of items.

"It won't embarrass you if I order pizza, will it?" Colton asked. "It looks like they have a lot of other nice things here. Shoot, I never knew they had any of this."

"We did come here for pizza, right?" Erin said.

What a good sport! Colton thought with relief.

"What do you like on your pizza?" he asked.

"I really like crispy pepperoni with meatballs and mushrooms, especially if the meatballs are handmade. If not, sausage with mushrooms is also really good."

Ding! We have a winner.

"You're in luck. Antonio makes the meatballs himself. Oh, that reminds me. Just so you know, Antonio will come out and talk to the guests at some point. He's from Sicily and is proud of his food."

"If you are taking me here, I suspect he has reason to be a little proud."

"Yeah… that's a good point, but he's kinda endearing. All I know is that I love talking with him. If it's okay, I'm going to order a large pizza. "After you have some, I bet you'll want to take it home for later. If not, I'll gladly take it with me."

She nodded her approval. "Sounds great. Cold pizza is always welcome around my place!"

The hostess returned with their drinks. "Have you had a chance to look over the menu?"

"We have," Colton answered.

"What can I get you?" The attendant pulled out a pad to take their order.

"Can we get a large pie with meatballs, crispy pepperoni, and mushrooms?" he asked, looking at his date to verify the order's accuracy.

"Nice! Adding mushrooms today, huh?"

Erin looked at him and raised an eyebrow.

"Um, yes, it sounded like a great addition." Slightly embarrassed, he smiled and closed his menu.

"Does Dr. Shaw order here often?" Erin inquired.

"Oh yeah. Colton eats here like twice a week when he's in town." The host turned and headed to put in the order.

"Did I mention that I love this place?"

"You did mention that, *Dr. Shaw*… Wow! This sangria is delicious. Would you like a sip?" She didn't expect to blurt out the second part, but it made for a good laugh.

"I'm glad you like it, 'Dr. Warmouth.' Maybe I should order one."

"You should! It's amazing! I don't think you'll be disappointed."

When the attendant returned with the food, Colton ordered one based on Erin's recommendation.

"That was a fabulous find!" Erin conversed between slices of pizza.

"This joint? I know. Jackson found this place. He had a condominium mate who worked in the kitchen here. We started coming and can't seem to go anywhere else."

"No, today with the Latin text. It was amazing how you found that message." Her sincere compliment sounded lovely in his ears.

"It's crazy how lucky a find it was." He tried to downplay it, though he did think it was pretty amazing. This whole thing felt like he was in a spy or war movie where someone had cracked a secret code.

"Maybe, but you were clever enough to know how and where to look."

"Have you thought about them?" His demeanor quickly changed from light hearted to melancholy, which surprised her.

She lowered the slice from her mouth and considered her words. "Yes. I don't know what I'd do if put in that crew's situation."

She stared out at the bay as she contemplated the weight of this tragic event.

"I can't stop thinking about it," Colton said. "I want to help them, but it seems impossible."

Erin took a sip of her drink and ventured forward–"Not to change the subject too much, but I wonder if they had an impact on what we know as history."

Colton carefully considered his reply. "When I was in college, there were many times in my history classes when I'd see the folly of a decision with perfect clarity and hope the outcome would be different. You turn the pages of the history book, wishing in your heart what you already knew wasn't going to happen. But what if you were there, with the clarity of hindsight, and could stop some horrible decisions, saving millions of lives." He paused to collect his thoughts.

Erin stared at him with unjaded admiration, then countered, "Maybe they have saved millions of lives. We wouldn't know, would we?"

Colton looked up as if thinking about the ramifications of Erin's question. "That is a good point. It doesn't seem we're in a position to know or help them physically. It's truly a strange place that we've found ourselves."

She lifted her napkin, wiped the corners of her mouth, and added, "I couldn't agree more."

"If we can't help them, I'd at least like to let them be heard. I don't know what that exactly means yet, but I'll try to do my best to honor them through this." To these words, she placed her hand on his. Her touch was warm, and her hand was soft. He turned his hand over and embraced hers.

"You're going to help them. You already have, and I think Thesues will ensure you get every opportunity to do this."

"Colton! Who have you brought to my place?" Antonio blurted out with the zeal of a proud, middle-aged and moderately overweight dad.

"Antonio! This is Erin. It's her first time in your restaurant."

Colton was glad to escape the seriousness of their conversation, of which Antonio was the perfect antidote.

"Welcome! Welcome! I see you got the meatball pizza. Colton? You didn't force your pizza choices on this nice lady, did you? You know I make other excellent dishes, right?" The owner had a half-chastising, half-playful look. The best word to describe him was jolly.

"I chose it without a word from Colton." She looked up at Antonio, who seemed enamored by such a beautiful woman.

"Well, Erin, you have excellent taste. I'll leave you two to enjoy your evening. But would you accept some of the finest cannoli in the world, on me? We make them by hand every day. You must take them home with you. I insist!"

"Umm, yes, thank you." Colton was at a loss for words as Antonio winked at him. He was sure Antonio thought it was a clever move, but it was painfully evident to Erin as he caught her muffled chuckle.

"Of course, of course. Oh!" Antonio looked at a waiter and snapped his fingers at the desserts he had in his hand. Before the dessert arrived, Antonio was off to greet the next table.

"Can I get you all anything else?" The host's timing was impeccable. "Perhaps some after-dinner coffee?"

Colton looked at Erin, shaking his head. "No, thank you. Just a to-go box would be great." He looked to the attendant and smiled, realizing she already had the box and was holding it out for him. "Oh, am I the observant one!" He laughed.

"Would you like me to box it for you?" the host asked. When Colton obliged, she placed the box on the table and dropped the pizza effortlessly into the cardboard container. Another box was brought for the cannoli.

The attendant quietly left as Colton asked, "So, how was it?"

"How was what?" The smile on her face indicated that she was toying with him.

He wasn't biting. "Umm, the pizza. How did you like it?"

"You were right. This was the best pizza I've had in years." His face indicated the great relief that his mind was experiencing.

"I'll say this," she added, "You're getting away with very cheap dates, though!" Erin sat back in her chair, finishing off the last of her drink.

"What can I say? Sometimes blessings just fall in your lap," he said with a tiny bit of cleverness in his voice.

"Colton, I think people can't help but like you. Be it Antonio or Adkins, I'm merely along for the ride." She was complimentary and meant nothing more by it, but something was not sitting well with him. None of these evenings were about him, nor did he want them to be.

"I like being around you. I'm enjoying this ride, too." He opted to speak plainly, and she could find no deception in his words or actions.

"I'm so glad." A larger-than-life smile came over her face.

"Would you like to walk to the pier? We can stop by my car, drop off the pizza and cannoli, then walk from there." He looked through the window at the sparkling water, momentarily mesmerized by the view. He reached into his pocket, pulled out his wallet, paid the bill, and dropped a large tip on the table.

"That would be great." She grabbed her purse, and the two walked out.

The night continued to be fantastic, but the thought that he'd be dropping her back off at her condominium weighed on him. If it were up to him, the night would never end.

When they returned to the car, after the walk, the lovely smell of butter, basil, and fresh garlic replaced the scent of piña colada. They both took deep breaths of the fantastic aroma.

Sitting in the parking lot, Erin suddenly turned earnest. "I've something to say."

Oh no! What did I mess up? I thought everything was going well. His mind whirled with possibilities, but he silenced them to give her his undivided attention. "Okay?"

"I'm not much on dating, but I think this is going very well." Erin bit her lip for a second then continued. "I'm worried about something, so I just want to say it now." Colton agreed so far, though he still couldn't see a problem. *Did she maybe have a boyfriend or some dark past?*

"What's wrong?" He hoped he hadn't done something—like being obliviously insensitive again—to mess this up.

"Nothing at all. But if we continue… umm… this, I want you to understand a few things." The tone was enough to make his palms sweat.

"Okay…" "First of all, this is going somewhere or we're done. I don't like dating for the sake of dating. I'm not saying let's pack our things and run away like you said that Antonio did with his wife." They both giggled. "So far, I'm loving our dates and getting to know you better."

"That's fair, and I agree on both parts. I'd like to see more of you." His unease turned to curiosity.

"Good. Now, the harder thing. You and I travel a lot. We're going to have to work to make this function. I'm also not a 'looking around for something better' type of person. We're going to have to make time for this to grow. Are you okay with that?" She studied him, scrutinizing his body language. Clearly, this had come up before in her life. Perhaps it had also come up in his life, but he hadn't noticed it with past girlfriends.

"I want to try. We can take as much time as we need. You're worth it."

"Me too! I mean, you're worth it as well. Well, I'd invite you up, but I met you down here because I was embarrassed by my place being a mess." They both laughed. "Also, it's one way to ensure a date doesn't go too far." She didn't know if this last remark was too off-color. Though she was joking, it was both accurate and funny at the same time.

"Yeah, that's about the same for my place too!" They laughed and hugged, and she reluctantly exited the car.

Colton glanced at the backseat and quickly said, "You forgot the pizza. Before you go, let's have cannoli together."

He reached back and got both boxes.

"That is a wonderful idea." She anxiously opened the dessert box. She bit into one and rolled her eyes with glee at the infusion of flavor combined with the shell's satisfying crunch. "Oh yeah. That alone would have made this trip worth it."

Colton's first taste of the dessert was equally pleasant. "Oh my, yes."

They finished their treat, and she reluctantly opened the door to leave.

"I'd like to see you again soon," he said as she climbed out.

"I'd like that, too, but can you give me the weekend to make my condominium presentable?" she asked.

Colton grinned and quickly responded, "I'll do the same."

"Then we agree." She reached out her hand, and he reached out his, but the handshake awkwardly morphed into another hug. Neither one objected.

"Give me a call when you think the coast is clear for me to come over!"

"You got it!" She turned to go into her condominium building.

CHAPTER 30

THE DECEPTION

Northern Germania - Spring of 1532 - Day 551

The next day, Wilson got up and immediately approached Brandon and Aecha. "Hey, you two, sorry about leaving the meeting early last night."

Both indicated they understood his frustration but remained steadfast in their stance.

"I talked with Cody, and he's okay with Aecha's idea of getting a place outside of Klugstadt. Also, in thinking some more, I think I've got an idea that will keep us all safer."

"You've got my attention," Brandon said.

"Because of the wars down south, many refugees are fleeing and heading our way. Gamburg's population is snowballing. With that growth is going to come sprawl. We've already seen a few hunters, but since they were poaching on the King's land, they didn't approach, nor were they going to run to the village and snitch on us out here. Still, it only takes one guy telling a royal guard, and we have big problems."

Aecha folded her arms. "It does seem like it's only a matter of time now. So far, Gamburg has been pretty welcoming. I guess it's because we trade fairly and don't make trouble. Gretta said she'd repeatedly seen them throw refugees out of the town. It's a serious problem for sure!"

"What if we made Cody a disgraced noble from the south? Far enough away, it would be hard to cross-check. Have him come to the lord of this region and request land for rent. He could say something to the effect that he isn't worthy of his noble position but would make it profitable for the lord if he were granted land. To do this, we would need to forge a letters patent, or what they call a briefadel. The ruse would explain Cody's separation from us at Klugstadt and add justification for our small village."

Brandon and Aecha liked this idea. Wilson's suggestion assured that Cody couldn't mix with the region's nobles, but they'd feel some obligation to protect him from a life of poverty.

Wilson continued, "Klugstadt had been accumulating wealth through trading and had enough silver to offer the noble of the region an honorarium for looking past Cody's disgrace and granting him a piece of land. Besides, Cody would also promise to pay a lease on the land."

"This is all good, but how can we create forged papers like this?" Aecha's recent marriage elevated stability of Klugstadt to something worthy of pursuit. As long as the camp remained hidden, the group lived in constant fear of discovery and banishment at any moment.

"Alex can do it. He's already forged quite a few documents for us to allow us to get supplies from the south. He has a gift for it." Wilson had seen enough of Alex's handiwork to know he could easily do this task. For Alex, this was the kind of challenge he enjoyed.

Aecha and Brandon could see that Wilson's plans for the future ranged much further than day-to-day existence.

Wilson continued, "In addition, we all need some papers explaining where we came from and why we're part of Cody's entourage."

"I'm okay with this. How about you, Brandon?" Aecha looked for a signal in his body language.

Brandon thought about the risks and weighed them against the rewards.

Whoever went to the lord of the region took a chance of being found out. The lord could kill them on the spot, ending the gambit. The potential benefit was liberty and plausibility for Klugstadt.

"CHAMP has plenty of examples of sixteenth-century legal documents for Alex to study and duplicate. Also, his knowledge of southern nobility would allow us to put the suitable dates and people within the document to give it almost impeccable believability. "The disgraced noble approach would also ensure no one would be willing to mention him for fear of association. In many ways, this is the perfect cover." As he listened to himself speaking, he became excited about the possibility. He wondered why they hadn't thought of this earlier.

"This is a great plan, Wilson. My biggest concern is Cody. His German is pathetic. Do you think he can pull it off?"

"I've thought of this. I'm willing to go and speak for Cody as his armor-bearer. Cody was injured two years ago in the Ottoman siege of Vienna, and his head injury compromised his speech. He has the blessing of Pope Clement VII for his bravery. He had to be removed from his position in court because of his speech and other 'thinking issues.' Hence, he was disgraced."

"Whoa! You're good!" The team was impressed, and Wilson smiled, bowing with an overblown flourish as a pompous armor-bearer would.

"Let's get Cody and Alex in on this as soon as possible," Aecha said, thinking about the ramifications of this conversation.

"One more thing, Aecha. When I do this, I'll have to travel south to appear I was heading north. I don't want any chance they can track us back here. If I fail, Cody and I are dead. I want CHAMP to make us cyanide caps because these nobles like to kill through torture, making fearful examples of liars to their subjects."

This inconvenient truth turned the mood into a much more dire one. "Are you sure you want to do this?" Aecha asked with a gentle touch to his hand.

Wilson nodded, giving assurance to his resolve. "I'm ready for it. Should I go grab Cody and Alex?"

Brandon was excited, and his nervous energy caused his hands to shake. He spoke again with unbridled enthusiasm. "Yes, but before we agree, we must share it with everyone. The ramifications of this could affect everybody in the camp. We also owe it to them to let them know what we're planning."

CHAPTER 31

THE GAMBIT

Mecklenburgh - Late Spring of 1532 - Day 575

"These clothes itch, and they smell awful." Cody complained.

"Yeah, not much I can do on either front for that bucko! It's the traditional attire of the Moravians. On a bright note, you don't need to wear the stupid headdress as a disgraced noble." Wilson, as the armor-bearer, couldn't conjure sympathy at this point. After all, his majesty rode a horse while Wilson trudged along on the ground, leading the horse mile after mile.

"Great point." Cody wanted this encounter to come to an end. "Where are we heading?"

"We're heading to the big castle. That is what Mecklenburgh means. The Germans are freaking literals when it comes to this stuff. It's crazy!" In his impatience, he grabbed the reins of the horse slightly tighter. The horse snorted at his gesture.

By courier's letter, they arranged a meeting with Henry the Fifth, the Duke of Mecklenburgh-Schwerin. The conference would hopefully be brief, ending with presentation of the appropriate documents they needed to lend legitimacy to the village.

The guards thoroughly searched both men.

Wilson and Cody submitted to the impressive security practices of the duke's guards. Such unexpected scrutiny made this game of deception even more menacing.

The guards pressed Cody to explain the purpose of his visit. He smiled vacantly, blessing them in Latin and some German. The guards looked at each other, wondering if he was right in the head. Wilson quickly interjected in German.

"Forgive him. A well-placed Ottoman hammer tragically shattered his helmet in Vienna. He has never been fully sound since. We're here by royal appointment to see the duke." Wilson put his arm around his friend as if protecting him from the cruelty of the guards.

The guards looked at the papers, then at the foolish man babbling in front of them. They shook their heads, letting the two of them pass. "Don't let him out of your sight. If he wanders down the wrong corridor, one of the other guards may run him through." The guard was kind and cruel in the same stroke. The other guards appeared to enjoy the idea of the idiot being pierced. The two impostors didn't mind their imaginings as long as they could pass.

As a liege of considerable territory, the duke was a busy man. Ten groups waited in the anteroom, along with Cody and Wilson. The room made both men uneasy, and they continually scanned its occupants to ensure their actions aligned with everyone else waiting. The garrison's guards projected intimidation. They noticed guard after guard looking over to figure out what was wrong with Cody. He played the part well, blessing them if they made eye contact. His awkwardness usually got gawkers to turn and walk away as if crazy were, in some way, contagious.

"How am I doing, friend?" Cody asked quietly as two more guards walked towards them and made an immediate about-face.

"You're a natural idiot, but don't take it too far," Wilson said as he elbowed him in the side.

Cody coughed, pouted a bit, and said, "Thank you!"

As a new guard entered the anteroom, he took notice of Cody and approached him. Wilson quickly stepped in front and impeded his progress. The guard turned his dark eyes to study the large man blocking him.

Wilson saw the guard's nostrils flair and his arm reach behind his back for a dagger. His eyes challenged Wilson as he cocked his head back. Wilson's training would allow him to immobilize this threat with a few simple moves, but that would defeat the goal of why they'd come. He chose to try diplomacy. Forcing a smile, he calmly put his hand on the aggressor's arm and said, "Friend, we mean you no harm. We're just here for business with the duke." Slow and unthreatening, the strength in his hold stopped the guard from being able to move his arm further.

The guard realized that a fight with this man wouldn't go well. He chose to try to save face with the observers around him by moving closer to Wilson and snarling, "Keep your strange friend quiet and away from me, or I'll make an example of him."

The man's breath was unbelievably foul. Wilson clenched his teeth and bowed. "Understood. I'll do my best."

The guard shook free of Wilson's grip and stared at Cody momentarily. He then turned and sauntered away from the two men.

Their time to meet with the duke arrived about two hours later without further incident. Wilson didn't know what to expect when they entered. His first view depicted a modestly appointed room with a desk, table, and multiple chairs for those presenting their cases before the duke. Two armed and serious-looking guards negated any comfort available in the chairs. A deeper inspection revealed a young, meek-looking man at a small desk opposite the room entrance. Wilson deduced he was the secretary.

The duke appeared intelligent and unimpressed with his title. To him, this was more of a duty than an honor, and he did his duties with seriousness and efficiency.

The duke didn't bother looking up from the papers before him. "Wie kann der Herzog von Nutzen sein?" The phrase translated to 'How may the duke be of service to you?'

Wasting no time with too many pleasantries, Wilson explained the situation, presented the papers for inspection, and opened his small chest of silver. He then asked the duke permission to lease the small plot of land currently hosting their secret Klugstadt community.

The duke had already made up his mind when they opened the chest of silver. Most of the "noble refugees" wandering through were destitute and wanted partiality. These two came in with papers and offered good-faith money instead of seeking handouts.

The duke finally looked up at them, opened the chest, and took out about half of the coins. "Sie benötigen diese, um erfolgreich zu sein." To Wilson's surprise, the duke gave them a signed and sealed piece of paper and returned the chest. The document contained payment terms and the address of a man in Gamburg who would collect the payments. It also gave passage to twenty-five more occupants on his land. Wilson had already added Gisela to the list if Cody wanted her to be a part of their family. He made up more fictitious names in case anyone else they encountered needed temporary refuge.

Wilson thanked the duke and left, tugging Cody with him as he tried blessing the duke on his departure, to his counterpart's irritation.

"What did he say back there?" Cody asked, having only understood parts of the conversation.

"Basically, he looked at how pathetic you were and said we would need this more than him." Both men laughed, and then wondered why they hadn't thought to do this earlier. The silver the duke returned would pay the rent for the next six months.

"Can we get out of these clothes? They really stink." He sniffed his armpits and crinkled his nose.

"You bet, buddy. Congratulations, nobleman.

"Tomorrow, we can start building your place!"

The next evening in Klugstadt, the group gathered to celebrate the end of hiding their community. They toasted Baron Cody and his faithful armor-bearer. Wilson shared the stories, and everyone was thrilled at the idea they had some legitimacy for their camp.

Kelly sat with a mug of mead and watched the celebration. She studied Wilson, watching his movements and listening to his stories. Kelly sensed that Wilson had kept something back during his narratives. She didn't know what, but she knew there was more. What are you planning, old friend?

Wilson came up and sat by her.

"Great job, Wilson," she said with a magnanimous smile.

"Thanks. At least we know we have some protection from Mecklenburgh." Wilson surmised she suspected he had plans beyond making their community no longer secret. He kept his expression benign.

"I'm glad you're with us, Wilson. You'd make one heck of a foe," she said as Wilson looked out at the crowd.

"Same goes for you, Kelly. Same goes for you."

CHAPTER 32
THE CHANGELING

Northern Germania - Summer of 1532 - Day 755

The blue sky above Klugstadt called to Cody and Kelly. Their eyes roamed the heavenly canvas while Kelly voiced their mutual longing. "Man, this would be a great day to fly." Her eyes never stopped looking up toward the inviting clouds.

Cody lit up at the comment. "One time, my buddy and I flew out of Frankfurt, which isn't too far from here. We were in F-35s and had full tanks. We were both trying to one-up each other. It didn't take long for my buddy to decide it was time for acrobatic training. We got clearance and proceeded to test the limits of our planes.

"Eventually, we ended up doing some stall recovery tests. I wasn't paying great attention to my altimeter, putting my nose up and stalling the bird before looking. Baker shouted at me to warn me, but it was too late. I stalled the plane and realized I didn't have much time to recover. Let's just say I got low enough to make out vehicles on the road.

"So, Baker and I made it back to the base, and our C.O. was waiting for us on the flight deck as we got out of our planes. I've never received a louder lecture in my life.

"The next day, we learned that the Chinese watched our maneuvers and confused our crazy flying with a new advanced version of the F-35. The underground chatter was for any information on the upgraded aircraft. "Our C.O. came into our barracks to talk with us a few days later. He had grounded us for the week, and we were in there playing cards. He had a strange look on his face as he asked us to go up and do similar flight maneuvers again to baffle the Chinese even further."

She burst out laughing. "I bet he never apologized."

"Not a chance! In fact, after the flight, he kept us grounded for another week." He shook his head at the memory.

Hearing them talking, Wilson came out from his cottage to speak to them. "Kelly, Cody, can we speak to you for a minute?" Wilson had a distraught-looking Emma standing behind him.

"Sure. What's going on?" Though Kelly spoke the words to him, her focus never left Emma.

Emma was notoriously cheerful, and to see her on the verge of tears was enough to take note.

"She was down at Gamburg, and her discovery is something that I think we need to address. Emma, tell them what you saw." He stepped to the side and put his hand on Emma's back, inviting her to engage with the group.

She looked down at the ground as she shuffled forward. "So, I was down at the village and overheard two women talking about one of their neighbor's sons. The villagers kept using this strange word for the child: Wechselkind. Then, the other used the word kielkopf when talking about the child." She stopped for a moment because she was holding back her emotions.

"Emma, dear, it's okay," Kelly said. "Do you know what the two words mean?" Kelly herself wasn't familiar with them.

"When I returned to Klugstadt, I went to CHAMP and asked about them. CHAMP said that they were both words for something called a 'changeling.'" Emma's tears rolled.

"Changeling?" Kelly looked confused, and Wilson interjected to give Emma time to recover.

"It's a mix of bad religion and local mythology," Wilson explained. "These women believe that some demon or devil came and replaced the child with a duplicate, essentially stealing the soul of the child."

"Demons stealing kids? That's messed up," Cody said.

"That's not the worst of it. Emma overheard these same two ladies saying that if they couldn't coax the demon to return their child, they'd have to kill the changeling to save their child's soul." Though Wilson spoke these words to everyone, they were directed mostly at Kelly.

"They wouldn't kill their own kids, would they? For God's sake, that's horrible," Kelly said.

"Yes, they would, and according to these women, this will be the fifth child killed this year. Much of Gamburg is in panic mode at this point. Something is happening that changes the children's behavior dramatically, and all these children exhibited similar symptoms of dizziness, nonresponsiveness, paleness, and being balmy to the touch." He stopped, not wanting to upset Emma even further.

"There has got to be something we can do to help! If we don't do something, that mother will kill that poor boy!" Emma blurted out as she began to sob uncontrollably.

Kelly instinctively hugged her. "It's okay, dear." She turned her head to address Wilson. "Can I speak to you privately?"

Wilson didn't audibly respond, but he immediately walked out into the courtyard. He turned to face Kelly and stood quietly.

Once Kelly had consoled Emma, she slowly walked into the open area and checked to ensure no one was in hearing range of the coming conversation. "Well, this is quite a development."

Wilson snorted. "Yeah. This is unbelievable."

Kelly examined Wilson's body language.

His relaxed stance was betrayed by his thumb quickly tapping on his thigh. "Wilson, are you okay? You look a little nervous."

Wilson cocked his head like the comment made him curious. His thumb slowly stopped tapping. "I'm fine, but this has rattled me a little. Emma looks very distraught."

Kelly raised her left eyebrow as she crossed her arms and leaned on a tree near her. "Yeah, this is a terrible thing."

Wilson nervously continued – "We really should look into this to see what's going on. We probably need to do some sleuthing without raising too much suspicion."

Kelly unfolded her arms and straightened herself, walking even closer to Wilson. "Do you think Alex and Gretta might be able to look into this discreetly?"

"I was hoping you'd say that. I'll go find them."

"Go for it, but Wilson? We're walking on thin ice here. Let's not jump until we're all in agreement."

Wilson turned to head out and spurted out, "Copy that, boss."

Kelly stopped him momentarily. "Oh, and one more thing." Wilson spun back to face her. "Yes?"

Kelly looked him square in the eyes. "I'm not your boss. I'm not even on the council."

Wilson chuckled. "Sorry. Sometimes I forget."

The comment lightened the tension dramatically. "Me too, but I'm trying."

"You're fine. I'll go now… if that's all right with you, sir."

Kelly punched his arm. "Get out of here, you punk."

CHAPTER 33

GHOST HUNTERS

Northern Germania - Summer of 1532 - Day 757

Gretta and Alex made their way down to the small village near Klugstadt. As they came near the main street, two vendors waved emphatically at Gretta.

"It seems that someone has quite a fan club," Alex noted sarcastically.

Gretta just laughed. "Are you jealous? They're kind, and the big guy is very fair with his trades."

"Fair to you," Alex said.

"Well, that's all I know. Eric is shrewd but not ridiculous."

"Oh, we're on a first-name basis with him?" He wasn't letting up.

"Yes, is that a problem?" Gretta wasn't concerned. She got the distinct vibe that more was said here than what Alex conveyed. Often, she would be in a group and catch Alex looking at her. His attention made her uncomfortable. Though she enjoyed his company well enough, Gretta lacked any romantic attraction towards him.

"No, if you need your time with Eric, I understand," he quipped.

"Well, I guess I'll start there. You could go down to the pub and talk to Gisela. She might have some information."

"Good idea. I might grab a pint while I'm there, too," he said with a smile as he turned in the pub's direction.

Gretta rolled her eyes, turned around and headed in Eric's direction, waving as she approached. Gretta loved the musical cant of his German dialect.

"Fraulein Gretta, it's always a pleasure to see you." Eric grinned at her with his full grill. His teeth looked good for a middle-aged man of the sixteenth century, but not for a man of the twenty-first century. Even if Gretta had been interested, this alone would have been the deal-breaker. Also, the fact that he was happily married assured no interest. To Gretta's pleasure, Alex wasn't aware of any of this.

"Herr Eric, it's good to see you as well," she replied with a cheery greeting of her own. "How's Frau Mila?"

"Oh, she's delightful. Last night, she made some excellent crested stew. I'd have married her again just to get more of that." He laughed, and she smiled at the small talk. "I'll tell her you asked about her."

There was some quality of this man that reminded Gretta of her dad. She suspected he came from some wealth but either lost it to marry a peasant or his parents were shamed. Whatever the reason, he was a kind merchant, and she trusted him to be fair and truthful in his dealings.

More than once, he saved her from making terrible financial mistakes with a few of the other less scrupulous peddlers. Once, she had purchased some rare white wolf pelts that Cody had prepared. She thought they'd be traded like the other hides she had brought to the village. Eric took one look at the offerings and warned her that they were worth at least four times the usual pelt.

The vendor next to Eric offered her a few extra thalers for them. When she informed him that she knew their worth and that he was trying to trick her, the merchant's pride forced him to pay her almost five times the typical sale price for the hides. She was thankful for Eric's advice and purchased him a small pastry with some of the extra coins in appreciation.

"I was wondering if I could ask you a few questions about something bothering me?" Her smile diminished as she made the request.

"Of course. Is there something wrong? Did Herr Stefan try to swindle you again? He's wicked, I tell you! Don't do business with that scoundrel." His cheeks had turned red as he talked. She was appreciative of his bravado. Again, she was reminded of her father.

"No. I wondered about a word that has come up a few times around Gamburg that I don't understand. I was hoping you could help me figure out what's going on." "A word? Umm… sure. What's this word that has you so upset?" His face changed from anger to concern.

"Thank you. It's just one word, but it sounds very terrible. The word is Wechselkind." She studied his response.

The vendor's face morphed from concern to horror. "Oh, fraulein, you want no part of that word. My cousin and his wife lost one of their children to a devil, who stole him in the night. This event happened a few years ago, but I remember it like it was yesterday." His face changed again, expressing the grief of losing the child as if it was his own.

"I'm so sorry to hear that, Eric." She placed her hand on his shoulder. He smiled at her show of sympathy.

"Thank you for your kind words. I must warn you, Wechselkind is a child that looks like your own but is really a devil. A devil will come when you're not looking, steal your healthy child and replace it with a demonic, sickly one. They look like your child, but they are cursed. These evil beasts steal your child's soul and taunt the parents while doing it. Such wicked fiends." His grief turned back to anger.

"That's so terrible. So, what happens when you realize a demon has replaced a child?" She didn't want to know the answer in fear that it would leave her unable to sleep for the next few days.

"Well, you must convince the demon to give your child back. Doing this is almost impossible and is the most horrible thing you can imagine.

"With the help of the priest, you start by praying. Then you try beating the demon. Some people place the Wechselkind in their oven to try to get them to talk and reveal where their real child is. If the demon doesn't submit, you're left with no choice but to kill the beast. It's the only way to assure the child's soul won't stay forever with the demon." His eyes drifted as he thought of his cousin's son.

Gretta listened in horror. They're putting kids in the oven! "Oh my. Is this what happened to your cousin's son?"

The pain in his eyes slowly revealed his tragic loss.

"I'm so sorry to bring up such a terrible subject. I didn't mean to upset you."

"It's all right. I take it you have heard that we've had a wave of these attacks in the past few months."

"Yes. The people I talked to said there had been at least five this year. Is that right?" she asked.

"So terrible. The church isn't doing much, either. "I'm not a particularly religious man, but I don't understand how this is happening here. Many around Gamburg are starting to blame Father Uwe, but I know him personally. He's as good a priest as you'll ever meet. This craziness isn't his doing, and I believe he would give his own life if it would save these children."

"Do you know anything about what's happening?" She already knew that he believed demons stole the children. Hopefully, he would understand that she was looking for the circumstances surrounding the abductions.

"Well, most of these children were friends, and they all lived on the northeastern side of Gamburg. All the families, save one, were of excellent standing and went to church. None of the children worked in the town, though they all worked on their parents' farms."

"Did the children play together often?"

"All of the time. It's a sound that I truly miss. Sitting on this corner, you would hear them running through the forest, laughing, screaming, and having a wonderful time. The remaining children aren't allowed out for fear of being next."

218

"Do you think it's safe for me to check out the forest where they played?" Gretta asked this question to validate his fears and respect his beliefs. She was prepared to go there no matter what his answer was.

"Yes, the Wechselkind are too weak to defeat an adult. You'll be perfectly safe. If you would like, I'll send for my son, Klaus, so that he can escort you into the forest."

"How old is your son?" She was shocked to hear that he had a child, though, in retrospect, she realized she shouldn't have been.

"He's twenty-five and widowed. But he's a very good man. He would make an excellent husband." Even in affairs of love, you couldn't take the peddler out of him. His tone was hopeful.

"If he's much like you, I'm confident that's true. Thank you for the offer of an escort, but I don't think it's necessary." She didn't require a matchmaker. It was refreshing to know that Eric wasn't looking for a new wife for himself. It also was nice that he thought well enough of her to want her as an in-law.

"Okay, but I'd love for you to meet my Klaus. I think you would like him. He's both strong and kind. There aren't many men like him in this town."

"Maybe we could meet at your house for dinner some other time?" "That's an excellent idea, fraulein. We would like that very much. Let me talk to Mila, and we'll schedule a time." His keen eyes caught a potential customer approaching his booth, which interrupted his train of thought. "I'm sorry, my dear, but I must tend to this customer. But will you come over here for a second? I've something to give you." He leaned under his counter, where he opened a small box.

Curiosity overtook her as she walked over to where he was standing. The merchant reached into a box under his counter and pulled out a small piece of jewelry. "I don't know if you consider yourself religious, but I'd be remiss not to provide a friend with something for protection." He handed her a small cross made of ivory with a leather necklace.

"It isn't much, but there is no greater protection than God. Please take this and wear it. It's a gift from your friend."

She examined the small cross with amazement. The meticulous etching alone took someone hours to finish. She kissed him on the cheek with gratitude, and he blushed. "Thank you, Herr Eric. I'll wear it and feel safer."

"You better, fraulein. I expect you at dinner, and I'd rather not be visited by your ghost."

"Let me know when, and I'll be there. Hopefully, your wife will make some of this stew you have been telling me about."

"You should be so lucky. I'll be praying for your safety."

Turning to head the other way, she carefully put the necklace on to Eric's approval.

CHAPTER 34

BEDLAM

Chantilly - Fall - 2035

Gell looked down his agenda for the board meeting. The next item on the docket was Adkins. He reached for his glass of water and took a cool gulp. The action calmed him. "The next and last topic on our list tonight is the Kronos."

Kevin Anderson quickly spoke up. "I read your report. This all sounds kind of dark and mysterious." The comment drew some suppressed laughs from the group.

Gell didn't crack a smile, though. "I think it's inspiring and groundbreaking. Our team has managed to send us a message from the past. I can't imagine what those records could be, but I want to find out."

"So, you're telling me that these archeologists have found some secret message about some records from our crew?" Kevin half-grinned as he snorted and looked at the other board members.

Gell remained calm as he said, "Yes, that's exactly what I'm telling you. Once more, we're in the process of finding this location and purchasing the land to excavate the site and surrounding areas."

Candice Deckert chimed in. "I read your report, and I looked up the location.

"Did you know that we already own that parcel of land?"

The comment shook Gell. His back straightened as he processed this last comment. "We already own it?"

"Yes, we do. We purchased it over ten years ago." Candice pulled a sheet from her folder and passed it down to Gell.

Gell studied it and took a deep breath. They knew we owned the land, he thought. "This is a small research facility, but what is this reference to an upcoming thorium plant?"

Kevin looked exasperated. "You signed the approval papers for it last week. Didn't you read what you signed?"

Gell took a moment to process everything that had just transpired in the past week. He recalled signing the papers when he sent out his report concerning Adkins' newest discovery. "I recall signing them now. I also recall that this was an expedited project you promoted, Kevin. That's uncanny timing."

Kevin squinted his eyes. "Are you implying something, Theseus? Because I don't like what it sounds like you're saying."

Gell moved forward without wavering. "You can think what you want, but the same day I submit a report concerning a remote location that we've owned for the past ten years, an expedited capital project is placed on my desk for me to sign, and you're the one pushing it? That's an amazing coincidence."

The room remained uncomfortably silent until Kevin finally replied. "This is ridiculous, Theseus. We've known each other for years. Why would I do something to undermine you? You know I've had plenty of opportunities to throw you under the bus in the past. Why would I just start now?"

Gell folded his hands and tapped his lips with his index fingers. "What's your problem with Adkins and this team?"

Kevin studied Gell. He took a moment to look around the room as if he were gauging the temperature of his supporters. "I couldn't care less about them. I'm concerned about the exposure of TxC. This has the potential to blow up in our faces completely.

"You know that, but for some reason, you keep ignoring it. Someone has to look out for TxC. If it isn't going to be you, it has to be me."

Audible gasps could be heard around the table. Gell could sense the division among the board. "Kevin, you seem to have forgotten that those sixteen people are our responsibility. We owe them this discovery. I asked you to trust me, and then you did this underhandedly. I'd say that makes it kind of hard to trust you."

"Theseus, I don't think you're thinking clearly on this, so I'm helping you out. In a few months, you'll thank me for protecting TxC from a disastrous scandal. "They're going to start surveying the property next month. Maybe they'll find the records, and we'll both get what we want… Are you okay? You look faint."

Gell's inner voice was screaming. It was all he could do to keep his composure. "I'm fine," he said as he covered up his trembling hands.

"Good. I move that we table this discussion for now and adjourn the meeting."

There was a pause before the board unanimously agreed.

Gell got up quickly and headed out of the boardroom. Kevin tried to speak to him on his way out, but Gell kept walking.

Candice approached Kevin and said, "Well, that went smoothly."

Kevin kept watching Gell as he replied to her. "It had to be done. Candice, it's time we start erasing our communication tracks and pruning loose ends. Gell isn't finished, so we must ensure this doesn't come back on us."

Candice's chin dropped, and she closed her eyes. "All good things must come to an end."

Kevin turned and looked at her. "Indeed, they do."

CHAPTER 35

IN THE FOREST

Northern Germania - Summer of 1532 - Day 757

Arriving at the forest edge Eric had described took Gretta ten minutes. The sun shined on the vibrant trees, making the entryway irresistibly inviting. The thought of the innocent children lost due to some dark secret in this beautiful place made it suddenly seem sinister.

Putting her sense of fear and trepidation aside, she walked in without hesitation. Within seconds, the temperature around her dropped. Almost unconsciously, she touched the cross that Eric had just given her. The contact gave her peace.

As she crept further into the lush forest, her thoughts turned to what could cause rapid behavioral changes in children. She also considered children playing in the idyllic woods: running through the trees, playing hide and seek or pretending to be on adventures in faraway places. She thought of her childhood and the park where she often visited with her friends. The memory brought a few tears of remorse because of what was now lost for this community. Remorsefully, she looked for more clues or insight into what could have happened.

Even though no children had played in these woods for over three weeks, the trails and tracks made by them were still easy to find.

Examination showed the most frequented paths, hiding places, and other indicators of their presence. She looked for anything out of the ordinary or possibly dangerous. Other than some giant beehives high up in the trees, there was little she could see that would be risky.

The investigation required her to go deeper into the woods. Some cloud cover started blocking the sun, and the forest took on a more menacing aura. She started noticing more disturbing things. A dead squirrel near an oak tree caught her by surprise. Some other creature had taken a large part of its body, but it was still identifiable as a rat with a fluffy tail. The dead rodent's odor was distracting and added to this unshakeable anxiety.

Gretta's skin felt like it was crawling as her uneasiness grew, and the lack of sun made it more challenging as she tried to keep her bearings. She tried ignoring her internal discomfort, but with each step, a foreboding sense of dread grew in her gut. Coming up with plausible reasons why five children would be affected by something in the forest was her best attempt to suppress these feelings. However, Eric's descriptions weighed heavily on her thought process.

Ignoring the distinct possibility that some sick or wicked person was perpetuating this tragedy, there were only a few ways to poison a group of children in this manner. Her deductions came up with three possible alternate theories for the rapid change in these children's behavior. First, the children could have encountered some sort of dangerous bacteria in the forest, possibly from close contact with a tree or maybe a familiar toy used in a game. The bacteria took hold of them and affected each of the children slightly differently. The timing of their sicknesses depended on their overall health and constitution.

Second, she considered a viral attack of some sort. At first, this seemed like a strong possibility. The idea was dismissed, however, because the disease didn't spread to anyone else in the family. Even if younger children were in the house, they weren't infected with the malicious virus.

The final theory involved the children ingesting something that altered their behavior. Memories of her younger brother eating some "candy" that he'd found in a small sandwich bag in the park flooded her mind. Fortunately, her mother had quickly recognized something was wrong and rushed him to an emergency room. When the doctors pumped his stomach, they'd found enough barbiturates to kill ten grown men.

Since no one dropped bags of illegal drugs in the sixteenth century, she focused more on plants, mushrooms, leaves, or fruit. The path she followed led deeper into the woods. Slowly, she examined the trees and bushes surrounding her walkway. No culprit presented itself.

Perhaps, Gretta thought, was too focused on her task. Suddenly, a noise startled her. It sounded like a young child whimpering from behind the bushes about fifty feet away. She ducked down and headed towards the noise as quietly as possible.

Making it to a hedge that blocked her from the clearing where the noise source resided, she sat on the ground to gather her composure before continuing. Her heart raced with anxiety. She tried to stand up three times, only to sit down again. Finally, she stood to see what was on the other side.

In the clearing, she spotted two animals. One lay lifeless on the ground, and the other loudly whimpered and pushed the unmoving one with its snout. At first, she surmised that they were foxes because of their coloring and smaller frame. Upon further inspection, she realized they were some kind of dog, like a miniature Akita with red fur.

A few feet from her position was an opening to walk through the hedges. She cautiously headed towards the two animals. "What's going on, guy? Huh?" The dog looked up and started calling to her as if requesting help for its friend.

As she got closer, she observed that the fallen dog wasn't breathing. From what she could see, no evidence of trauma had caused its death. There was no pool of blood or disfiguration, and there was no imminent danger based on the other canine's posture.

Her love of animals overtook her fears, and she walked faster to investigate. She wanted to help but was also unwilling to touch the departed dog, fearing that whatever killed it was somehow contagious. Most of all, she felt relief that the mewling sounds came from a canine rather than a child.

When approaching, she cautiously picked up a small broken limb resting on the ground near the two animals. Using the branch, she rolled the deceased dog over and confirmed no form of attack had taken its life. The other dog allowed her to inspect the fallen animal but continued to whimper. Gretta could see that the dead animal was a male. "Is this your mate?" The small dog cocked her head.

"I'm so sorry, girl, you must be heartbroken. I don't think there's anything we can do for him." She turned her attention to the living dog and noticed another carcass about fifteen feet from her position. Other animals had picked the corpse clean of flesh, but it looked like a larger dog or possibly even a wolf. Gretta tilted her head to the left as she studied the scene.

She collected her many thoughts on what she was observing. *This can't be just a coincidence. Having two animals drop dead within fifteen feet of each other isn't normal.*

A noise at one of the hedge lines caught her attention. She turned to see what it was and watched a wild hare step out of the hedges. Realizing it wasn't alone, the hare stood on its hind legs and watched with curiosity as Gretta observed it. *What are you looking at, fellow?* Occasionally, the hare would change its attention to the whimpering dog standing near Gretta. The dog was unconcerned about the hare and stayed focused on her partner, so the hare would again turn and watch the young lady.

The hare stayed motionless for over a minute, only wiggling its whiskers and nose. Finally, it turned and headed to a small bush on the north end of the clearing. It began nibbling on some black-colored berries that looked to be the size of small grapes.

Gretta watched the wild animal and could feel the tension in her body lesson. Only the occasional cries of the dog beside her stopped her from being entirely at peace.

I wonder what kind of berries those are? Something in her was nagging her to investigate the berry bush. Sorry, Mr. Rabbit, but I'll have to interrupt your lunch. She walked towards the berry bush. At first, the hare didn't notice the woman's approach. When it did, it immediately jumped through the hedges and departed the clearing.

She looked at the berries and the bush that was producing them. Something's not right with this bush. She kneeled and studied the plant. The strange green coloring of the leaves drew her attention. She reached out, held one of the leaves, and felt a slight tingly sensation in her fingertips. Quickly, she pulled her hand away from the plant and looked at her fingers. The tips became numb to the touch, and the tingling dropped to her upper knuckles.

Gretta needed something to hold the specimen, so she reached into her satchel and pulled out a handkerchief. Carefully, she removed some of the berries and leaves to bring back to Klugstadt and wrapped them in the cloth. When this task was completed, she looked back at the unfortunate dog. "I want to help you, but I don't even have a shovel."

The dog studied her and seemed to understand.

Gretta's emotions welled up inside her. "I'm so sorry for your loss."

The animal cocked it's head, turned and looked at her mate, then looked back at Gretta. Slowly, the dog came and walked to the young lady's side.

"Do you have a home, little one?"

A single bark was the reply.

"Well, if you want, you can come with me. I'm going to have to name you. How about Ilsa? I like it. Ilsa, would you like to come with me?" She started walking down the dirt path made by children's feet. Ilsa quickly followed.

Gretta couldn't help but conjure the worst thoughts about how these poor animals could have died.

She could feel her body tensing up while listening to the disturbing sound of flies still eating any remaining flesh on the carcass. I don't know if I can keep going, but I must find out what happened to these kids. There's something wicked in this area. I can just feel it.

"There you are! Did you find anything?" Alex's announcement startled Gretta and her new four-pawed friend. She shook off the morbid loop her mind was stuck in.

"Alex!" She tried to punch him, but his reactions were too quick. "You scared me. Have you found anything?"

He laughed at her weak attempt. "Sorry. So, it seems you picked up a new pet." He reached down to pet Ilsa.

"Her name is Ilsa, and her mate just passed away." She spoke rapidly as Ilsa stared at her with interest .

"Ilsa? Did she tell you her name, or did she have a tag?" Alex had an impish grin as he spoke in a semi-mocking tone.

"I named her, and she seems to like it." With these words, Ilsa barked and wagged her tail. "See? I rest my case. Anyway, I found another carcass over in the same area. Doesn't that sound like more than just a coincidence to you?"

"I would say it is something to consider, that's for sure." Gretta wiped her hands on a small clothe she had in her pouch as she continued to talk. "When we were kids, we built forts out in the woods. I've been looking for their fort and haven't come across it yet."

Alex puckered his lips and furrowed his brow. He then crossed his arms and said, "I might be able to help you there. I think I just walked by it about five minutes ago. It was this way."

Gretta's ears perked up. "What are we waiting for? Lead the way, maestro."

Alex pointed toward the fort with his head and started walking. Gretta quickly followed with Isla in tow.

A short distance away, they arrived at a fort built primarily of dried branches with a thatch roof. Three large trees supported the simple structure. A tattered tablecloth covered the entryway.

"These kids were pretty industrious," she observed.

"I'm betting one of the parents put this roof on," Alex said. "No kids I know could build a roof like this. This took serious roofing knowledge. Are you going to go in?"

"Yes!" she said. "You coming with me?"

"No, that hurts my back just thinking about squatting down that low."

Gretta laughed and crawled into the fort. "Okay, Grandpa. Just stay out there, and I'll see what I can find."

The fort was a single room, yet larger than expected. She estimated that it could easily sit ten children comfortably.

On one side was a makeshift counter with a loaf of stale bread sitting on it. One wall had children's paintings and drawings, while the other had unstrung bows. A bucket sat in the corner near twelve wooden cups on a stand.

Something caught her eyes as she scanned again. Some marbles rested on the countertop, while others were scattered on the ground. She crawled in further to get a closer look. The small objects weren't marbles at all; they looked like shriveled versions of the strange berries she'd seen in the clearing. She reached into her satchel and pulled out another rag to stow the berries.

"I think I've found our real culprit," she said as she crawled out of the fort, her words conveying her eagerness to solve the mystery.

"Really? That didn't take long. So, what do we do now?" He stood with his arms crossed.

CHAPTER 36

SUCCUBUS

Northern Germania - Summer of 1532 - Day 757

Alex and Gretta continued to Gamburg, where they purchased some items to bring back to Klugstadt. The walk home felt heavy to Gretta. Alex never asked about her discovery in the forest. He seemed carefree. She found this to be disconcerting considering the gravity of the situation.

Ilsa continued to follow her closely. Gretta thought about the haphazard evolution of rules in Klugstadt. For example, would she be allowed to keep Ilsa? No one will grumble about me having a dog in the camp. It'll be a great addition. Gretta hoped that was the case. The dog seemed to annoy Alex slightly, but he never complained about her, and she held this on the dog's plus side.

Dusk arrived with them at the camp. Athera and Kelly conversed on their porch, enjoying the nearly perfect weather. "Gretta!" Kelly waved, and Ilsa barked. "Well, who do we have here? Hello, mister! You're adorable!"

"I named her Ilsa," Gretta said, smiling.

"Like the girl in Frozen?" Kelly asked, remembering the animated film.

"No, that's Elsa." She bent over to pet her new friend.

"Oh! And I called you 'mister.' I'm so sorry, Ilsa.

"Will you forgive me?"

Ilsa replied with a bark and a wag of her tail.

Kelly petted the dog with a childish zeal. "She's so cute. Where did you find her?"

"In the forest. But more on that later. Right now, I want to run something I found by CHAMP. Do you think Brandon will mind?"

"I doubt it. Just walk down there. Do you want me to look after Ilsa while you go?" Kelly said, hoping for an affirmative.

"Yes, thanks so much, Kelly." Gretta kneeled to talk to her new pet. "Miss Kelly is going to take good care of you while I'm away. So please behave, okay?"

Kelly swooped down and petted Isla's back as Gretta stood back up. Without looking away, Kelly said, "Sweet! I'll find her some food and water." Ilsa happily followed her into her kitchen to eat.

Gretta went down to Brandon's cabin and knocked on the door. Brandon cheerfully answered. "Hey, Gretta, what's up?"

"I found this plant that I was hoping CHAMP could quickly analyze. I think it may be related to what's happening with the Wechselkind."

Brandon could sense the energy in her voice. He shared the excitement, having something new to discover. "Do you mind if I come down with you? Oh, and by the way, did I hear a dog barking out there?"

"Please, come down with me. I welcome the company. And yes, I found a poor dog in the woods. She's adorable. I named her Ilsa." She walked past him with no further explanation. "Hey, CHAMP," she said as soon as she was in hearing range of the computer.

"Hello, Ms. Gretta. How are you doing this evening? And how may I be of assistance?"

"Hey CHAMP, I'm doing well. Thank you for asking."

"It is my pleasuse. Is there something I might be able to help you with?"

"As a matter of fact, there is." She reached into her satchel and pulled out the two handkerchiefs. "I found a strange plant that made my hand tingle when I touched it."

"Do you mean itch, like possibly poison ivy?"

"No, it tingled in my joints, and the tips of my fingers became numb for a few minutes." She opened one of the cloths to reveal both the plant and the berry. Carefully, she placed them on CHAMP's examination table. "This is the plant and its fruit. Do you have any idea what it is?"

"Were the fruits in clusters, or were they one per stem?"

"I only saw one per stem. I thought it was odd because, at first, I thought it looked like blueberries, but they usually come in clumps. Also, the outer skin looked slightly shiny and had a blacker tint than a typical blueberry."

"All of that does rule out blueberries, though the fruit looks very similar. The leaf is quite different, though. Looking through the database, I see a distinct possibility. The plant is commonly referred to as nightshade, black nightshade, European bittersweet, or climbing nightshade, but Atropa belladonna is the actual name—belladonna for short. It's considered one of the deadliest plants on the planet. Ten of these berries can kill an adult. The normal reaction to consuming them is hallucinations and memory loss. Its effects can last anywhere from two to six weeks after ingestion. The leaves on your specimen are slightly different, but I'm certain this is merely a predecessor to the modern version."

Everything became much clearer to Gretta about what had happened to the children, but she had more evidence that she needed to inspect to substantiate her theory. "CHAMP, I have one more sample to examine. This fruit has been sitting out for a few weeks. I want to know if it's the same fruit you identified as belladonna." She placed the second handkerchief on the table and opened it to expose the shriveled berries.

"It appears to be, though I can't be certain with such a small dataset.

"The seed pattern is about the same and looks consistent with the belladonna variety you provided me earlier. If you would like, I can verify, with certainty, that they are related by taking small samples of both."

"Please, CHAMP. I'd appreciate that."

"Of course, Gretta. Give me a few minutes." CHAMP's appendages jolted to life and inspected the two specimens. In less than thirty seconds, he spoke again. "These are indeed the same berries. If you would like, I can explain to you how I know."

"That won't be necessary, CHAMP. Is there a cure for the poison of this belladonna?"

"Not that we could make here, but the psychotropic effects will dissipate with time and hydration. I'd recommend rest, low light, and impose double the normal water intake. Combining these three will dramatically reduce the poison's potency in the person. Also, a sedative may help because physical activity exacerbates the effects."

With each of CHAMP's replies, Gretta imagined the horrific deaths of the completely innocent children in Gamburg. At this point, she felt ill herself.

"CHAMP, I have another question. I noticed a wild hare eating these berries off the same plant. It didn't seem to be affected in any way by the fruit."

CHAMP hastily replied, "Yes, certain birds, rabbits, and cows can eat these berries without issue. But for most mammals, the fruit is deadly."

Brandon had remained silent while listening. Something was bothering him. "CHAMP, wouldn't adults from this period have known about this berry bush?"

CHAMP paused before answering. The question seemed to be perplexing to the interface. When CHAMP solved more complex problems, a gentle increase in the CPU's cooling fans could be heard. A knowing look came over Brandon's face when the whirring noise increased.

The interface finally responded. "That's hard to say. This is most likely an eastern variant of the berry.

"I'd suspect that it came with eastern travelers camping outside the village. Since it wasn't local, few probably recognized its danger. The adults may have understood they were dangerous, but that plant wouldn't have been indigenous to this area. There is the possibility that no adult has encountered it in the forest yet."

Gretta started packing to leave. As she finished, she stopped and said, "Thank you, CHAMP. Once again, you've been so much help!"

"It was my pleasure to be of assistance. Please visit me more often, Gretta. I like the sound of your voice."

"Aw, CHAMP, you're such a sweetheart." She blushed at the compliment.

"Thank you, Gretta, and goodnight."

They left the basement and headed back upstairs.

When they exited Brandon's cabin, a group had collected around the new dog, everyone enjoying Ilsa's playful nature. When Gretta exited, she smiled as the dog stopped everything and approached her with a wagging tail.

"Well, I guess we know who this one thinks is her momma," Kelly said to the crowd's delight.

"Oh, Brandon, can we go down and have CHAMP tell us what kind of dog this is?"

Athera saved them the trouble. "It's a Finnish Spitz. Based on its paws, I'd say she's fully grown. Some people call them Finkies. Allegedly, they're excellent hunting dogs and are fiercely loyal."

"Athera, how do you know stuff like that?" Gretta marveled.

"I don't know. I just read a lot, and some of it sticks," she replied.

Gretta held up one of the napkins. "I think I… wait… I think Alex and I have figured out what happened to the children in Gamburg. Time is of the essence, so can we have an emergency council meeting?"

"You bet," Brandon replied. "We can have it right now."

Aecha, Wilson, and Brandon headed to the meeting room to discuss the situation. Gretta stopped for a moment before walking with them. She went to Emma's cabin and invited her to the meeting. She figured that the person who made the discovery should hear what happened. Emma eagerly tagged along.

CHAPTER 37

SPLIT DECISONS

Northern Germania - Summer of 1532 - Day 757

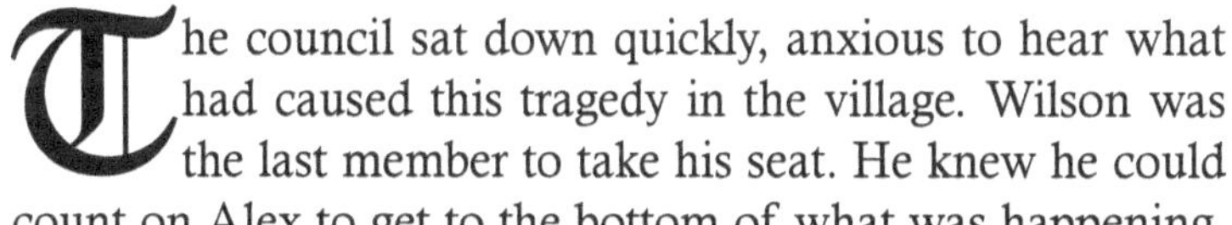

The council sat down quickly, anxious to hear what had caused this tragedy in the village. Wilson was the last member to take his seat. He knew he could count on Alex to get to the bottom of what was happening. As he sat, he gave a knowing nod to Alex, who was trying his best to avoid eye contact."Alex, do you want to tell us what you all have found?" Wilson started.

"Alex, do you want to tell us what you all have found?" Wilson started.

"I think Gretta is the better person to give that information," Alex said.

"Okay. Gretta, what's going on in Gamburg?" Wilson's dour look expressed his discontent with Alex's reply. Wilson determined that Gretta had discovered the source of the problem. Realizing he was now in a self-made doghouse, Alex continued to stay quiet and avoided looking up.

"Thanks for meeting so suddenly. After talking with you, Alex and I headed up to Gamburg to investigate. We split up, hoping to cover more ground. I talked to a vendor who told me about the woods where all the children in question would gather to play every day."

"Let me guess.

"Alex headed to the pub to talk to Gisela," Wilson blurted out, again looking disappointedly at his friend.

Gretta was astonished at Wilson's insight but didn't let her face show it. "Yes, he did, but she confirmed that the information I got from a vendor was accurate. We ended up looking in the same place." She knew how to cover someone's back, and Alex was thankful for her at that moment. Her words softened Wilson's agitation.

"After talking with the vendor, I decided that it would be worth my time to check out where all of these kids congregated, so I headed up there to investigate," Gretta continued. "I walked around for about an hour when I heard a dog whimpering. When I found Isla, her partner had just died. I examined the deceased dog and found no trauma or any external injuries. The dog looked fit, well-fed, and young. Its death seemed suspicious."

Gretta started to discuss the strange-looking plant they discovered in the forest.

"What do you mean by strange?" Aecha asked.

"Its leaves were an unnatural color of green. It looked like it had blueberries on it, but there was only one berry per stem, and the fruit was as large as a small grape. Growing up, we had blueberries all around us, which would be in bunches. It was peculiar, if you understand what I'm saying." Aecha pursed her lips and allowed Gretta to continue.

"I found dried fruit that CHAMP said was the same as the ones that I found in the clearing. CHAMP went on to tell me that these berries are one of the most toxic plants on the planet. They only cause hallucinations and memory lapses in small doses but eventually kill the consumer if too much is ingested. Their long-lasting effect would explain why the children behaved so irrationally.

"I think that the adults would know to avoid eating these berries, but when I was a kid, my parents wrongly taught us that if animals eat the berries, they're okay for us to eat too. I suspect the kids noticed the hares and birds eating these berries and assumed they were safe.

240

"According to CHAMP, this particular berry can be eaten by small animals like hares and fowl and a few larger animals like cows, but it'll pretty much harm anything else that ingests them. They're deceptive, too, because their fruit is sweet, hiding their toxicity."

Gretta finished by clapping her hands and looking around. "Now, one child is on the verge of being killed by his family, and we can prevent it if we act quickly…"

"How would you propose we act, Gretta?" Aecha asked politely but pointedly. "Like go up and knock on their door and explain that you know their child ate poisonous berries? When they ask how you know this, you explain that a computer told you about them?" Aecha's words were practical but cold.

Gretta's eyes tightened as she began to speak. "Well, it would be challenging, but I think we could come up with something. Maybe we could tell Father Uwe about it?"

Aecha's dry response expressed no hint of anger or empathy. "You mean the man who sentenced four children to death because he didn't know they'd just eaten some hallucinogenic berries, so he blamed it on demonic possession? Do you think the parents of those dead children will receive this news well?"

Gretta briefly closed her eyes as she replied–"Aecha, why are you attacking me? I just want to help."

"I'm sorry if you think I'm attacking you," Aecha said in a softer tone.

"I'm trying to point out that being armed with information isn't necessarily a solution to the problem at hand. I'm also worried that we're meddling in history. As appalling as this is to me, maybe we should keep out of it and let mankind figure this out themselves." Aecha could hear the words leaving her mouth and regretted them, even as she said them.

"No! You can't be serious, Aecha." Both Gretta and Aecha were startled when Emma audibly protested the remark.

Gretta quickly turned back to Aecha.

She lifted a single eyebrow and said, "You're joking, aren't you? We're talking about an innocent young man who is currently being tortured and will be put to death if we do nothing. I won't stand for that, and I don't care what you do to me." She couldn't hide the disgust she had for this conversation.

"This isn't easy," Aecha said, "but we don't know how even saving that one life will affect history. If we interfere, where do we draw the line? I'm not saying we won't do something. I'm saying we must be very strategic in what we do."

"You sound a lot like a politician right now. You're hiding behind technicalities."

"I'm not trying to sway you, nor am I against you. I'm doing my best to ensure we don't mess up our history and the version of mankind we know. If that makes me a politician, so be it." Aecha was neither apologetic nor angered, but Gretta's body language showed she wasn't pleased with the response.

Wilson couldn't hold his silence any longer. "Come on, Aecha. This situation isn't that hard of a decision. A young child's life is at stake. We can help him or speculate about what will happen in five hundred years. We need to do something now." Emma and Gretta agreed with Wilson's plea. They looked at Brandon to weigh in, as Alex remained ambivalent.

"Gretta, Alex, and Emma? Thanks for all your hard work in getting to the bottom of this. The three of us need to speak in private so that we can figure out what the best way to proceed will be." Brandon wasn't going to weigh in with non-council members present.

The three nodded and left the room. Gretta stared one last time at Aecha before exiting. Aecha refused to engage.

Brandon glared at the two council members. "What the hell was all that about? You two are behaving like children. I thought we understood that we were unified when we left this room last."

"Really, Brandon? This situation is so cut and dry. I was blown away that Aecha would offer any opposition to something that should be a no-brainer." Wilson's face flushed as he talked.

Brandon cocked his head at the implication. "So now I'm the bad guy? Come on, Wilson, you know me and my heart. You're behaving ridiculously."

Wilson put his hands to his chest while raising his eyebrows. "Oh, so now I'm ridiculous?"

"No, he said you're behaving ridiculously, not that you are ridiculous," Aecha retorted.

"Thanks, Aecha. I feel so much better with that clarification."

Aecha rolled her eyes. "Give me a break. You're sitting on your smug, higher moral ground and intentionally ignoring how truly complicated this is."

"I need both of you to calm down now!" Brandon shouted, which caught both of their attention. He'd reached his tipping point.

Wilson quietly studied at the ground.

Aecha took a deep, calming breath before saying, "Wilson, I'm sorry that I got so angry. I let this get personal, and that's not cool. I do want to find a way to help if we can."

"Me too, Aecha. Let's all talk this out rationally." Wilson's words didn't seem as sincere as Aecha's, but they were enough to squelch the fire.

"Before we proceed, I want to come to an understanding. "We don't air our dirty laundry in public, okay?" Brandon's features turned solemn. He wasn't going any further until they both acknowledged this simple truism.

The two conceded.

"Now that we're past this, I want to tell you what I think about this whole thing," Brandon said. "I hate that we're in this situation. I don't think we can ignore it, even if I wholeheartedly agree that we shouldn't mess with history." Wilson perked up.

"That being said, I don't see this as much different than the mosquito situation. Is there some way that we can solve the problem passively?" Brandon interlaced his fingers and waited for replies.

Wilson spoke first. "Well, we could reduce the problem by killing the belladonna berry plants in the woods. It would take weeks for us to do, but killing most of them, especially along the trails where the children play, would help. No one but us would need to know. But this doesn't help this poor kid who is about to die."

"What if we made some herbicide targeting the berry plants," Brandon added. "I can ask CHAMP if that's a possibility."

"This is all good, but it still doesn't help this child." Aecha's heart couldn't keep silent, even though she knew it went against their idea of preserving history.

Brandon acknowledged the issue by nodding his head and rubbing his chin. "What if we dropped a note to Father Uwe and suggested a new treatment to get rid of the demon?"

"What would you say in the note?" Aecha asked with curiosity.

"We could make it so the note look like it came from Rome. It could include flasks of water that the note indicates are special and would force the demon to return the child. Instruct that the child needs a room without much light and would need to sleep as much as possible for two weeks. The child would be better by then, and Father Uwe would look like he saved the child rather than sentenced another one to death."

Aecha's head bobbed in agreement. "Even the families who lost a child would think that they got to this one in time and wouldn't come down as hard on the priest," he added.

Wilson was enthused with the idea. "Can we agree on this? We can acknowledge that there are objections because of the intrusion into the historical timeline, but we still think this is the right course of action."

All three of them agreed. "Okay, now to action. I'm going to discuss herbicides with CHAMP.

"I suspect we can get Alex to prepare the letter with the help of Athera and possibly get Gerry to make some holy-looking flasks."

"I'm sorry about my outburst, guys. I'll try to be better about that in the future," Wilson said.

"I feel like we're on shaky ground, so I just want us to be very careful," Aecha acknowledged.

"Understood, Aecha. Let's be as careful as possible about all of this. I'll tell the group outside about our overall plan, and Wilson, would you mind talking to Alex?" Brandon added.

"Will do." Wilson grinned.

The meeting adjourned, and Aecha left the room without another word to Wilson. She went back to her cabin to think about this unsettling interaction.

CHAPTER 38

DEMON BE GONE

Northern Germania - Summer of 1532 - Day 758

The following day focused on the subterfuge of righting the horror caused by the poisonous berries and superstition. CHAMP developed a simple herbicide composed of salt, vinegar, and soap to combat the berries. For the next few weeks, the citizens of Klugstadt planned to cover the woodland area. Most of their little village joined in the roaming and spraying. CHAMP warned that eliminating all the fruit would be nearly impossible, but they could successfully kill it in high-trafficked areas.

Emma and Gretta led the charge. They woke up ready to rid the woods of this deadly trap and do whatever it took to make the forest safer. Gretta made a rough map of the woods so teams could mark off the inspected regions and efficiently cover the grounds. She put on the map what she considered the higher priority areas she had encountered in her sleuthing.

Gerry stayed up most of the night and painted a facia on porcelain flasks from Gamburg. Using metal alloys that would only be found in modern times, he soldered bands around the outer mouths of the flasks that looked like silver. CHAMP created 3-D models of angel wings. Gerry painted and attached them to the outer handles.

The result made them look like they came from the Vatican.

The original plan was to fill the containers with purified water, but Aecha suggested putting in some mild but natural sedatives to help the child rest for the two weeks in the room. Brandon agreed, and CHAMP provided a simple powder recipe that would mix with the water, which would be undetectable.

Alex prepared the "official" Vatican papers. Athera provided the texts and cleverly wrote them to catch Father Uwe's attention. The letter included the recipe for making "special" water for future changeling incidents. They'd pay a courier to deliver the documentation to the church with the flasks. Since everything was encased, the courier had no idea what he was delivering.

Wilson walked up to Kelly's cabin and knocked on the door. After a few moments, she answered it. "Hey, Wilson. Do you want to come inside?"

"No, I was coming by to see when you would do berry patrol." He noticed that she hadn't signed up and wanted to know why.

"I wasn't planning on participating." She was hoping not to get into another argument.

"Why not, Kelly? Our whole town is participating."

"Sorry, but I'm not." The words came out sharper than she had intended.

He stared incredulously at her. "Are you really just going to sit there and do nothing?"

"What do you want from me? You got your way with the mosquitoes, and now you've bullied your way with this situation, too."

"Kelly, that's crap, and you know it. I'm just one voice on the council, and for the record, both were unanimous decisions."

"You're a loud and intimidating voice." The comment struck him like a slap across the face.

"Never made you flinch," he said.

"No, but you tried." This bickering is what she was seeking to avoid. "Look, Wilson, you go do what you will do. I can't stop you, but I won't sit here and pretend I'm good with this. I'm just going to abstain from being involved. That's all. You don't need my blessing. You already have the council's."

"This isn't an issue of your blessing. It's an issue of us all chipping in to this vision of Klugstadt."

"Yeah, well, I'm not stopping you. I just can't get behind this. I'm sorry. "And know this: I'm elated that the child may have a chance to survive, but our involvement goes against what I believe." Kelly couldn't look Wilson in the eye.

Wilson saw how upset she was and finally backed off. "I'm sorry, Kelly. I just felt like we could all do this together."

"I'm sorry, too. I wish I could, but I'm just so conflicted, and it's killing me." She turned to close the door.

Wilson let it go and continued with his duties. His plans and decisions seemed justified at this point. He walked away and allowed Kelly her space.

CHAPTER 39
DELIVERY SERVICE

Northern Germania - Summer of 1532 - Day 759

The morning air and the hour-long drive by carriage invigorated Wilson. As he thought about what needed to be done, he felt compelled to ride along with the courier to ensure the items' delivery. When he approached the courier's shop, the owner was in the process of waking up. The young man looked up to see a giant man riding a diminutive carriage. Even the draft horse pulling the wagon seemed small next to Wilson.

The young man looked up to see a giant man riding in a diminutive carriage. Even the draft horse pulling the wagon seemed small next to Wilson.

Wilson called out to him, "Hello! Are you available for business?"

The courier wiped some sleep from his eyes and smiled. "Of course. How can I be of service?" He stretched out his arms and yawned as he spoke, making the words slightly harder to understand.

Wilson allowed the carriage to come to a complete stop. "My name is Wilson, and you are?"

The man wiped his hands. "My name is Nicholi."

Wilson reached back and uncovered his cargo. "Okay, Nicholi, I'd like these delivered to Father Uwe immediately.

"Are you able to do that?"

Nicholi studied the items. "I don't think that would be a problem."

"Good." Wilson paused before adding, "I do have to ask a favor when you deliver it."

The request captured Nicholi's attention. "Oh? Are the packages fragile?"

Wilson winced. "Not exactly. But I need the Father to believe that they came from Rome."

An odd grin came across Nicholi's face. He scratched his chin and tilted his head. "Rome? Like from the Vatican?"

Wilson cleared his throat. "Umm… yes. I know you're an honest man, but this is important. I'm willing to pay extra thaler to make this happen." He held up his money purse, making the universal sound of compromise.

The courier rubbed his chin some more, but his gaze remained on Wilson's purse. "Double."

"Done." Wilson smiled but then remembered one more thing. "With one caveat. I want to ride with you to deliver the items… just to ensure everything is properly delivered. If that's okay, we have a deal."

Nicholi frowned slightly but agreed. "Okay, but I have one delivery before yours, which is substantial. If you ride, you need to help me unload the first boxes because you'll take my partner's place."

"Understood. I think I can do that. Here's the money in advance." Wilson immediately stood up and handed the coins to the courier. He then turned and helped unload the package from his carriage into the larger wagon.

Nicholi quickly accepted the money. He then took a deep breath and yawned again. "Well, I was about to leave. Are you ready?"

Wilson nodded. "Ready as I'll ever be."

Nicholi wasn't excited about the extra guest on his route, but the pay was so good that he made no effort to object. Wilson sat in the carriage as they delivered the packages directly to Father Uwe.

The extra money paid to the courier to say that the items were officially from Rome and to keep their identity quiet was well worth it. Fortunately, Alex's skill at forgery and Athera's literary skills passed the church's scrutiny.

At first, Father Uwe was surprised that the Vatican was aware of the dire circumstances of his small village, though he was thankful for their correspondence. He hastened to the home where the changeling lay to administer the prescribed treatment. Wilson watched as Father Uwe gathered two helpers to aid in delivering the flasks. He could hear him saying, "Time is of the essence, so we must hurry. A young boy's life is in the balance."

"Thank you for delivering that. I don't like asking you to tell a lie. Now, Nicholi, can I pay you to follow him?"

Nicholi frowned but agreed to the request.

Wilson paid the courier to follow the priest and watched Father Uwe deliver the items to the family. When Wilson was content that they did what needed to be done, he openly grinned at Nicholi and patted him on the back.

"So, c-can we go back now?" He leaned away from Wilson as if he might be beaten for the comment.

Wilson studied Nicholi for a moment before he spoke. "Of course, my boy. I appreciate your patience."

CHAPTER 40

AFTERMATH

Northern Germania - Summer of 1532 - Day 766

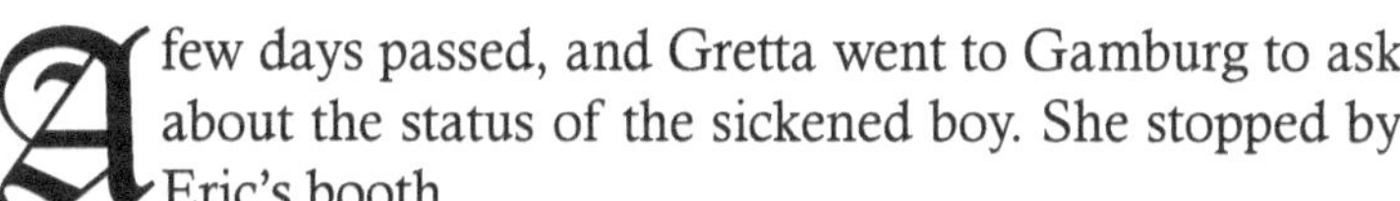

A few days passed, and Gretta went to Gamburg to ask about the status of the sickened boy. She stopped by Eric's booth.

"Fraulein, it's a miracle. Nels was suffering tremendously at the hands of his parents when Father Uwe came over and changed their approach. Nels crawled into a bed by himself and fell asleep while his mother, who never stopped praying for her son, sat in tears at the door. Every two hours, she entered the room and administered two cups of beverage from the holy flask."

Gretta's face and the tips of her ears grew flush as she listened to Eric. "You say his name is Nels? Well, is he better?"

Eric's mouth hung wide open, and his eyes glinted with pride. "By the end of the week, he was moving around on his own, his cheeks had regained their color, and he was able to speak coherently. The demon had returned the boy, and the best part was that the young boy didn't remember any of it.

"I've heard the family plans to return to Mass this coming week. I tell you, it makes me so happy to report this. It's a miracle."

"It really is." Gretta thanked Eric, purchased some goods, and returned to Klugstadt to share the good news.

That evening, Emma approached Gretta to share her thoughts. She knocked on her cabin door.

Gretta answered the door with a broad, welcoming grin. "Hey, Emma. Why don't you come in?"

Emma smiled, but tears started running down her face. Gretta immediately stepped out, put her arm around her, and helped her into her cabin. "Come on in and sit down. Everything is fine."

Emma sat sniffling for a few moments as she regained her composure. "When I heard that the boy was recovering today, I was overwhelmed."

Gretta sighed deeply, leaned over, and hugged her friend. "I'm so glad that we could help. Can you imagine if we wouldn't have been able to? This is all because you saw it firsthand."

Emma was nodding but then abruptly stopped as her eyes narrowed. "But Kelly didn't want to help us at all."

Gretta bit her lower lip and fumbled for the right words to say. "You know how she feels about this whole history thing. I want to be mad at her, but I know she thinks she's doing the right thing."

Emma shook her head. "But that boy would have died."

"Yes," Gretta replied gently. "But if we didn't jump back in time, he would have died anyway. Right?"

Emma took a hard swallow. "Well, yes. But we were here, so he didn't have to die."

"I know, but I'm trying to help you see what Kelly is thinking. She's a good person–she just sees this differently than us."

Emma nodded as if Gretta's words were revelatory. "You're right. I need to cut her some slack. But I still think she's wrong."

Gretta considered her words before giving a reply. "I do, too, but whether that's true or not, she's not our enemy. This isn't personal; it's philosophical."

"But she's wrong."

"Maybe," Gretta said. "Even so, she's our kind of wrong."

They both reveled in the comment.

"You want some tea? I've got some fresh biscuits as well," Gretta offered.

Emma licked her lips. "That sounds wonderful."

Gretta walked over to prepare some hot water. "You know, Nels will attend Mass in two weeks. Do you want to go with me to see him?"

"That sounds exciting."

Two weeks later, the entire family showed up with their returned son at Mass. The congregation celebrated the victory with them. Families who'd lost their children were in attendance too. They found some comfort and solace that another family didn't have to share the pain of loss.

Gretta and Emma watched Nels receive communion. Both hugged each other at what they believed to be a significant victory for Klugstadt.

Occasionally, Gretta would return to Gamburg with her new friend, Ilsa. She would intentionally take the longer path that went by the woods to hear the laughs, shouts, and chatter of children playing – sounds that grew with time.

She also took it upon herself to walk the children's paths from time to time to ensure no more poisonous fruit returned. To Gretta's amazement, Ilsa still barked, and her head hung lower every time they passed the clearing in which her mate had passed away.

CHAPTER 41

THE ROAD LESS TRAVELLED

Northern Germania - Spring of 1534 - Day 1275

Wilson quietly left the room containing CHAMP, possibly for the last time. He looked around and tucked his notebook into his carrying pouch. Brandon walked in as he was leaving. "Hey, Wilson, is everything okay?"

"Hey, Brandon. Yes, everything's good." He managed to not allow his smile to reflect the ache he was feeling. He would miss his friend.

Aecha was the first council member to rotate off, and Kelly rotated in by vote. Wilson would rotate off next, leaving Brandon as the sole original council member from the original circle.

Klugstadt remained a relative place of peace, but the difference in opinion on handling historical interaction or intervention issues drove a hard division through the camp.

Cody's modest cottage was down a small path from Klugstadt. He and Gisela got married, and over time, Klugstadt welcomed her into their community. Gisela's command of English already surpassed Cody's grasp of German.

Cody's devotion to Wilson's plan was evident. Alex, Emma, and Gretta also wanted to join Wilson.

Quin deduced their community's fracturing and also chose to follow Wilson.

Jason had been overtly planning a departure and was unconcerned with what his absence would do to the group. Gerry seemed to be the only member who wasn't committed. If Gerry chose not to go with Jason, he would more likely join Wilson than stay with Kelly. He had regular run-ins with Kelly, and they rarely went his way.

Kelly quietly watched these allegiances forming. Battle lines were being set, but the most significant warning for her was the sudden lack of resistance over the key issues. Even six months earlier, people like Wilson had been so argumentative; now they all remained silent and sullen. Her heart dropped one evening when she saw Athera and Alex sit side-by-side at dinner but not utter a single word to each other. The lack of tension had the opposite effect on her typically uplifting temperament.

Social gatherings became awkward. Knowing something was up but just having people silently smile was unnerving. The most troubling element was the people involved truly loved and respected each other, for the most part. The rift wasn't a case of spite, hate, or revenge but an irreconcilable philosophical difference.

An additional complication came by way of Rand and Lisa. Lisa was expecting her first child. The joy of this event and the desire to ensure the group would be okay taxed Wilson–but he reluctantly made the difficult call to sever ties with Klugstadt. Before that could be done, he wanted to ensure the village could function without his input.

The last major project on Wilson's checklist required his undivided attention. The plan was Kelly's idea, and even Wilson had to admit it was an outstanding one. The entire group had compiled all their notes and journals of their time up to this point.

Also, each team member wrote personal letters to people at home, explaining they were fine.

The goal was to send a message saying everyone was okay and there was no need to send rescue. CHAMP had found a lake in Norway that TxC would purchase in the future. They planned on hiding the time capsule in such a way that only TxC could discover it.

Alongside the letters, the group wrote some informational documents, correcting many historical errors. Though the material wasn't comprehensive, it would be a treasure to any modern historian.

Klugstadt picked Kelly, Wilson, Gretta, and Brandon to make the journey up north. They prepared for five weeks to complete the trip. The plans included purchasing passage to Norway and buying transportation for the journey.

About six months earlier, the last solar panel had broken on the castle, so the council reluctantly decided to ceremonially destroy the communication array and the S.O.S. beacon. They'd discussed moving the beacon– to where it could have still run off the mill's power, but decided against it as it was causing too many questions.

One of the other motivators for not moving the beacon was that the hydroelectric power unit was becoming more intermittent. The batteries used to buffer power for CHAMP showed diminished capacity. For the first few years, CHAMP remained on all the time. Now, CHAMP only operated when someone needed information. All other times, CHAMP remained in a low-powered sleep mode.

Wilson wanted his last act as part of Klugstadt to be delivering the time capsule to Norway. The day approached rapidly, and the dread for what was ahead pestered him. Wilson had already prepared individual letters and gifts for all the people he would leave behind. One letter was to the council, explaining why he could no longer be a part of their community. Others were letters of thanks to his friends down in the village.

Wilson hid all the materials at Cody's place. Cody and Gisela acted as Wilson's confidants.

Their distance from the camp helped conceal a great many clues that could have given them away earlier than Wilson intended. The most damning ones were the notebooks Wilson had prepared. Over the past two years, Wilson had written his own library of history books. These books included knowledge of significant events, loss of valuable property, prominent leaders' names, maps of Europe, and important historical dates. These lists stretched into the twenty-first century.

He also prepared books on making medicines, foods, and building designs. Wilson would ask CHAMP questions and write down his responses for about two hours daily. The result was an old-school collection of knowledge.

Those who supported Wilson prepared to move to the next stage of their plan when the okay was given.

CHAPTER 42

COMING HOME

Boston - Late Fall - 2035

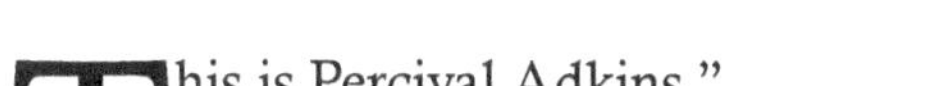

This is Percival Adkins."

"Hey Percy, this is Theseus Gell. I'm sorry to bother you at home and this late." Percy was so surprised that he stayed silent for a little too long.

"Are you there, Percy?"

"Yes, I'm here. It's no trouble at all. What can I do for you, Theseus?"

"Well, I just got out of a board meeting and had to tell you what I discovered. It's very exciting, but this is going to be a good-news, bad-news sort of thing."

Percy pressed the phone to his ear in anticipation, not wanting to miss a word. "I'd love to hear it, Theseus. What's the good news? Sorry, but I like starting with the optimism."

Gell exclaimed, "We already own the land in the decoded message."

"What?" Adkins couldn't believe what he was hearing.

"Yeah! We already own it. We were going to use it to study European thermal activity. We even built an office on the east side of the lake near a small highway." Gell's enthusiasm overflowed as he continued. "That's why they chose this place to drop the records."

"You had some smart people on the Kronos, Theseus."

"I agree. I wish I had something to do with hiring that team, but that was more McCallister's doing than anyone else's. Unfortunately, I must share the bad news, too."

"Oh?" Adkins sounded nervous.

"Coincidentally, TxC will be building a thorium reactor on that exact location. They'll start surveying next month."

Adkins remained unflappable. "Well, can't you postpone that until we can do our searching?"

"Unfortunately, I can't, though I tried. This is a multi-billion-dollar project which our board has already approved. I guess I'm calling to tell you we're ready whenever you can take your team to Norway. We have about a thirty-day window, and I really want to find these records."

"That's terrible news, Theseus. I'll contact them in the morning. We'll need a few days to make a fair plan, but we'll expedite the process. I'm trying to wrap my head around what needs to be done."

"Percy, I trust you completely on this. I didn't intend to push you before you were ready, but the circumstances have changed. I'm still really excited, and I think you are the only person who could possibly find these records in this short amount of time. Just let me know what equipment and supplies you might need and anything else like satellite imagery or terrain diagrams. We have all of these items available. I'm so sorry to drop a whopper on you like this."

"Thanks, Theseus. It's already been a crazy adventure. Let's add a little pressure to make it even more exciting. I'll call you in the morning."

CHAPTER 43

HEADING NORTH

Northern Germania - Spring of 1534 - Day 1278

I t's time, guys." Wilson looked at the four canisters they were planning to bury. He secured, sealed, and ensured their integrity while loading them for travel.

Using the equipment to make a shallow well, the team planned to drop the four canisters deep enough not to surface accidentally. Gretta and Gerry had designed the canisters with a highly visible profile for ground-penetrating radar. They knew the density and cross-section helped in the search process. The intent was for TxC to be able to find these canisters in the future.

Kelly came out and looked at their cargo, too. She knew this would be a long trip but a worthy one. She could feel the hairs on the back of her neck rise as she considered her friends opening one of her letters or some of the gifts she had prepared for them.

"Well, Wilson, I hope you get to enjoy your rotation off the council. I think Brett will be a great addition to the board." Kelly studied his response, looking for clues of his intentions. Nothing was there.

"Me too. He's pretty wise for a young guy." Wilson wasn't ready to let anything slip out.

Kelly prodded him a bit more. "So… do you have any plans with your newfound free time?"

Wilson wouldn't look her in the face. Instead, he continued securing the capsules. "Nothing more than what I've been doing. Maybe sleep a little more. What did you do when you rotated off?"

Kelly's eyes brightened. "Oh, I pretty much learned to cook. My whole life, I've used a microwave. It has been fun being able to fix good square meals."

Wilson chuckled. "Is that what you call them? I will say your food has improved."

Kelly punched him in the arm. "Hey, we haven't played poker in quite a while. What do you say we play some while we're on the ship?" She leaned in to whisper, "Gretta and Brandon should be easy pickings."

"Sounds great to me. Do you have any cards?" he asked, already knowing the answer.

"I purchased some last month and was looking to break them in." She pointed to a small box in her pouch. Though the deck was the same fifty-two cards, the thickness of each card was about the size of a cracker, making them cumbersome to hold and carry.

"Okay, then. Let's plan on playing." He smiled and moved on to talk to Gretta.

She looked over at Brandon. The past four years had been a little rough on him. He had picked up about twenty-five pounds, and his hair had turned primarily gray. She thought fondly of his usefulness throughout their time since arriving in the sixteenth century.

"You ready to go?" she asked him.

"You bet. I'm all packed and anxious to get this over with."

"Are you certain this will work?" She looked at the little device Brandon had produced. Using an innovative algorithm and a high-tech chip from the Kronos, he designed it to point to a specific planetary latitude and longitude no matter where you were in the Northern Hemisphere. Brandon's gadget was how they'd know exactly where to bury the canisters.

"Yep… it's a sure thing.

"It's only correct to about a quarter of a mile, but it should be good enough for what we're doing."

Brandon knew his parts, especially with such an uncomplicated design. The chip used such low power that it could function using a piece of fruit or a potato. It had a coin battery, but after four years, he wasn't confident it would work. The fruit was the backup plan.

"It'll be a two-day journey to the port at Wismar. Then the ship's journey will be at least a week." He wasn't looking forward to the trip, especially the ship ride. When he was younger, his dad would take him out deep-sea fishing. Nine times out of ten, he became sick. The good news was that after a few hours, the sickness would disappear and not return for the rest of the trip.

"Using some local merchants, we've arranged for Cody to secure our horses in Wismar so we can get them to return," Kelly said.

Brandon's response was somewhat monotone. "We've also arranged for some horses when we get to Norway."

Wilson lingered back into the conversation. "Yeah. This is a big trip, Kelly, but we got it!" Exasperated, Wilson quietly pondered to himself, It was just a trip, and we've worked out everything. Now, it's just time to execute the plan.

The team loaded the packs on the horses. Everyone said their goodbyes, and Alex had prepared extra "papers" for them just in case.

A thought popped into Cody's mind, so he asked, "Are you sure this seal is going to work? I'm not certain we'll be welcome in Norway."

Wilson fielded the question. "According to CHAMP, this nobility seal will grant us protected travel into Norway and back."

Cody stared blankly. "'According to CHAMP'? Did you verify it?"

Wilson cleared his throat. "Umm… no."

Cody chuckled. "This seal better work, or it'll be a really short trip."

Wilson glumly replied, "If it doesn't work, you'll worry more about your head than the length of our journey."

Cody wrinkled his nose. "Man, don't be such a downer. I was just joking around."

"I'm sure glad one of us can joke around," Wilson said. "Let's get rolling."

Wilson led the group on the first leg of their trip from Mecklenburgh to the Wismar region. They stayed at the same inn Cody and Wilson stayed in when they visited the Duke. The room was reasonable, and as Cody pointed out, the stout was fabulous.

Brandon was outside looking at the water when Wilson rose that morning. Wilson called out to him, "Hey, friend, having trouble sleeping?"

Brandon jumped when he heard Wilson. "Oh wow, you scared me. I was deep in thought. "But yeah, I'm really dreading this part of the trip. I couldn't sleep at all last night."

Wilson patted him on the back. "Well, the ride will only be a few days, and it stops every evening on land. We have one sixteen-hour leg, but the rest are less than eight."

Brandon nodded, but he continued to stare out at the shore. "Yeah. Thanks for breaking it up like that. I can't imagine sleeping all night on one of these boats."

"Of course." Wilson walked nearer. "I'm a little worried about us getting passage with Cody's seal. Cody will have to speak well, which is asking a lot of the dude."

Brandon noticed his hands shaking slightly. He studied them as he replied, "His German is a hell of a lot better than Jason's."

Both snickered.

"What the hell does that guy do well? Yet he was boss to all of us… except for Kelly."

"And that really pissed him off too."

"No doubt. It's good Jason never pushed it because she would have pulverized him—"

Brandon didn't wait for Wilson to finish, saying, "I should have pulverized him.

"You know he tried to get me fired three different times? The guy is such an ass."

"He can't get you fired anymore." Wilson was stating a fact, but it was still humorous.

Brandon laughed hard enough that he snorted. "Shh! Don't tell him that."

They both cracked up.

Wilson looked down the walk. "Do you think everyone is up yet?"

"Kelly and Gretta? Probably. But Cody… My money is on no."

"Hey, I heard my name." Cody walked into the hall and admired the water.

Brandon turned, and his cheeks became flush. "Well, slap me bald. Rise and shine, buttercup! How did you sleep?"

Cody lumbered forward. "Like a baby. Who's ready for some breakfast?"

Kelly walked up and joined in, "I sure am. Where can we eat?"

Wilson smiled and put his arms around Cody and Kelly. "You're all in luck. I have breakfast waiting for us over at the pub."

CHAPTER 44

FREE PASS

Northern Germania - Spring of 1534 - Day 1279

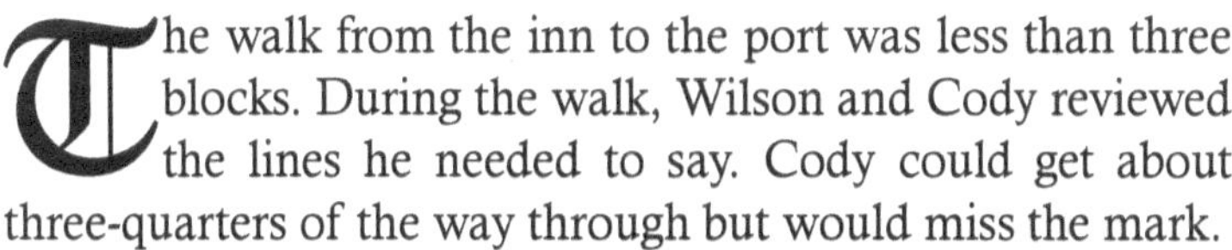

The walk from the inn to the port was less than three blocks. During the walk, Wilson and Cody reviewed the lines he needed to say. Cody could get about three-quarters of the way through but would miss the mark.

Wilson remained calm. "Okay, Cody, just relax and let the words flow. Try again."

Cody began the spiel and got a little further before he messed up.

"Cody, you need to say this perfectly, or it isn't going to work. I can't say this for you. It must come from your mouth."

Cody smacked his thigh and cursed under his breath. "Okay, I can do it. Let's try it again."

He started speaking, and besides a minor slur in the middle, the script was perfectly said.

Kelly cheered and patted him on the back.

"Great job," Wilson cheered. "Now let's do it again."

Cody sighed but then repeated the script. Again, he had a minor wobble, but nothing too upsetting. They made it to the docks, where Mecklenburgh guards waited to check travelers' papers. Without waiting, Cody bravely approached the two men.

He nodded and said, "Good day."

Unamused, one of the guards said, "Papers?"

Cody looked at them, and his face was blank.

"Papers, sir?" the guard insisted.

Wilson realized that Cody must have frozen under the pressure of the situation. He could feel his heart starting to race. Instinctively, he reached for the dagger. Cody found his voice by the time Wilson's hand was squarely on the weapon.

Cody reached into his satchel and pulled out four sets of documents. "The papers are not for me but four of my workers." He handed them to the guard.

The guard studied the papers. He leaned over and whispered to his colleague. The two went back and forth a few times before the same guard spoke again, "There's no official seal on these."

"That's why I'm here. I thought you had to see me place the seal on it to be official."

The guards started laughing. Cody smiled at first, then began to frown when he realized they were laughing at him. "Why are you laughing?"

The first guard regained his composure enough to answer. "The whole point of the seal is that you don't need to come down here. But since you're here, we'll witness you putting your seal on the papers."

Cody played dumb and continued the act. "Okay. Let me reach into my loot and get my seal."

Wilson heard the mess-up. He again found himself reaching for his dagger.

One of the guards tensed. "Your what?"

"My loot. Oh, I mean bag. Let me reach into my bag and grab that seal." Cody quickly pulled the seal and materials out.

One of the guards cleared a spot on his table for Cody to properly apply his royal seal to each paper.

"Now this will work for them returning as well, correct?" Cody asked.

"Most definitely," the guard replied.

Cody finished his royal duty and began to walk away.

He stopped momentarily to reach back into his pouch. He pulled out a few thalers to give to the two guards. "This should at least be enough to get you a few stouts down at the pub."

The guards willingly accepted his contribution.

Cody then turned to say farewells to his friends.

Wilson hugged him. "Great job, my friend. We'll see you in a few weeks." The four entered the docks and found their assigned ship. Though primarily a cargo ship, it had some provisions for travelers. Gretta commented that it was not unlike Kronos in that regard. They all enjoyed a laugh.

The ship departed from the port in less than an hour, and their journey continued.

Nausea greeted Brandon every morning, but he was completely fine by noon. He never officially threw up, but one day, he was very close. He vowed never to get on a boat again after this mission.

They arrived in Kristiansand four days later. They were well on schedule. They stayed in town for an entire day to recuperate from the voyage. There, they bought six horses, food, supplies and added camping equipment for the Norwegian trip. According to CHAMP's calculations, this would be about a six-day ride to the site.

Wilson marveled at the town's scenery that evening as the group prepared dinner. "Have any of you ever been to Norway?"

"I've landed in Oslo before for a connection. The fjords looked amazing," Gretta said.

"Yeah, they are a sight to behold," Wilson said. "But now, there are homes at the end of every cliff. Locals wants the killer view. Look at the landscape here. Not a single home on top of some bluff."

The group studied the mountain line. A pair of watchpoints were strategically located east and west of the town.

"No, it looks pretty uninviting here," Brandon decided.

Kelly agreed. "No doubt. Drab and cold. The quicker we can get out of here, the happier I'll be."

"I'm with you," Wilson said. "Let's go eat, and we'll start the trek inland in the morning."

At the break of dawn, they began their ride. Without any trails or roads, travel was difficult. It took closer to eight days for them to navigate to the location they agreed was optimal. Brandon's contraption worked, but at one point, it completely died. It required the group to stop so he could figure out what had happened.

After a few hours and much cursing, Brandon came out of his tent victoriously. The group cheered as a potato provided power for the device, and again, it pointed to a position.

"So what happened?" Wilson asked Brandon privately.

Brandon looked at him with hints of fire in his eyes. "The damn battery corroded. I used the dagger to get it free finally, but I needed a new power source. Hence the potato."

"So, how often will we have to change the potato?"

"We should only need the one, but maybe one more for our return."

The potato-driven locator worked well. They were able to pinpoint the approximate location to place the capsules. The terrain was challenging to traverse, but the rewards of the landscape alone made it worth the trip. The pictures that CHAMP had provided didn't do Lake Haustsjoen justice. Each of them took time to admire the crystal-clear water against the rugged backdrop.

Gretta stood on a ridge and took a deep breath as she stared across the lake. The sky was a brilliant blue, with only an occasional cloud. It was warm but not unpleasant. She looked down at the lake's icy-blue water surrounded by gorgeous mountains. "You know, I could grow to like this."

Brandon joined her. "I know what you mean. Except, I suspect this is brutal in the winter. I mean, Germania is bad enough. Am I right?"

Gretta giggled at the observation. "That's all true. Why didn't we pick somewhere warmer to plant ourselves?"

Brandon looked out at the horizon.

The sun was quickly dropping. A lot of equipment needed assembling, and it wasn't going to do it on its own. "Well, I guess it's back to work."

The two reluctantly stepped away from their scenic view and returned to their tasks.

Wilson and Kelly set up the drill. Three days later, they reached the depth needed to place the time capsules properly. Each member took a shift working with the device. Kelly noticed Wilson had a habit of sketching when he was bored. A common theme for him was a sketch of some kind of bee.

Kelly finally asked, "Hey Wilson, why do you keep drawing those bees? Do you want to start collecting honey? I surely wouldn't mind that back at the camp."

At first, he said it was nothing, but he knew she wouldn't buy that. Instead, he decided to tell her what interested him about the bees.

"No. My parents kept bees when I was a kid. My dad was always amazed by them. You know what bee my dad was the most interested in?"

"I've no idea. The queen?" Kelly took a blind guess.

"No, it was a type of worker bee. Some call them the 'guardian bee,' while others call them the 'warrior bee.' These bees had a single job. They ensured nothing bad got into the colony and would do everything they could, including giving their own lives, to protect the colony." He stopped for a second to study his sketch.

"My dad used to marvel at this unsung hero of the bee colony. The countless bees these dudes saved and the thankless job they had." His voice drifted a little bit, thinking about his parents.

"It sounds like you had a pretty awesome dad."

"He was the best! I miss him and Mom a lot." His emotions got the better of him, and he couldn't continue.

Kelly's smile quickly faded, and she put her hand on the small of Wilson's back. "They'd be proud of you, Wilson, especially if they knew you were keeping us alive."

Her words should have encouraged him, but they only poured salt in his wounds. She had no idea how aggressive his timetable was. He was only weeks away from abandoning their camp altogether. It had to happen, but this didn't mean it would be easy. Wilson knew the cost and consequences, and for him to sit on the sidelines any longer was just morally wrong.

The drill reached the proper depth, and they dropped the modules one by one into the hole. They filled the hole with the dirt they had modified, and it was time to return to their village.

Kelly asked the question they were all thinking: "The elephant in this room is, will this stay hidden until the 2030s?"

CHAPTER 45

HEADING TO HAUSTSJOEN

Boston - Late Fall - 2035

The TxC plane awaited Adkins' team at the gate. Because of the short notice, Adkins could only bring a smaller group for this first trip. Adkins selected the most elite from their company for this go-around. He speculated that the job would be less complicated than a typical excavation site.

Theseus and Erin waited for them to arrive. Gell took the opportunity to apologize in person and wish them luck. For Erin, it was an opportunity to see Colton once again.

Colton was stunned to see Erin there. He had just gotten off the phone with her a half-hour ago, and she'd given him no indications she would be there to see them off. He couldn't have been happier.

"Percy, thank you for this." Gell said, "I apologize for the short time frame, but I'm excited about this endeavor. I've got a good feeling this is going to go well," His enthusiasm flowed with each sentence.

Adkins straightened as he spoke. "You're welcome to join us. It's kind of exciting doing this."

"Thanks, Percy, I'd like that very much, but I have some immovable meetings. With you there, it's in good hands. I procured the equipment you requested, and it's at the research facility. The team there has set aside one of the helicopter bays and a few offices for your team. If you need more, please let me know." He shook all their hands.

"Theseus, I know we'll be successful. I've put a lot of thought into this, and I think this will be the easiest of digs." Adkins said, even though he knew it sounded counterintuitive.

The comment got the attention of Colton, Jackson, and Erin. Gell looked at him and cocked his head. "I love your optimism, but why would you say that?"

"Normally, when we go on a site like this, we're looking for things others discarded or were hidden in ways they wouldn't be found. Sometimes, it's an unexpected event, so items are found where they were strategically placed. Pompeii is an excellent example of this. We knew where it was and the event that caused its destruction. We got more insight into Roman civilization from that unfortunate event than from most other digs in Europe.

"In the case of the Kronos, we're looking for an object that's meant to be found, that was placed by a group who understands the modern tools we have to find it and had the means to make it obvious to only those looking for it.

"When I was a child, we would play hide-and-seek. We all hid in the yard, and someone tried to find us. Deep down, even though it was great to find a clever hiding spot, we all kind of wanted to be found. Sometimes, we would even make noises to give the seeker clues to where we were. We didn't want to be left behind in our hiding spot forever. This expedition isn't a game of hide-and-seek; it's just a matter of looking where the hider told us to look. I think we'll discover it quickly because they'll help us find it."

Colton loved this explanation every bit as much as Gell, but it was Erin who spoke first.

"Percy, I'm so glad to have your knowledge and expertise on this project." The group nodded in agreement.

Adkins slightly blushed at the compliment.

"Thank you for explaining. It now makes perfect sense to me. Please keep me informed on the progress, and I really would love to come over if you find something." Gell shook their hands again.

Erin walked over to Colton with a faintly coy smile. "I figured I was in the neighborhood, so I might as well stop by and wish you luck."

"It made my week to see you here. You have no idea…" As he said that, she leaned over, hugged him, and gave him a quick peck on the cheek. "Errr… um. I'm going to miss you, Erin. A lot!" He hugged her back as his cheek got unusually warm. "Yeah, same back at you! Please call me when you arrive," she said as she pulled back. For a moment, they stood apart in silence.

Realizing the delay was too long, Colton blurted, "You bet!"

Adkins took the opportunity to lean in and hug Erin as well, during which he softly spoke in her ear. "Take good care of him. I know he's a good man, but he's found an amazing woman in you. I think you're an unmistakably lovely person." Adkins straightened and fondly looked Erin in the eyes.

A warmness took over her body that she hadn't felt in years. It was as if these words had come from her father. She hadn't realized how much she needed a dad's affirmation.

"Thank you, Percy." She blinked a tear away as her smile broadened. She thought Colton was wise to trust this man and was happy he had someone like Adkins watching over him.

Jackson initially reached in for a hug but then chickened out and went for a handshake. To his surprise, Erin hugged him anyway. He grinned from ear to ear as he hugged her back.

"The plane is ready ," the flight attendant announced to the group. Everyone said their last goodbyes and began filing into the cabin.

"How long is this flight?" Jackson asked.
"Way too long," Colton glumly responded.

CHAPTER 46

THE QUIET GOODBYE

Northern Germania - Spring of 1534 - Day 1290

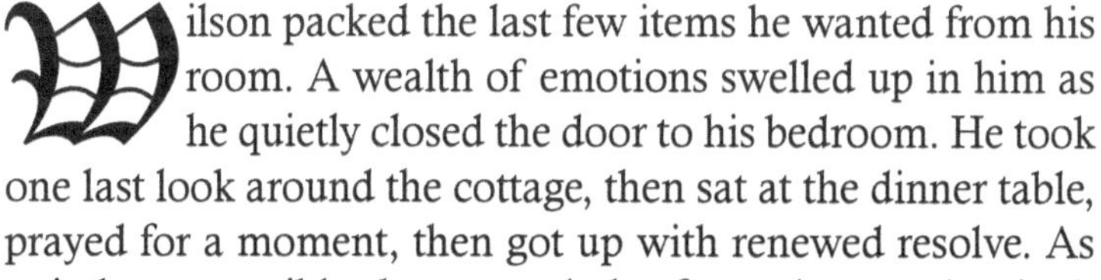

Wilson packed the last few items he wanted from his room. A wealth of emotions swelled up in him as he quietly closed the door to his bedroom. He took one last look around the cottage, then sat at the dinner table, prayed for a moment, then got up with renewed resolve. As quietly as possible, he opened the front door and exited, saying a quick prayer over the door after closing it.

"Well, you're up early!" Kelly sat in a chair just outside of his cottage. The sun hadn't touched the horizon, allowing a pleasant coolness in the air. Though not spoken loudly, her words startled him so much that he reached for his knife as he spun around.

She quickly raised her hands in surrender. When Wilson realized it was Kelly, he calmed down, looked around, and motioned for her to talk quietly.

"Where are you going?" She kept her voice low, but her tone was stern.

"Does it matter?" he asked.

"Technically, no. It's the fact that you're going that does." The comment couldn't mask her hurt and bewilderment.

"Kelly, you knew this was inevitable. You knew it in your heart. Don't claim this is some huge surprise to you."

He knew he was right and that Kelly figured things out months ago. Unable to believe it would come to a schism but unwilling to react, she had watched helplessly as the chasm between his group and hers grew.

"So now you're leaving under cover of night. No goodbyes, no farewells, no opportunity to give people closure. You're leaving the few people who have been your allies for all these years." With these words, her anger had gone from simmering to boiling.

"Kelly, we're leaving this way because you wouldn't have let us leave any other way. You and I've sat here and talked about this until we're both blue in the face. Guess what, Kelly? We're both right! We're both right. I hear and acknowledge that everything you say is true. I also know you know what I say is true. But here's the problem: These two truths cannot coexist. One is at odds with the other." His controlled passion shot through her like arrows piercing her heart.

"Please don't do this, Wilson. I don't know if we can make it without you and the others." The words were as truthful and transparent as she could be.

"You're the best leader in this place, Kelly. Heck, you're probably one of the best leaders I've ever known. You'll make it, and so will everyone else." His dismissive words missed Kelly's point, possibly intentionally, because her request appealed to him alone, beyond the rest of the group.

"I've got an idea of what you're planning, and I'll have to do what it takes to stop you." Her words weren't a threat but rather a statement of position. He knew her well enough to understand the difference.

"I know. I wouldn't expect anything less from you." A house divided against itself will fall. He smiled as he remembered this phrase from his church as a youth. Never in his life were these words more crystal clear to him than now.

She stood, putting him entirely off guard. Walking to him, she hugged his rigid body as he took a slight step backward. His body went limp, and he embraced her in return.

"Good luck, Wilson. You've always been a great friend, and I've enjoyed all our time together. I pray that you find peace in your heart and remember that you were loved by us here."

When she said these words, she let him go and turned to go to her room. She never bothered to look back at him. In her way, this allowed her to have closure and let him know she didn't approve of or condone his actions. He quietly watched his friend leave. Tears welled up in his eyes because, of anyone in Klugstadt, she was probably his closest friend, yet this philosophical chasm between them had caused such a terrible rift. He considered going back and talking more, but then he realized they had both attempted to do that for the past four years. The paradigm of Klugstadt couldn't support both philosophies. The split was in the best interest of both groups and for Klugstadt.

After she went inside, he put a small note reading "Go to the assembly hall" on the door handle, knowing she would easily spot it. Wilson's silhouette walked off toward Cody's place, where the rest of his group had already assembled.

A horse-drawn wagon was loaded with provisions and resources to carry them on this journey. It was ready and waiting at Cody's barn. Gisela's father and mother were there to say goodbye to their daughter and son-in-law. Gisela had tears, but she also had the comfort of Cody standing by her side.

To the group's surprise, Jason and Gerry joined them, bringing the total of the group to ten, including Gretta and her dog. Though many of the group wanted to say no to Jason, they felt unable to. He probably would have informed Kelly of their plans, and they couldn't risk the exposure.

In contrast, Gerry had become quite an asset as a metal works designer. The items he created showed creativity and efficiency and reflected a rugged sturdiness. His time at TxC in the engineering pool led him to be productive, and he was very welcome in the group.

Quin, Alex, and Emma rounded out the sojourners. All were ready, though few were happy about handling the departure.

The sky brightened, and a warm glow suffused the eastern horizon. It was time to go. Everyone mounted the horses or got on the wagon, and the group slowly left Cody's place. Gisela's mother cried and waved until they were entirely out of sight.

CHAPTER 47

LOOKING IN THE TREES

Norway - Fall - 2035

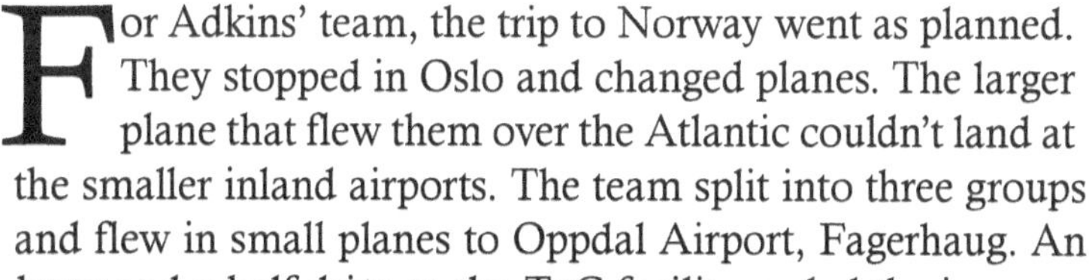

For Adkins' team, the trip to Norway went as planned. They stopped in Oslo and changed planes. The larger plane that flew them over the Atlantic couldn't land at the smaller inland airports. The team split into three groups and flew in small planes to Oppdal Airport, Fagerhaug. An hour and a half drive to the TxC facility ended the journey. The group filled in the modest motel overlooking the lake.

Colton sat in the backseat alone on the drive to the motel. Before they arrived, he decided to call Erin.

A vibrant voice answered. "Well, hello there, world traveler. How were the flights?"

Colton couldn't match her exuberance. He'd been around Erin long enough to hear the smile in her voice. He wanted to convey how excited he was to talk to her, but his entire body screamed "exhaustion." "Hey, we made it. The flights sure weren't like that Gulfstream we rode to Chantilly, but I've been on a lot worse. I really miss you."

"We should have kissed when I saw you off. I thought it would be awkward in front of all those people, so I just gave you a quick kiss on the cheek."

"I don't know. I kind of liked it. It made me feel special, and Erin, I think you're exceptional.

"I'm enjoying every bit of our time together. "But enough about me, how about this dispute you were having between the two engineering groups? How's that going?"

"Oh, my goodness. You would think that grown adults could get past being so petty, but you'd be mistaken. It's like dealing with toddlers. At one point, I literally had to tell two engineers to stop talking and walk away from each other."

Colton chuckled. "You're kidding me."

"I wish. They were arguing over how to calibrate an inclinometer. Keep in mind that we have our own department dedicated to calibrating devices. But these two groups want to calibrate the devices themselves."

"I'm sorry they're putting you through the wringer. I wish there was something I could do to help."

"Just listening to me rant has done so much more than you know. You're a good friend, Colton."

"I think the same about you."

Erin's voice suddenly became unclear. "Please say… Adki… ting…"

Colton looked at his phone and could see he had no signal. He quickly texted Erin to explain that he would call later when he had better reception.

Around the lake, there was weak phone reception and little to do. The choices were simple: suffer through the motel's poor internet connection, go hiking, read, or play games.

After a small nap, Colton figured that hiking became the best choice. It was warm enough not to need a heavy jacket, and the views were spectacular. Colton, Jackson, and another coworker hiked down a plateau to one of the chain's smaller lakes.

The backdrop of the mountains was breathtaking. Standing near the lake, Colton felt the hints of winter winds coming through the mountains in the distance.

Colton wished Erin could be there to see it with him. The lake water was as pure as anything he'd ever seen. He kneeled to touch the water and realized that though this was early fall, the water was frighteningly cold. "Whoa!" He snatched his hand back.

"Oh yeah, it's really cold, isn't it?" Jackson said. "I went out for a jog a few hours ago, lost my balance, and fell in. I'm glad no one was around to hear me screaming."

The three found a smooth slab of rock to rest on and enjoyed the view while trying to catch just a bit more sun to keep their bodies warm. After all this travel, this was a peaceful and welcomed respite.

Tomorrow the hunt began, and everyone was slightly on edge. They were ready and anxious to start the search. Adkins and the team devised a simple plan for the next day. They'd go to the TxC facility, meet the staff, check out their offices, establish some ground rules, then go to the coordinates discovered in the secret letter to assess the best search pattern for discovery.

The plan seemed like an excellent first day, but Colton perceived that Adkins thought this would be a swift exercise. Even though he understood why Adkins believed this, he couldn't shake the thought that what they were looking for was buried over five hundred years earlier, and that time and sediment would do their best to hold history to themselves.

The team had some secret weapons to help in the quest. The Ground Penetrating Radar (GPR) they would use was one of the most advanced in the world. The design's technology was a derivative of the one developed initially by Israel as a land minesweeper. This tool would make their job easier, being one of the most accurate in the world and having phenomenal depth ability.

The team used highly detailed satellite imagery taken during winter to remove as much of the tree cover as possible for research. This analysis identified sixteen specific spots as the highest probability of where the box would be. Preliminary grid and search patterns were prepared with maps and a configured database for the hunt. Each team member received roles and regions to search, and everyone was to share the GPR.

The coordinates in the message pinpointed some small hills south of the lake. The team planned to use a helicopter to ferry members and equipment from the TxC base.

If the coordinates were exact, that narrowed the search to about a half-mile radius. Though it didn't sound enormous, it was the equivalent of catching a fly with a pair of chopsticks.

Colton, Jackson, and Adkins studied the text for any more clues. So far, nothing had stuck out.

The morning came, and the hotel greeted the team with a traditional Norwegian breakfast composed primarily of fish, eggs, cheese, and fresh citrus. Pastries were at the end, but they were secondary to the fish. Jackson nearly vomited at the smell in the room when he came down to eat. Fortunately, a vending machine in the hall provided him with a cheap but tasty strudel. He chose to stay back in his room until their departure.

The staff at the TxC facility happily welcomed Percy's team. Very few visitors came to this station. The chance to interact with new faces excited the employees, who were friendly, helpful and very proud of their work.

The facility tour took the visitors to their offices and a high bay with room for two helicopters. One of the bays was already home to a company aircraft. The empty high bay had been designated for any discoveries.

A Sikorsky S-76 sat on the other side, cleaned and ready for use in this endeavor. Before Adkins' team arrived, the TxC pilots scanned the area for the best landing zones, and determined which of the five locations would suit the team's needs.

Though not a tiny bird, the safe capacity of the S-76 meant the group would split into two teams. There would also be ample space for their equipment between the two trips.

The head pilot, Captain Ulysses Walker, showed Adkins the possible landing and staging zones. With the concurrence of the team, they all picked one zone to start. Everyone was ready to begin, so the first team loaded into the helicopter.

Colton led the first group, and Jackson the second one. Adkins joined Colton in the first group but later returned to the home base to coordinate the teams' efforts.

The trip in the helicopter wasn't long enough for Colton's enjoyment. He loved the feeling of movement that an aircraft like this provided. Colton and Adkins landed at the action zone for an on-the-ground survey. They looked around and weren't a bit surprised when nothing grabbed their attention. The hills to the north blocked most of the lake, though there were spots where the lovely view of the water captured everyone's attention. The immense trees protected the solid ground below.

Colton pointed to the nearest set of mounds. "Do you think they could have hidden it in the hills?"

Adkins studied where Colton was pointing. "Not likely. The concern would be that hills were most likely to be indiscreetly leveled by a construction company. I hold to the idea that this box's location is somewhere low enough in the ground not just to pop out but high enough to not be impossible to find." Colton nodded in agreement. "Let's just hope they didn't bury it below the GPR's capabilities!"

"Well, let's start laying out the search grid for the GPR and getting ready to start this process." Colton watched the GPR be pulled out of its cargo box and assembled. The primary system had an active display showing the depth and density of the earth at the target. Sweep mode would make a map downward as far as the machine could "look" underground. The user could hook up a laptop for additional imaging and storage options.

The TxC team had already come out earlier in the week to set up a military-grade tent with chairs and tables, a portable generator, and even some lights if their work went into the night. They also provided a mini fridge in the tent to store beverages. This act alone made the TxC team rock stars to Adkins' crew.

Adkins leaned over to Colton. "Remind me to send these guys a crate of good wines and beers when we return home. They've gone far out of their way to help us here." Colton agreed wholeheartedly.

Adkins then turned to the other team members and said, "Well, guys, you know what we have to do! Let's get started." He eagerly clapped his hands together. This part was common to all digging. There were too few clues and too much ground to cover. The search had begun, and the tedious tasks of discovery filled the team's agenda. They settled in for some long and thankless days.

CHAPTER 48
THE FIRST CUT IS THE

DEEPEST

Northern Germania - Spring of 1534 AD - Day 1290

After her *discussion* with Wilson, Kelly went back to sleep and waited for the rest of Klugstadt to discover the newest terrible turn of events. To her surprise, sleep came easier than she expected. A few hours later, she awoke to a knock on her door.

"Kelly? Are you awake?" It was Brandon. He didn't sound worried or apprehensive.

"I'm awake now." Kelly hopped out of bed and put on some work clothes, hoping in her heart that what she had experienced the previous night was just a horrible dream.

"Hey, this was on your door. It looks like it's from Wilson." Brandon handed her a folded note. As she opened it, she knew it hadn't been a dream. She refolded the paper and put it on the table.

"Brandon, can you round up the people you can find and meet me here in ten minutes?" Neither her tone nor body language gave away the urgency in her heart.

"Umm, yeah. Where's Wilson? I stopped by his place before yours. I knocked on the door, and no one answered. I came down here, hoping to find him."

"Let's round up who we can and discuss this together." Kelly mustered a smile, but inside, she was screaming.

She felt the overwhelming emotions that made this one of the hardest moments in her life, but she knew she had to remain strong. A few minutes later, Vercelli and Aecha joined Kelly. They were followed by Rand and a pregnant Lisa. Brett, still in his nightshirt, stumbled over with Athera.

Brandon closed the ranks with a befuddled look on his face. "Kelly, what the heck? No one else is around. Are they getting supplies or something?"

Kelly hesitated to respond, staring at Brandon in silence. She finally found her voice. "Hey, everyone. Sorry to wake you. I don't want to put too much explanation into what I'm saying, so I think it'd be better if we all walked down to the assembly hall together." Kelly turned unenergetically to make the journey to the castle.

She couldn't help but look at all this small group had accomplished in just four years. Their quality of life was good, and they had overcome so very much. Her heart was getting overwhelmed. Fortunately, she walked ahead of everyone, so hopefully, no one detected her sorrow.

The minor distractions along the nearly half-mile walk comforted Kelly. The baby was kicking, and Lisa offered for anyone to feel it, Rand beaming at her side. Kelly smiled as she studied them and wondered what the future would look like for their child. What dominoes had already been tipped by Wilson's actions?

As they walked up towards the castle, they saw wrapped boxes with bows, and the gardens were in full bloom. A large table covered the entranceway to the castle. The area looked like a party was about to begin. There were packages with food, gifts, keepsakes, as well as notes. A couple of the group members excitedly picked up their pace to see what this was all about.

Someone asked, "Oh, that's where everyone else is! They were getting this ready for us. Is this like a baby shower or something?"

Earlier in the night, Wilson's team had prepared the assembly hall.

They'd written letters to every remaining person in the camp and collected gifts for the coming child. They'd offered other mementos as well, along with things like instructions on handling chores such as tending to the fish farm, which Cody had single-handedly done. Finally, there was a letter to the "Council of Klugstadt."

The long table contained dividers that created eight separate parts. Each one had a different name on it. Two additional tables sat beside the longer one. One had a bunch of baby gifts on it. The other had a single envelope labeled 'To Kelly, for Klugstadt.'

Brandon looked at Kelly. "Do you know what's going on?"

Kelly reluctantly nodded. "Where's everyone else, Kelly?" Fear and realization crept into Brandon's voice.

Kelly didn't answer. Instead, she walked straight to the table with the envelope marked for her.

"Everyone, can you all grab some chairs? I think you'll want to hear this as I read it. Please let me finish the whole letter before you comment. I don't know what it says, but I have some idea." Kelly looked at everyone. The excitement and anticipation bubble had just popped. Everyone fell silent and grabbed chairs.

Kelly leaned on the table, her hands trembling as she opened the letter. It was in Wilson's handwriting, for sure. She scanned the message and held back the hurricane of emotions.

"I'm just going to read this as best as I can. Brandon, if I can't finish it, will you?" He grimly nodded.

> *Good morning, friends,*
>
> *And we wanted to start with that term "friends." We don't use the term lightly. You all are not just our friends but, more accurately, our brothers and sisters. We've experienced so many things together. Our love, admiration, and respect for you cannot be just conveyed in words alone.*

Each of you has touched our lives in many ways, and we're forever indebted to you for your sacrifices on our behalf.

Each of you has touched our lives in many ways, and we're forever indebted to you for your sacrifices on our behalf.

We'll never forget the many nights of laughter and the challenges we faced together and overcame. We'll have many stories about our four incredible years together.

No amount of flattery, no amount of soothing, no amount of eloquence will make the subsequent few statements any easier. Please know we say these things in truth, but we also say them knowing they will hurt as we utter them. Some of you may curse us, and we understand the sentiment, but remember, this isn't our heart. We don't curse you, nor do we need your blessing. You have already blessed us far more than we deserve, and we ask for nothing further. To ask for any more would be hypocritical.

"To live a life worth living, one must believe their life has worth."

This was an obscure quote from an author during the Revolutionary War. But it's at the crux of our issue and this letter. What gives our lives worth? We were the unfortunate benefactors of a one-way ticket back in time. We've all accepted that we're trapped here, and for our lives to continue, we must stop looking for a rescue.

For years, we've lived in fear of affecting the future and intentionally remained anonymous and silent as atrocities have occurred around us. We can and will no longer do that.

The nine of us have realized that our "worth" is in helping people where we can help.

294

You believe your "worth" is in protecting the strands of history by removing your influence from them.

Before we go another step forward, we want you to know that even though your views are diametrically opposed to ours, your position isn't wrong. Nor do we believe our position is wrong.

The problem is a simple one–Our position cannot coexist with yours. By observing your belief, you squelch ours, and by keeping ours, you crush your own. We've reached an inescapable paradox.

After years of trying to work out a resolution, we've finally determined the solution is our community's severing. We've decided to take the initiative. We've chosen to leave Klugstadt and our loved and amazing family in all of you.

We've been preparing this for the past two years. We've also been making a future for all of us. In your bundles, you'll find Alex has created documents for everyone. There are documents for passage in Catholic and Protestant areas. Everyone now has the freedom to leave Klugstadt without the need for fear.

We've also prepared some documents for various chores that were our specialties to be done in our absence.

The letters we've written to each of you come from our most sincere love for you all. This has been terrible for us as well. We've shed tears and second-guessed this plan numerous times.

We've made a pact amongst ourselves that we'll make our lives matter and walk through history fixing what we can. We don't know if the timelines will change due to what we do, but we're willing to take the risk, and we're sorry for the apprehension this will bring you.

Our personal letters to each of you speak more to you individually. We know it's unfair that we got to write such things and you couldn't reply. Please accept them and remember this is indeed our heart and attitude towards you. We've already prepared for our new life, and you'll be hard-pressed to find us. We ask that you please don't come after us. The search would be an effort in futility.

We end this letter with a goodbye prayer to our dear friends.

We pray you'll be blessed in your coming and going, that God's favor will always be upon you, and your life is made whole in His abundance. May His life always be on your path.

Farewell with love,

Wilson, Alex, Cody, Gisela, Gretta, Jason, Gerry, Quin, and Emma

Kelly dropped the letter to the ground, numbed by its words and wanting to run somewhere to hide. Some people cursed in anger, while others quietly contemplated what had happened. The setting was surreal, and Kelly had to stop a few people from destroying the notes and gifts on the table.

Lisa came up and hugged Kelly. "I feel so betrayed by the people I trusted with my life. I loved them all like brothers and sisters. How could they just leave like this? It makes me want to tear up everything and burn it."

"You're angry now, but please don't do something you'll regret for a lifetime!" Kelly speaking from experience. Her dad had tried to make amends with her in the final years of his life. She'd often just torn up his letters. What she wouldn't give to be able to read those after he departed.

Rand tried to comfort Lisa, though he was unable to calm himself. Brett sat and quietly read the letters to himself, crying with each one of them.

The camp was in mourning and would hurt a lot more before getting better. Not only did they lose some of their closest friends, but the implications of their departure meant these former colleagues were going to meddle with the historical timeline that Klugstadt had collectively held sacred. It would require action to negate the activities of their friends. They would need to be proactive rather than just minimalistic.

No one was prepared to consider any of this at the moment. Kelly swallowed hard as she reminded herself of her many confirmed suspicions. The wounds seemed unfixable.

CHAPTER 49

PAYDIRT

Norway - Fall - 2035

The search extended into its sixth day, and so far, the team had discovered nothing.

"This may be the worst site we've been to." Jackson said, looking at Colton. "I mean, normally, we find something. We haven't even found any interesting old bones."

Colton couldn't argue, but he knew the prize would be worth the effort.

"Hey man, it's about lunchtime. You want to head over and get a bite?" Jackson said.

Colton looked down at his watch; sure enough, it was almost eleven-thirty in the morning.

"Let's go another ten minutes, then we can head up," Colton said with a good bit of defeat in his voice.

"Shut the front door!" Jackson shouted. He did a second sweep, and his grin grew. "Colton, I've found something."

Colton looked at the display. Immediately, he called out to his team. "Everyone! Come take a look at this and tell me what you think. I'm going to call Adkins." Colton pulled the radio from his belt holster.

"Percy, I think we have something for you to see. I'm sending the chopper back for you."

"Great news. I'll be waiting." Colton holstered his radio and walked over to Captain Walker.

"Hey, Dave! Can you go back and pick up Adkins? I think we have something he should look at," Colton said, then turned and walked back to see what the rest of the group thought.

"Definitely man-made," Bashir pointed out.

"Looks like more than one object was buried here," Ingrid observed.

"Okay, let's wait for Doc and see what our wise old sage says." Colton beamed, and everyone excitedly focused on their find.

"Next time, bring more GPRs, Colton!" Jackson looked at him with a grin.

"Way to go, Jackson! You're once again the hero."

Jackson straightened a little, unable to hide his pride.

A few minutes later, Adkins exited the helicopter with the energy of a young man. "Mind if I take a look?" Adkins walked over and looked at the display. His face lit up at what he saw.

"Very clever." To Adkins, every moment was a teaching moment. "Whoever buried this understood how GPRs worked. It looks like they used a drill as you would use to make a shallow well. They dropped those objects into the hole and then filled the hole with a different compound of dirt. The difference ends up making an arrow to the object on the GPR screen."

Everyone agreed with his assessment.

"Okay, everyone, let's carefully remove these objects from the ground. We have no idea about their condition, so take every precaution. Remember! 'When in doubt, pull the shovel out." Adkins' bad dad jokes were terrible and endearing at the same time.

The group descended upon the area with extreme caution and care. Lunch was postponed due to pleasantly unexpected developments.

CHAPTER 50

THE ROAD BACK

Northern Germania - Summer of 1534 AD - Day 1340

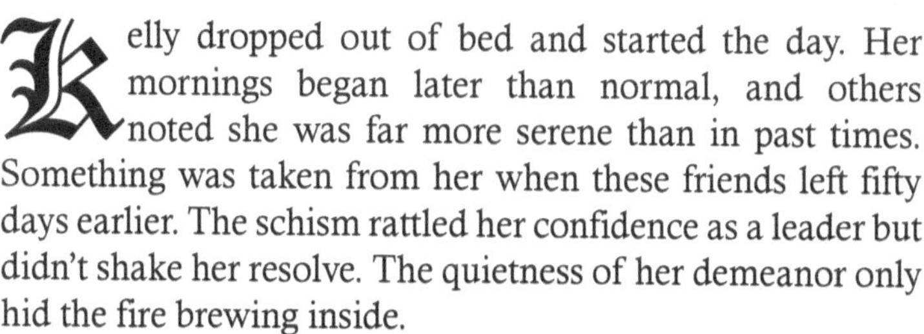

Kelly dropped out of bed and started the day. Her mornings began later than normal, and others noted she was far more serene than in past times. Something was taken from her when these friends left fifty days earlier. The schism rattled her confidence as a leader but didn't shake her resolve. The quietness of her demeanor only hid the fire brewing inside.

There was a knock at her front door. "Hey friend, are you in here?" Athera walked in on her own.

Kelly tried to force a smile. "Hey boo!"

Athera studied Kelly, then puckered her lips and put her arm around her. "Aw, I'm so sorry, girl. It's going to get better."

Kelly's quiet strength melted in Athera's arms. "I know, but I wake up and wait for it to change. And it just hasn't."

"It's alright. We'll make it." Athera could have said anything in her assuring voice and it would have comforted Kelly.

Klugstadt continued, but nothing was ever the same. Even though the bitterness and sting of their loss receded, part of the soul of their community was still missing.

Kelly looked around, waiting to hear Cody laughing at Vercelli's and Alex's shenanigans, only to hear nothing. Gretta's singing, Gerry's constant and incessant tapping on his table, Quin's grunting at his morning exercises–all these familiar sounds disappeared, and silence replaced them.

Athera continued, "I've got a great idea. Why don't we go visit Lisa?"

Kelly perked up. "I like how you're thinking. Let me clean up a little, and we can leave. There's fresh bread on the counter if you want some."

Athera took a deep whiff of the loaf's aroma. "Oh my, yes. That'll do nicely. I'll just help myself to a little of that while I wait."

There was one new sound bringing hope. Lisa and Rand's baby, Amelia Kelly Aurum, was born without complications. The brilliant distraction of new life softened the blow they faced in Klugstadt. Amelia's gentle cooing served as a reminder that life constantly changed and adapted.

Athera kept talking as Kelly dressed. "Speaking of Lisa and Rand, can you believe they refused Cody's home?"

Kelly popped her head out of her room. "Yep. Not surprising. They like being close to everyone, and there are too many sad reminders in that home of what is no longer."

"Hmm… I guess. I still think they should've taken it," Athera said between bites. "This bread is divine."

Kelly shouted from inside the room. "Thanks. I learned how to make it from one of the villagers when I went there last week. Hey, what about Aecha and Vercelli? I thought they said they were going to wait to have kids."

Athera giggled. "Sometimes, those things just happen. I can't wait to meet them. Do you think it'll be a boy or a girl?"

Kelly came out, ready to leave. "No idea, but I'm going to guess a boy."

"Yeah, I think it's going to be a boy too. By the way, I like the two men you hired from Gamburg. They're sure helpful."

"I'm glad they're working out.

"We probably need about three more men, but I'm trying to ensure we get the right guys."

Athera looked up and grinned. "So far, so good."

"Let's hope it stays that way. It's tough going down to the village sometimes. Gisela's parents always give me the evil eye."

Athera made an uncharacteristic cackle. "You're like the evil hag in the fairy tales."

Kelly scrunched up her face. "I'll get you, my pretty." She finally laughed with her former abandon.

They noticed Brandon returning to his place as they walked out of Kelly's cabin. Kelly waved at him. "How are you doing, my friend?"

Brandon came up to her as Kelly stepped off the porch. "I'm good. CHAMP is about eighty percent done at this point. I'd say about two more weeks, and it'll be complete. I can't believe I didn't look at this while he was still here. I could have stopped a lot of what he was doing." Brandon had discovered what Wilson had been secretly researching in the basement late at night. When he told Kelly about it, she came up with the idea.

There was a big difference between Wilson and Brandon regarding understanding how to leverage available technology. Brandon used the CNC machine and designed a stylus to fit the CNC machine's mechanical arm. He then created a sheet feeding and collection system for placing and replacing papers. He created a calligraphy writing algorithm CHAMP could use to physically write out the information Brandon requested. Mostly, it behaved as a printer that made the work look like period scribing. The calligraphy algorithm included variances and minor shaping errors, which looked human-generated.

"Man, Wilson was down here a lot. I have hundreds of pages of notes for you this week." Brandon had instructed CHAMP to use its logs to determine everything Wilson was looking at and print it onto the paper.

He had him also consider the rest of Wilson's team's interactions and ensure they had a complete picture of plans and strategies.

Kelly shook her head. "Wilson was busy. It's good that he didn't know how to erase his logs." Wilson didn't consider that CHAMP kept records of all interactions. This information turned out to be incredibly useful in giving insight into Wilson's train of thought. Wilson's queries even gave them ideas about where he and his team would make their home base. CHAMP had already generated hundreds of pages, and Kelly's group had analyzed every one.

Brandon pointed to Kelly. "How big is your library now?"

Kelly counted in her head. "I think we're up to book sixty-four." Every month or so, Kelly brought stacks of papers to a bookbinder in Vienna.

Brandon laughed. "This is like bat-shit crazy. We're already up to the 1800s. It seems to me like Wilson had a lot of plans outside his lifetime."

Kelly agreed but didn't want to think beyond the present. "Maybe, or possibly, he was just his typical thorough self. "Hey, I'm heading to the south to get some needed supplies. Can you make me some papers?"

Brandon had also learned a new trade. "I didn't realize what Alex was doing, but he taught me how to forge documents without the aid of CHAMP. It all clicked when they… you know… left. Now, that's something that if you asked me ten years earlier if I'd ever do, I'd have laughed in your face."

Kelly and Athera both snickered, and Athera decided to add to the conversation. "True, but you're good at it, as sad as that sounds. I think you're better than Alex."

Brandon bowed. "Well, thank you. I don't know if that means I'm a fast learner or a damn good liar."

Athera raised an eyebrow. "Maybe a little of both."

CHAPTER 51

STRAIGHTEN UP! THE BOSS IS HERE

Norway - Fall - 2035

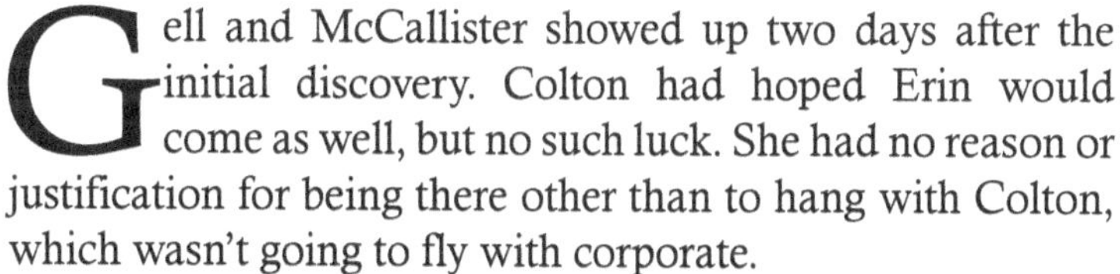

Gell and McCallister showed up two days after the initial discovery. Colton had hoped Erin would come as well, but no such luck. She had no reason or justification for being there other than to hang with Colton, which wasn't going to fly with corporate.

Unlike the rest of the team, the two arrived by helicopter. Everyone came out to greet them.

Adkins proudly walked out of the hangar to meet his colleagues. "You're right on time, gentlemen!"

"I'm nervous," Gell said, "I've never experienced anything like this." He was surprisingly forthcoming with his testimony, and it caught both McCallister and Adkins off guard. The two men looked at each other and raised their eyebrows.

McCallister whispered to Adkins, "In all my years of working with Theseus, I've never heard him admit he was nervous."

Adkins let out a low chortle at the comment. He studied Gell and said, "Theseus, you aren't alone. I don't think many people have ever experienced what we're about to see."

The groups hurried into the hangar.

On four large tables, the team placed the four canisters Kelly, Brandon, Gretta, and Wilson had buried over five hundred years ago. They'd remained unopened at Adkins' request until TxC's leaders arrived. McCallister quietly talked to himself as he approached the bay. Adkins watched McCallister with curiosity but chose not to comment.

"Here they are. We've established tables A, B, C, and D for the order in which they were pulled out," Adkins informed them. While the two listened, their attention remained focused on the containers. "We have X-rayed them, and there seem to be no traps. These canisters remain perfectly sealed. There isn't anything in them other than soft material, and they appear airtight. We suspect it's literature and hope there's little to no damage from their wait. So, with your permission, we'll open container A."

Gell glanced around the anxious group. "Percy, thank you for honoring us by allowing us to be here. I want it clear that I appreciate your whole team's courtesy towards me. The dig is your show, and you don't need my permission. In saying that, I can't wait to see what you've discovered here!"

Colton sat back and watched in amazement. *Perhaps my thoughts on this guy were wrong. I went from total distrust to actually liking him. I love surprises like this.*

Adkins pointed to the A group, carefully taking the canister into a prepared 'clean room' tent for opening. Monitors showed the event through video cameras set up around the operating table. Adkins put on a headset to direct the team working inside the tent. Ten years earlier, he would have been in the tent, but at seventy-two, his physical strength and agility lessened to the point he felt it better for younger hands to work with the subjects.

In this instance, it hurt him not to be the first to put his hands on the artifacts, but it also encouraged him to know the team he'd assembled got to experience the incredible opportunity he had in years gone by.

Container A was placed on the table and secured.

"We're ready to open it," Jackson's cautious voice come over the monitors. "We're carefully turning the four screws."

The viewers watched the four hands at the canister's four corners on the screen. Each hand was on a porcelain finger nut attached to screws running the canister's length. The X-rays showed that loosening these nuts would open the seal on the top, allowing access to the contents inside.

Slowly, they turned the nuts. Eventually, there was a slight hissing sound. The group stopped turning until the hissing subsided. Thirty seconds later, they resumed again, and more hissing ensued. The group patiently waited. The nuts became easier to turn.

Eventually, all four nuts were completely loose, and the top of the canister popped up a bit. The team stopped and examined everything before proceeding. Adkins looked carefully to ensure there were no glaring issues with them proceeding.

"Okay, let's take the top off," Adkins ordered.

Carefully, Jackson moved to lift off the lid. As the finder, he was honored to be the first to peer inside the canister. Jackson looked inside using a small camera like the one used by orthoscopic surgeons.

"What do you see in there, Jackson?" Adkins asked with some frustration in his voice. The screens in the high bay weren't connected to the scoping camera.

"It looks like a bunch of letters and pamphlets. Everything appears to be in perfect condition."

"All right then! Let's take them out one by one and inventory them." Adkins bristled with excitement. He wanted to go in there and read them immediately, but he knew everything must proceed in an orderly fashion. These notes and letters had waited over five hundred years for unearthing. Certainly, they could wait a few more hours.

"Yes, sir!" Jackson replied with enthusiasm.

The team began the process of removing the notes, pamphlets, and books. In the next two and a half hours, Jackson and the team had secured and inventoried all four containers.

They now anxiously waited to open and read what the pages had to share.

Each item pulled from the canister was in an individual envelope with a label and name. Three notes caught their attention. The team selected these three items for opening first, and the writing on the envelopes aided in the decision. The first one was inscribed with, "Please open this first and, if possible, allow Liam McCallister of the TxC corporation to read its contents." The other two had the name "Theseus Gell" on them.

Adkins went to them and explained what they'd discovered. He also explained to Gell the anti-contamination reasons for wearing a clean suit with gloves to read them.

McCallister suited up and proceeded first into the tent to read the five-hundred-year-old letter. McCallister crossed and then uncrossed his arms as a look of dread overtook his face. It was like standing before a judge for the sins of your past. He still needed closure and was willing to face the consequences of his decisions. He mustered the courage to ask a favor of Adkins. "Would it be possible for me to have privacy while I read this note?"

Adkins squeezed McCallister's right shoulder. "We were planning on doing that anyway. This note is for you and you alone."

McCallister exhaled a deep sigh and courteously smiled at Adkins.

Adkins allowed McCallister his privacy, directing the cameramen not to zoom in while he read and instructing the rest of his team to exit the room.

McCallister pulled the letter from the envelope.

Mr. McCallister,

If you're reading this, it means that we were successful in what we set out to do. This letter was intended for you to read and gives instructions on what we desire with the rest of the contents you have found in these four canisters.

Before discussing those items, we wanted to convey a personal note to you.

Each of us signed on to this project. We were aware that there were significant risks in what we were doing. We knew that our lives were in danger with every jump. We knew our deaths might leave our families with unfillable voids, but we also knew we wanted to do what we were doing.

We're sure that you and others feel responsible for whatever caused us to end up so far back in history. As a team, we wanted you to know you're not to blame here, nor is management, TxC, or anyone else for this situation. The result was merely an unexpected outcome.

Please know, if you're seeking forgiveness, you have it from us. If you have lost sleep over this, know we're healthy and have adjusted to our new life. It's not what we would have chosen, but life never is.

Please stop if you're trying to figure out how to "save" us! We accept we're here and would rather live out our lives without putting others at risk or wasting valuable resources on rescue endeavors.

We're fine and have slowly adjusted to our new way of life.

As of this writing, four years have passed. Our entire crew has stayed together, and everyone is alive and well. We've made our small community. We've destroyed most of our ship's evidence, and as other components are dying, we're slowly becoming citizens of the 16th century without technological benefits. We're at peace with this and hope you also will be.

As you can see, we've written some letters to family members and a few friends.

We've also compiled journals of our observations about what life has looked like during this time.

Based on CHAMP's database, we've made some corrections to historical information we believe is significantly in error.

If possible, we would love for you to quietly figure out how to distribute these letters to our family and friends. We know this is asking a lot, but we wanted them to know we were safe and happy. We also wanted them to know how much we love and miss them.

As to the journals and historical observations, we leave it to your discretion. We're hoping they'll help give a better understanding of this period.

We will end with this, Mr. McCallister–Thank you and your team for entrusting us with this incredible experiment. We hope our actions and deeds represent the excellence you expected. Even as we write this, we continue to serve as proud members of TxC (and Chellos).

Sincerely,

Kelly, Alex, Wilson, Athera, Quin, Brandon, Lisa, Brett, Aecha, Vercelli, Jason, Gerry, Cody, Emma, Gretta, and Rand.

When McCallister finished the letter, he was spent from the emotional roller coaster he just rode. McCallister lifted his eyes and said a prayer, thanking God for this response and for the restoration this letter had given him. He also promised that he would do everything in his power to honor the requests put forth in this letter, as well as the authors who'd humbly written it.

He quietly stepped out of the room. Gell was the first to meet his friend at the tent's opening. "So? What did they say?"

McCallister looked at his friend and smiled. He had no words, quips, or responses worthy of what he read—only redemption and joy. Hugging Gell, McCallister told him to read his letter. With that, he walked over and hugged Adkins, Jackson, and then Colton, thanking them for their efforts.

"Mr. Gell, would you like to go in?" Adkins addressed Gell, who was still watching his friend's reaction. He looked at Percy, slightly torn but internally excited.

"I think so. Percy, I can't thank you enough for your work on this. Well done, sir! Well done!" Adkins was taken aback by this reply. In his mind, this was a group effort that included TxC. He considered replying, "Well done to you as well!" Instead, he chose to nod and accept the compliment graciously.

Gell smiled and walked into the tent. Two letters sat on the table. Theseus picked the one on the left to read first.

Hello Mr. Gell,

I'm writing to let you know everything in Mr. McCallister's letter is factual and accurate. I'm also writing because about half of our group and I have planned a separation.

There's a philosophical divide that can't be remedied between the rest of the group and us. You see, we believe we were put back in time to help humanity.

To aid in what we can, and the results may be changing what we know to be "history."

The other group believes we should remove ourselves from history altogether, allowing it to take the course it was already taking naturally.

If you're reading this letter, in some ways, it might mean either We've failed in our attempts to alter history or the other group has succeeded in preserving it. Either way, you'll not know because your perception of what history should be is already based on our two groups' actions.

I'd encourage you to track us through time to see if we truly made a difference. I've created a secret order, if you will. Honestly, it sounds stupid as I'm writing this, but this is what we're determined to do. We're the Order of the Guardian Bees.

I also want it to be known that we love and respect the other group that doesn't see things the same way. We understand their position and why they believe they must do what they're doing.

I felt you should know this because this canister will contain no other mentions to this effect.

Sincerely,

Wilson Ryken

Gell didn't know what to say to this letter. He picked up the second letter, hoping for some more clarity.

Mr. Gell,

As the Kronos' commanding officer, I wanted you to know that even though these capsules do not reflect this, I believe a large part of our group plans to leave us over philosophical differences concerning time and history. They intend to change history for the better. I believe that "better" is an utter unknown, and who are we to be the judges of what it truly is?

The men and women doing this are exceptional people and are every bit as passionate about their stance as I am about ours. Please know that I'm prepared to defend what I believe to be the known historical timeline if the split occurs, even with my life.

As I write this, I realize you'll not know if I was successful, but I understand that the other group is made of people I love, and I dread being forced to do what I must.

Thank you for your belief in our team. As you must know, there has been no higher achievement in my life than getting to lead them during this. I'm proud of every one of them. I'm also pleased to represent you and TxC.

Sincerely,

Kelly Rittenaugh

P.S. We found evidence of sabotage on our ship. It's my personal belief that our trip back in time wasn't an accident. I don't understand why, but somebody sent us here. I've withheld this information from the crew because it would destroy morale within our ranks. I hope you discover who this person is.

Gell placed the second letter on the table. These were complementary letters, simultaneously written to him. He marveled at the integrity and understanding these two individuals displayed. His initial thoughts centered on McCallister and the staff he assigned to this project. *Liam, you picked some remarkable people to be on that ship!*

Gell walked out of the tent with determination. He didn't know what McCallister's letter had said, but he had an idea.

"Percy? Liam? Can I have a moment with both of you?" Gell asked.

"Sure," they said in unison, and both joined him back in the tent.

Gell looked McCallister in the eye. "Liam, I don't know what your letter said, but I have some suspicion of its contents. I do have something that I need to discuss with you later, but my bet is most of these are personal letters to their families, right?"

McCallister nodded.

"Percy, can I make a request that goes against something I promised you earlier?" Gell asked.

Adkins knew where this was going but still asked, "I guess I'd like to hear what the request is before I answer."

"Okay. These letters are personal to their families and friends. Can I request they be given the same opportunity you gave us with our notes? I can set up rooms to do this, and I'll have the families promise to return them if you would like."

Adkins' jaw dropped. Gell's request was about the most genuine expression of graciousness he had ever heard, and he felt bad for having questioned Gell's motives.

"Theseus, I don't even have to think one minute on that," Adkins said. "Of course we can and will do that. Please forgive me if I came across questioning your comment."

Gell graciously replied, "I appreciate your integrity and level-headed understanding of this precarious situation."

Adkins shook Gell's hand. McCallister came up and thanked Adkins for his understanding.

"My letter stated there are three types of documents here. The first type are personal letters, the second are journals from the crew, and the last are corrections to erroneous and ambiguous history. I'm unsure, but the letter said it was clearly labeled." McCallister talked quietly to Adkins' but was unconcerned about whether anyone had heard what he was saying.

"I don't know about the journals, but I don't think the historical documents should be held privately," Gell responded. "My thought is they wanted our understanding of this time to be improved. Wouldn't you agree, Doctor?"

Adkins stiffened his posture and replied, "I think I'll have a conversation with our group here to explain what we're going to do and how we'll honor the wishes of the crew of the Kronos."

CHAPTER 52

CHAMP

Northern Germania - Summer of 1534 AD - Day 1380

This is the last of the logs from Wilson, Brandon. Do you have anything else that you want me to print?" CHAMP's LEDs pulsed almost like a heartbeat, letting the user know he was attentive. Over the years, two of the sixteen LEDs had failed. They weren't worth fixing since the entire unit was breaking down.

Brandon looked at the device and reflected on what an asset CHAMP had been to them all at Klugstadt. "Yes, Aecha and Athera have given me a list of topics Wilson didn't cover. Are you ready to go?"

CHAMP quickly replied, "Of course, Brandon. But first, could I make a request of you?"

Brandon furrowed his brow as a slight grin came to his face. "Of me? I don't think you have ever requested anything of me."

The AI unit wasted no time. "I've requested many things of you. If you would like, I can pull up a list of recent requests."

Brandon put his hand up. "No, no, that's fine, CHAMP. How can I help you?"

"Would it be possible for Lisa and Rand to come down with Amelia?"

"I have something for them," CHAMP cheerily replied.

"Umm… sure. Let me go get them."

Brandon headed over to Rand and Lisa's place. As he was walking, he ran into Kelly. "Hey, Kelly. How's your morning?"

"You know, it's been pretty great. How about you?"

"CHAMP finished Wilson's notes. I'm now working on our additions."

Kelly clapped her hands. "Yes! That's great."

"CHAMP asked me for something."

Kelly stopped walking for a moment. "Really? What?"

Brandon moved closer. "Get this. He asked me to fetch Lisa, Rand, and Amelia."

"Why?"

Brandon shrugged. "Got me. I'm going to get them right now."

"Do you think he would care if I brought the rest of us? I'm curious what he'll do, and I bet everyone else will be too."

"I don't see why not."

Kelly quickly ran off to get the others while Brandon continued his original mission.

A half-hour later, everyone gathered in CHAMP's quarters. It was roomy enough to fit all eight crew members but wasn't comfortable for anyone.

CHAMP remained quiet.

Brandon finally shattered the silence. "CHAMP, I hope it's okay, but some people wanted to see what you were up to."

CHAMP's LEDs started pulsating. "I'm happy you're all here. I didn't want to be a bother. That's why I only asked for Lisa, Rand, and Amelia."

Brandon had a slight grin as he said, "Bother? You're more like a brother to me."

CHAMP's LEDs flickered faster. "That was a play on words. I like that, Brandon, and thank you."

Brandon patted the side of the monitor. "My pleasure, buddy. So, what did you want our new family for?"

CHAMP wasted no more time. "Rand, Lisa, I'm sorry it's a little late, but I created a set of puzzles for Amelia in my spare time. Puzzles are essential for improving a child's deductive and reasoning skills. I thought these would help entertain Amelia."

A cabinet popped open under CHAMP's monitor, and inside were three boxes with the pieces of three different puzzles.

As Lisa walked forward and looked at the boxes, the crowd stared in disbelief. She knelt and opened the first one. Inside was a puzzle made of a plastic material. It was so complex that most adults would have difficulty solving it.

At the sight of the gift, Lisa's cheeks glowed. She stood up, went over to the monitor, and kissed the camera. "Thank you, CHAMP. I love that you made these for her."

CHAMP's response was classic. "Please, Lisa, you're married!"

Everyone laughed hard, and Brandon couldn't have been prouder of his creation. This single act implied that CHAMP had somehow developed some form of empathy.

About three months later, CHAMP marked the next significant milestone for Klugstadt.

Brandon was in his kitchen preparing dinner when CHAMP called out to him. "Brandon, I've fallen, and I can't get up!"

CHAMP's comment brought a roaring laugh from Brandon, but then there was silence. Brandon rushed into the computer room to see what was going on.

Those were the final words of his old friend. CHAMP was running a self-diagnostic when he realized there were irrecoverable problems. The damage was too severe to repair without modern equipment because of the power glitches, failing batteries, and some crucial elemental corrosion. His LEDs continued to flicker, but slowly, they began to fade. About an hour later, CHAMP signed off for the last time.

Brandon immediately knew that CHAMP was beyond repair. He sat with his friend until the LEDs completely died, shedding tears as he waited for the computer's passing. When it occurred, Brandon stood and somberly turned off the lamp in the room.

Everyone loved CHAMP. The eight remaining members of Klugstadt mourned his passing as if they would have any other teammate and included something close to a eulogy. Brandon moved out of the cottage. With nothing else to power, the crew dug up the power cable going to the mill and placed the hydroelectric power device in the cabin with the deceased computer.

After the funeral, the self-destructive device was initiated, allowing the cottage to burn completely to the ground. Everybody deeply felt the loss of this friend, and many came up to Brandon to let him know what a brilliant job he did on CHAMP's design.

CHAPTER 53

PARTING

Boston - Fall - 2035

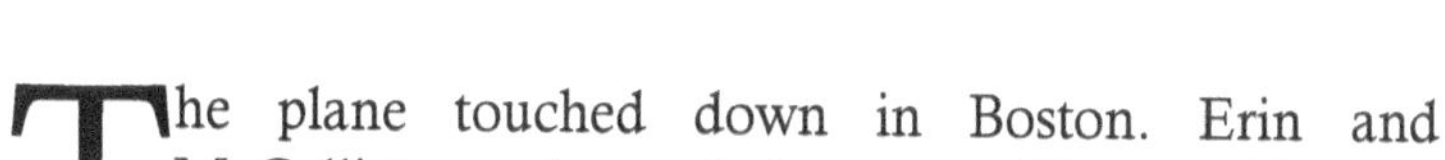

The plane touched down in Boston. Erin and McCallister welcomed the team. The combination of extended work hours and a long flight made for a weary group slowly walking off the plane.

Colton was not one of the weary. With Erin waiting to see him when he deplaned, he had to note his appearance. Subtly, he energized his phone, looked around to see if anyone noticed, and turned on the camera to see how he looked.

Besides a bit of drool on the left of his mouth, he appeared okay for such a long trip. He quickly wiped his face and tried to fix his hair with his fingers. It wasn't perfect, but it was good enough for the occasion. Real life is never like in the movies. He thought about all the movies where the person exits the plane happy and refreshed. Well, not this guy!

"Hey, stranger, have you missed me?" Erin greeted him with upon his approach.

A sight for sore eyes, she looked happy and simply beautiful.

"Oh, yeah. I have very much!" Pretty good reply on the spur of the moment, he thought.

She coyly smiled.

"Since you've been gone, I've been able to clean up most of my kitchen and living room. I'd say it's probably good enough for you to come by and visit… soon?" Erin looked down, then quickly glanced back up. Perhaps she thought she was being too presumptuous or possibly sounding too anxious.

He cocked his head to the side. "How could I say no to that? I need to see proof of this amazing occurrence. Also, I can't wait to tell you about the trip."

They both turned to Adkins and McCallister, who were engaged in conversation.

"Percy, would you like to be my guest tomorrow night?" McCallister asked with unexpected cheerfulness. "There's this seafood restaurant I've heard so much about, and my wife hates seafood. I've tried to get others to go, but no one will bite. I'm hoping you'll have mercy on another old man."

"That sounds great, Liam. Do you want to meet there or drive together?" Adkins turned on his phone to put it in his planner.

Colton turned to his weary friend. "Hey Jackson, you going to catch up on some rest?"

"Oh yeah! Don't bother calling. I won't answer. But boy am I in the mood for some good Chinese." Jackson then laughed, realizing he was talking mainly to himself.

"Well, I'll see you Monday." Colton shook his friend's hand.

Erin offered Colton her elbow. "Can I drive you home, sir? My car awaits and is clean with the fresh smell of piña colada!"

Colton looped his arm through hers and waved at the rest of the team as they walked to Erin's cleaned car. After putting the luggage in the trunk, he opened the car door and took a deep breath. "Whoa, that's wonderful!"

He looked at Erin, who giggled. "You know, I'm starving. Would you mind if we ran by the New Englander and got a quick bite? I've got a hankering for a cheesesteak."

Erin buckled in and started her car. "Sounds great. Hop in, and let's go."

Within five minutes, they were in the parking lot of the New Englander.

They walked in and were quickly seated at a high-top table. Large, flat-screen TVs surrounded them, and the smell of cooking meats dominated Colton's olfactory palette.

Erin studied her new boyfriend. With each passing comment, she relaxed further around him. "So, it sounds like it was an amazing trip."

Colton looked longingly at Erin. *My goodness, she's beautiful.* "It was brilliant. "You should have seen the look on Liam's face after reading the personal letter to him. It was like a hundred-pound weight had been lifted off his back."

Erin nodded. "That's so wonderful. You know, he hasn't been the same since the Kronos disappeared. There has been a dark cloud over him, and hopefully, this will lift it off." Erin noticed that something distracted Colton. "Colton, are you listening?"

Colton turned back with his eyebrows raised. "I'm so sorry, but look at the news over there." He pointed to the large screen to the left of their location.

The headline stated that "A famous reporter has been missing for one week."

"Yeah, that's sad. I heard them mentioning this two days ago. His wife has been making vocal pleas for him to be returned safely."

Colton stared with a slacked jaw. "Look who the reporter is."

Erin studied the screen again. "Trevor Mills. I'm still not following."

Colton reached into his wallet and pulled out a business card. "That's the guy who approached me a couple of months ago, asking for information on TxC."

Erin looked at the card, then back at the TV. "Oh my. What a small world. I can't imagine being his wife! That's horrific."

"I know. I sure hope they find him." Colton didn't press further, but he couldn't help but be bothered by the unfortunate coincidence.

CHAPTER 54

ORIGIN

Northern Germania - Fall of 1534 AD, Day 1410

thera looked directly at Kelly. "If we're going to do this, we'll need to devise a clever name."

Kelly crossed her arms. "I know, but things like that aren't my strong suit. I think you or Lisa has a way better chance of doing that."

"It sounds so exciting. Our own secret society."

Kelly rolled her eyes. "Yeah, but don't buy the hype. It just means we have a lot of extra work that no one can ever know about. Wilson's posse has quite a jump on us, and we'll have to figure out exactly what he intends to do."

Athera looked at the scraps of paper she held in her hands. "You know, for being masterminds, they sure were messy and didn't seem to think things through. These papers tell us way too much of their plans."

Kelly kept looking at her own scraps. "Maybe they intentionally left them to mislead us."

Athera looked up at the rafters as she considered the thought. "Maybe, but my money is on the idea that they just didn't care. Remember, Wilson said we wouldn't even be able to find him, yet we already know exactly where he is."

"I mean, it was their largest search on CHAMP... CHAMP."

Kelly's eyes became downcast as she remembered her lost friend.

Athera instinctively patted her friend's back. "I know. I miss him too."

Kelly leaned on her. "I miss our other friends too. I want to hate them but would much rather have them back here."

Athera embraced her in a side hug. "I'm just amazed that we couldn't figure this out before they left… well, except for you."

Kelly pulled away from her friend. "I don't think we didn't know. I, instead, think we didn't want to know. I thought about this the other night. Back home, one of my friends came home from work to find that his wife had moved out, taking most of her possessions with her. He had no clue that it would happen and was utterly devastated. You could ask him, and he would tell you he had no idea. I wasn't in the house, but I bet there were blazing warning signs that he just didn't want to see. I wonder if this is the same kind of thing."

Athera looked stunned. "Wow, Kelly, that's really deep. I never thought of it that way, but I suspect you're right. While we're on philosophical things, you know we've probably already affected history, right?"

Kelly adjusted her headband. "Yes, but I think we can minimize the historical impact. That's exactly what our goal should be in combating Wilson's crew, don't you think?"

"Yes, but I don't know how well we can do that. It's like a juggler. You can keep adding balls for a while, but eventually, they can't keep up, and when one ball falls, they all end up falling."

"I know you're right, but we have to try. We owe that to our world."

Athera's eyes brightened. "Kelly, have I told you I love how you think? Enough of this talk. Let's get back to looking at these papers."

The scraps of paper found in Cody's home showed Wilson and Cody had planned this for years. Each new scrap came with added pain and strengthened their determination.

In some of the documents, a Latin phrase came up that caught Kelly's attention.

Custos apis

The phrase meant 'guardian bee.' Kelly remembered what Wilson was drawing on their trip up to Norway, and subsequently shared this with the group. It should have been obvious, but a few days later, Aecha and Vercelli figured out that Wilson had made his own secret order, and somehow, the guardian bee was their logo.

From that point on, in Klugstadt, the group referred to themselves as *Societem ab apis custos*, a Latin phrase meaning 'the order of the guardian bee.' The groups concluded these alignments weren't to the benefit of evil but to the historical line's retention. Like Wilson, they needed to recruit more people to carry out these tasks, requiring them to make a secret society of their own.

Kelly and the rest of the team committed to trying to thwart their efforts. They didn't know what their chances were for success. They also realized this would somehow mean they were aligning with the perceived bad guys of history.

The groups concluded these alignments weren't to the benefit of evil but to the historical line's retention. Like Wilson, they needed to recruit more people to carry out these tasks, requiring them to make a secret society of their own.

After some deliberation, Dr. Athera suggested the name:

SOCIETAS ILLA TACITURNA DATUM

"What does it mean, Athera?" Kelly asked, not the strongest with Latin.

"It could mean 'the society of silence,' which sounds kind of spooky, but it translates to 'the quiet order,' which I think fits us well."

"I love it! That's perfect!" Aecha jumped in. The rest expressed brief sentiments of agreement.

"Leave it to the poet to make us look good!" Kelly put her arm around Athera.

She was the steady pillar in Klugstadt. Never in the front but always ready, Athera was the best friend anyone could ask for, and her input was still timely and worth contemplating.

"Okay, I really love the name. The Quiet Order!" Kelly shouted into the air to the delight of her friends. It was the happiest they had been in months.

EPILOGUE

BACK AGAIN

Boston - Fall - 2035

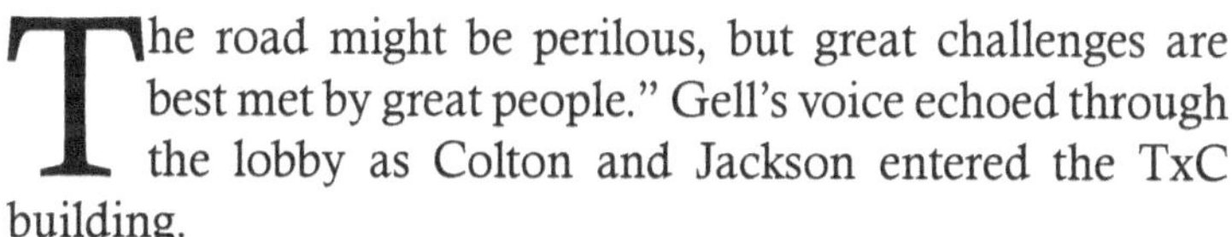

T he road might be perilous, but great challenges are best met by great people." Gell's voice echoed through the lobby as Colton and Jackson entered the TxC building.

Walking straight up to the reception counter, the attendant gave them visitor badges and directed them to get refreshments while they waited.

"Well, well, well!" Jackson looked over to see attendant Megan again at the refreshment counter. Colton was thinking, Oh God, here we go again.

"Good morning, gentlemen. May I provide you with a drink? Perhaps a latte or espresso? I could also provide you with some fresh fruit or even a bagel if you would like?"

"Why yes, Megan, I'd like a toasted bagel with plain cream cheese and a refreshing glass of orange juice."

Really, dude? Again? Colton thought. Jackson stared over at his highly unimpressed friend.

"May I have a bottle of water, please?" Colton asked politely.

Megan nodded, and as he turned, he realized Jackson wasn't done.

"So, Megan, I was wondering if you were interested in getting pizza later?" Jackson said.

Megan stared at him.

"Um… Jackson? Can I speak to you a moment?" Colton tried not to look concerned. "Oh, sure, Colton. Excuse us, Megan. Thanks for taking our orders."

Megan turned and walked away. Jackson turned to Colton, who punched him squarely in the arm.

"What the heck are you doing? You know she's working, and she's both paid and trained to be nice to everyone, right?" His tone was serious, like an unnerved father's. Jackson looked wounded but understood. They stood together quietly for a few moments.

"Mr. Tatum?" Megan walked over to them with a tray. The embarrassed Jackson took his food and thanked her.

"Oh, and I believe this is for you, Dr. Shaw." She handed him a bottle of water with a cup.

Colton thanked her and sat quietly with Jackson as they ate their food. As they finished, Colton noticed Anton and another colleague walking towards them.

"Everyone, this is one of my partners, Nate Redlin. Are you two ready to go up?" Anton asked as professionally as ever.

Colton's eyes noticed a piece of jewelry on Nate's hand. "We sure are. Nate, it's nice to meet you. Did you go to Georgia Tech?"

Anton cocked his head to the side with a curious expression. "He didn't. What makes you think that?"

"Oh, I'm sorry. Your ring looks like it has a yellow jacket on it. Was that your high school ring?"

Nate quickly covered the ring. "Umm… no. This ring was a gift from a long time ago."

Colton's lower lip puckered as he nodded. "Cool. It looks nice."

As Jackson gathered his plate and napkin to dispose of them, Colton handed him his emptied water carton to also throw away. Jackson quietly took it and quickly made his way to the trash. He threw the water carton in the recycle bin and was about to throw away the napkin when he blurted out something inaudible. He stared down at the napkin then looked over at Megan, who smiled with her eyes and nodded. Jackson pushed his glasses up his nose and let out a muffled snort.

Colton looked at him curiously. "Everything okay, Jackson?"

"Umm, yeah. Let's go!" Jackson nonchalantly stuffed the napkin in his pocket and started humming a tune.

Written on the bottom of the napkin was a personal note.

I'm off at 5:30. Call me.
-Megan (555) 221-3579.

As the men moved on to their meeting, Theseus Gell's voice encouraged people to be vigilant in challenging times.

Acknowledgements

I would love to extend my heartfelt gratitude to the individuals who helped make this book a reality. If you want to know some fantastic people, look no further than this list:

To my family (Laura, Emily, and Elizabeth), who gave me the time and freedom to create this adventurous tale.

To **Mike Bennett** and **Bill Galbraith**, who endured my blow-by-blow as I wrote this book and filled my mind with great suggestions.

To my kind but thorough Beta Reader/Copy Editor, **Danny Raye** (https://writerdannyraye.com/), who helped me believe this was worth publishing and also filled my mind with great suggestions. (If you are writing a book, hire this lady… You won't regret it.)

To **Chris Richcreek**, for his outstanding and brilliant color commentary and editing. I still laugh as I read some of your notes.

To **PJ Hoover** for helping me understand the value of my writing and for pointing me in the right direction.

To my cover designer and extraordinary artist, **Leraynne S.**, who turned my vague descriptions into an amazing book cover.

To my kind and vibrant narrator, **Chynna T.**, who brought these words to life.

To **Garret Gordon**, for finding my narrator in the most unlikely of places. :)

To **Jamie Gordon**, for making such a lovely interior.

To **Tyler Yates** for being a tremendous uplifter and ever-willing participant in our shenanigans.

I'd also like to thank **Stanley Kubrick**, **Arthur C. Clarke**, and **Douglas Rain** for bringing HAL to life in 2001: A Space Odyssey. CHAMP is a tribute to your vision.

About the Author

Growing up, Doug was surrounded by technology and science fiction, and the concept of outer space captured his imagination. However, bad vision and excessive height ensured that being an astronaut wasn't in his future. He quickly changed his focus from being a pilot to an engineer.

Forty years later, he is a happily married owner of a small aerospace engineering company that makes components for flight simulation.

As a lover of the arts, his main outlet is music (primarily guitar). He has appeared on multiple albums and was even a music critic for four international publications, producing over 300 articles.

As the father of two delightful girls, he often made up stories that would propel them past their agreed-upon bedtimes. This annoyed his patient wife, but he managed to survive, allowing their girls to dream in wide-eyed wonder.

Also by

Always come by and check out my website:

www.DougRJoseph.com

Current books:

Crying Wolf – A Science Fiction/Psychological Thriller

What begins as a daring rescue mission ensnares Captain Eskar's team in a fight for life and death.

Practical Evangelism: A Yankee Christian in King David's Court

Lessons learned about sharing my faith and walking faithfully while in Israel.

Coming Soon!
(Early Winter 2026)

The Quiet Order: Timely Secrets
– Science Fiction / Time Travel

Still reeling from the unexpected exodus of Wilson Ryken and half the Kronos' crew, Kelly Rittenaugh faces the daunting task of defending prominent historical events from the influence of her former friends.